SAFFRON'S TRIALS

By the same author
Novels in the same series:

SAFFRON'S WAR*
SAFFRON'S ARMY

633 SQUADRON: OPERATION RHINE MAIDEN
633 SQUADRON: OPERATION CRUCIBLE
633 SQUADRON: OPERATION VALKYRIE
633 SQUADRON: OPERATION COBRA
633 SQUADRON: OPERATION TITAN*
633 SQUADRON: OPERATION CRISIS*
633 SQUADRON: OPERATION THOR*
633 SQUADRON: OPERATION DEFIANT*

RAGE OF THE INNOCENT
IN PRESENCE OF MY FOES
YEARS OF THE FURY

A MEETING OF STARS
A CLASH OF STARS

THE PERSUADERS; Book 1, 2, and 3

Other novels:

OF MASKS AND MINDS
LAWS BE THEIR ENEMY
LYDIA TRENDENNIS
THE SIN AND THE SINNERS
THE GROTTO OF TIBERIUS
THE DEVIL BEHIND ME
THE STORM KNIGHT
WATERLOO
THE WIDER SEA OF LOVE
THE WAR GOD
A KILLING FOR THE HAWKS (American Literary Award)
THE TORMENTED
THE OBSESSION

Novels under the pseudonym David Farrell:

TEMPTATION ISLE; STRANGE ENEMY;
VALLEY OF CONFLICT; TWO LOVES;
THE OTHER COUSIN; MULLION ROCK

Non-fiction:

WRITE A SUCCESSFUL NOVEL
(In conjunction with Mae Sherrard-Smith)

* available from Severn House

SAFFRON'S TRIALS

Frederick E Smith

This first world edition published in Great Britain 1996 by
SEVERN HOUSE PUBLISHERS LTD of
9–15 High Street, Sutton, Surrey SM1 1DF.
First published in the USA 1996 by
SEVERN HOUSE PUBLISHERS INC. of
595 Madison Avenue, New York, NY 10022.

Copyright © 1996 by Frederick E Smith

All rights reserved.
The moral rights of the author to be identified as author of
this work have been asserted by him in accordance with the
Copyright Designs and Patents Act 1988.

British Library Cataloguing in Publication Data

Smith, Frederick E
 Saffron's Trials
 I. Title
 823.914 [F]

ISBN 0-7278-4877-1

With love to
Our close and dear friends of many years
Patty and Bernard Phillips.

All situations in this publication are fictitious and
any resemblance to living persons is purely coincidental.

Typeset by Palimpsest Book Production Limited,
Polmont, Stirlingshire, Scotland.
Printed and bound in Great Britain by
Hartnolls Ltd, Bodmin, Cornwall.

Chapter One

Bickers threw back the cabin door and halted. "Aren't you dressed yet?"

Saffron, seated on his bunk, was scribbling on a pad of notepaper. He closed it abruptly on seeing the Londoner and pushed the pad into his sidepack. Bickers gazed at him suspiciously. "What are you doing?"

Saffron's reply was short. "Nothing. What are you all dressed up for?"

Bicker sounded smug. "I've just sworn the oath. So I'm ready to go ashore and see what those Colombo women are like."

"Have you signed the liberty sheet?"

"What liberty sheet?"

"The one for the boat that takes you ashore. Didn't you hear what they said on the tannoy? If you don't sign, you don't go. And it's first come, first served. They're only taking a limited number of men ashore today."

Bickers looked horrified. "You never told me this."

"I didn't think there was any need to tell you. The announcement was loud enough."

"I suppose you've signed it."

"Of course I have. I want to take a look at Colombo."

The Londoner's voice was hoarse. "Where do I find the bloody thing?"

Saffron glanced at his watch. "On the messing deck but there's no point in your going now. Signatures had to be in by 13.30 hours. You've missed out, mush."

Bickers, a gangling corporal in khaki shorts, with lank black hair and a lugubrious face, collapsed on the bunk opposite. "That's terrible, Saffron. You mean to tell me that after all we've been through I can't get some comfort ashore."

Saffron shrugged. "You should listen to orders instead of feeling sorry for yourself."

Indignation mixed with dismay on the Londoner's face. "Feel sorry for myself. We've been through hell these last three days. So why am I feeling sorry for myself?"

"You've been lucky," Saffron told him, pulling on a clean shirt adorned with his sergeant's stripes. "If back in Mombasa that officer on the *Khedive* hadn't thrown us off his ship because we were scruffy and dirty after three months in the jungle, you'd have gone down in his ship like the rest of them."

The reminder made the Londoner shudder. Less than a fortnight ago, he, Saffron, and their draft of thirty odd delinquents, had been posted from their jungle huts to join a small convoy heading for the Far East. Refused permission to board the *Khedive Ishmael*, the only ship carrying white troops, because of their status and condition, the draft had been ignominiously sent to their present ship, the *City of Paris*, a smaller vessel filled with African troops.

Although not seen that way by the draft at the time, this switch in transports had proved to be their salvation. For five days later, not far from the Maldive Islands, a Japanese submarine had penetrated the convoy and sank the *Khedive* with a fearful loss of life. Although damaged in the attack, the *City of Paris* had made Colombo harbour safely.

Fortunate or not, Bickers, who like the rest of the draft had found no reason to love the Navy while under their sovereignty in East Africa, was not handing out any bouquets now. "He didn't do it as a favour, mate. Like the rest of his kind, he hated the RAF and thought we'd have a rough trip on this tub. You could say it served the sod right."

Saffron frowned. "Don't talk like that. Over 1500 men and women lost their lives in that attack."

"Do you think I don't know that?" the Londoner demanded. "That's why they've got a nerve to make us swear this oath to keep quiet about it for six months. You know the reason, don't you? They lost the *Prince of Wales* and the *Renown* to the Japs by being stupid and they don't want the world to know they've just had another cock up. Do you think one of our subs could get into the middle of a Jap or Jerry convoy and not be detected? It's a bloody disgrace and everyone should know about it."

Saffron, who had no cause to love the Navy himself, felt a certain sympathy with the Londoner's indignation. "That has to wait. Right now they don't know if that submarine managed to radio its High Command before the corvettes sank it. We have to keep our mouths shut in case it didn't."

Bickers looked anything but convinced. "That's their excuse. I've got mine." Then, as Saffron straightened his forage cap in preparation to leaving the cabin, his tone changed. "So I've got to rot in this old tub while you enjoy the fleshpots of Colombo? All because you hadn't the decency to tell me about this list. Some mate you are. It'll serve you right if you get the clap out there, Saffron."

Grinning, Saffron clapped his skinny shoulders. "Come on deck with me. You never know. Someone might take pity on you when they see the state you're in."

"Pity? The Navy? That'll be the day."

"Come on just the same," Saffron urged. "You never know your luck."

Grumbling, Bickers followed Saffron along a passage and up a companionway. Stifling heat met them as they emerged on the deck. Across the huge harbour, the dock cranes of Colombo stood up against a powder blue sky. With shipping crowding into the harbour as the Allies began building up supplies for their long awaited counterattack against the Japanese, the *City of Paris*, along with other ships of her size, was having to ride anchor and unload her cargo by lighters. Between her and the docks, the oily water flexed like plastic in the sunlight.

Not that the huge harbour contained only serviceable ships. Rusted masts and funnels rising from the oily water were evidence of the accuracy and ferocity of the Japanese Naval Air Force. Bickers was eyeing them apprehensively as Saffron led him towards a gangway where a midshipman and a huge marine were standing. "They've made a pig's ear out of this harbour," the Londoner muttered. "Let's hope the bastards don't try anything while we're here."

Saffron grinned. "They might if they find out you've arrived. They'll want to get rid of you before you turn the tide of the war."

"Funny, funny," Bickers muttered. As the two men approached the midshipmen, they heard voices and orders coming from the bows of the ship. Motioning Bickers to join him, Saffron went to the deck rail and gazed forward. He pointed at a small tug nuzzling against the ship bows. "You see that? They're sending divers down to see how badly damaged we are."

"Do you think they'll find anything?"

"There must be some damage," Saffron pointed out. "That sub hit us pretty hard when the depth charges blew her to the surface."

"Yes, but she crash dived right away. So she can't have been damaged."

"Maybe not but she was probably stronger built. And she did hit us below the waterline."

Bickers was looking brighter by the moment. "Let's hope you're right. If she'd badly damaged we could be here for weeks. They say there are some good-looking women in Ceylon."

Saffron eyed him with disgust. "That's all you think about, isn't it? Sex and pleasure. Never about the war effort."

Bickers sniffed. "We aren't all eager beavers, mate. Anyway, I didn't notice you keeping away from women when we were in South Africa. Or in East Africa for that matter. Who got us both beaten up by the Navy because he couldn't keep away from those two ENSA girls in Mombasa?"

"That was different. We weren't involved in the war effort then. Now we are. The sooner we get to Bombay, the sooner we get our postings. You should be looking forward to that."

"Looking forward to it? You're out of your mind, Saffron. Don't you realise we're part of a delinquent draft?"

"So what?"

Bickers almost choked. "So what? Why do you think this draft's being sent to the Far East? It's because those Brass Hats in Whitehall have decided to punish the poor bastards by sending them to the shittiest places they can find. And although we did nothing wrong, we were put on the same draft. So isn't it ten to one we'll get shitty postings too?"

"You're just assuming that. A pessimist like you would."

"I'm a realist, mate. I've as much faith in those clowns at Records as I have in the Navy giving us presents for Christmas. As far as Records is concerned, we're a part of the draft now and we'll be given the same treatment. Like a posting to Tokyo or Berlin. Just you wait and see."

"I'll bet those Japs are terrified. Can't you see the panic over there? Corporal Bickers of the RAF might soon be parachuting in! It's enough to make 'em commit hara-kiri."

"You can laugh now, Saffron, but wait until we get to Bombay. You'll be laughing on the other side of your face then."

A shout made them both turn. It was the midshipman addressing Saffron. "Are you two waiting to go ashore, sergeant?"

Saffron moved towards him. "Yes, we are. When does the next boat leave?"

Pulling a sheet of paper from his pocket, the young midshipman pointed at a lighter that was approaching the ship. "She'll be leaving in fifteen minutes. Have you got your names on this list?"

Bickers gave a low groan. "I won't forgive you for this, Saffron. I wouldn't do it to you in a million years."

"That's a laugh. You'd do it tomorrow if you thought you'd steal a girl from me. What about that time in Durban when you tried to make it with Marie when I had to return to camp?" Before Bickers could reply, Saffron turned back to the midshipman. "Yes, our names are there. Saffron and Bickers."

As the Londoner gave a start, the midshipman checked the list and then nodded. "OK. They're here. But you'll have to wait until the rest of our black troops are on the lighter. They're getting special jungle training here and have priority over men on liberty leave."

Bicker's face was a study as he turned to Saffron, who put a finger to his lips. Taking the cue, the Londoner drew him aside and then hissed in his ear. "Was it you who did it?"

Saffron nodded. "Isn't that what you wanted?"

Bickers was showing indignation instead of gratitude. "Why didn't you tell me before instead of leaving me miserable all this time?"

Saffron grinned. "I like seeing you miserable. You look so damned funny."

"Sod," Bickers muttered. The rest of his reply was cut off by a shout below as the lighter berthed at the foot of the gangway. At the same moment a platoon of black troops emerged from a companionway and began marching towards the midshipman. As the troops began boarding the lighter, Bickers turned to Saffron. "Are we supposed to go ashore with them?"

"Yes. Why?"

Bickers frowned. "I always thought they kept white troops and black troops apart."

Saffron stared at him. "Don't tell me you're a racist."

Bickers straightened indignantly. "Of course I'm not."

"Yes, you are. You don't like the idea of going ashore with all those black lads even although they behaved marvellously when the *Khedive* was sunk."

"I never said they didn't. I just don't think black and white mix well, that's all."

Saffron raised an eyebrow. "Is that so? Then remember that when we go ashore. Because from now on the only girls you're going to have a chance to lay your hot little hands on are going to be coloured. So what are you going to do? Stay celibate for the rest of the time we're in the Far East? That could be years."

"Don't talk like a prat, Saffron. I've nothing against coloured girls or anyone else coloured for that matter."

The midshipman and the marine, who had overheard the recent words between the two NCOs, were grinning at one another and moving closer to listen. Saffron, who had long accused the Londoner of hiding under the umbrella of Communism as an excuse to avoid work and danger, was enjoying the moment too much to stop now. "And you try to kid everyone you're one of Uncle Stalin's comrades. That you believe all men are brothers and equal, no matter what their creed or colour. You're just a phoney, mush."

Bickers was showing appropriate indignation. "Don't talk out of your trousers, Saffron. You're just resentful because I'm not brainwashed like you. Who else but a fool joins up to fight so that the Lord Salisburys and Lord Norfolks can keep the loot they've plundered from the masses. It's eager beavers like you who've got it all wrong, Saffron, not Communists like me."

Saffron grinned. "I still think it's a damned good excuse for scrounging and keeping out of danger. And so does everyone else who knows you."

With the last of the black troops now on board the lighter, the young midshipman winked at the big marine before turning to Saffron. "You can embark now, sergeant. Or doesn't your friend fancy a bit of Communist chit-chat with the girls in Market Street?"

Bickers' long ears pricked. "What's Market Street?"

The big marine spoke for the first time, his voice sounding like a file scraping across rusted iron. "It's the red light street, buster. But I wouldn't go there. It's only for real men. You Brylcream boys could get eaten alive by those Market Street women."

Bickers, who had an excellent opinion of his sexual prowess, forgot himself for a moment and gave a sniff of disdain. "If your lot are as handy with women as you are with Jap subs, the girls'll probably welcome us with open arms."

Seeing the big marine's face darken and aware Bickers had

touched on a sore spot, Saffron hastily took the Londoner's arm. "Never mind Market Street. Let's go and see what Colombo has to offer us."

The big marine's bellow followed them as they made their way down to the boatful of black smiling faces at the foot of the gangway. "Why don't you tell the girls you follow Uncle Joe? Then they might give you a dose of clap for nothing."

Chapter Two

Bickers pushed aside a bush and gave a grunt of pleasure at the scene that opened out before him. A large crescent of golden sand, fringed by palm trees and dotted by recumbent figures under umbrellas, lay below. The blue sea was as calm as a millpond, with its tiny waves nibbling at the bows of half a dozen canoes lined up at the water's edge. Saffron, standing alongside the Londoner, nodded his approval. "So this is Mount Nevinia. Aren't you glad now you came out here instead of crawling about Market Street?"

Bickers was not surrendering an earlier argument that easily. He jabbed a finger at the half nude figures lying on the beach. "I'll let you know later when we've had the time to do a recce. Come on. Let's get down there."

Saffron caught his arm as the Londoner started down a path that led to the beach. "Hang on. If there are any European women down there, you take it easy. Remember we're not in South Africa now. I don't want to get involved with any angry husbands or boyfriends."

Bickers gave a sniff of disdain. "You take care of your problems, Saffron, and I'll take care of mine. Like I always have."

Saffron nodded sarcastically. "Like you did at Clifton in South Africa. Or in Durban or Mombasa. I've got you out of more scrapes than you've had hot dinners, mush. So you watch yourself." The Yorkshireman nodded at a huge hotel that stood on a bluff on the northern tip of the crescent. "That place makes me feel this is an exclusive beach. So keep that ham act of yours under control until we learn the score."

Although Bickers scowled, he made no further comment. Reaching the beach, he pulled off his shirt and then his shoes and socks, only to give a howl and run back into the shade of a bush. "The sand's red hot, Saffron. I think I've burned my foot."

Saffron grinned. "Of course it's hot. Put your shoes on until we can hire an umbrella."

Obeying, the Londoner followed Saffron across the wide beach, an unconsciously comical figure with his scrawny arms and chest, thin legs, and flopping shoes. On their way they passed an umbrella giving shade to a couple of European girls. Both were in their early twenties, slim, sun-tanned, and wearing scanty bathing suits. As one of them caught sight of the blond Saffron with his powerful physique, she lifted her head from her towel to examine him further. Then she noticed Bickers, nudged her companion, and whispered something to her. A moment later a giggle passed between them.

Bickers, whose eyes had been devouring the two girls since they came into sight, had never been known to show diffidence with women, which possibly explained why he had been so surprisingly successful with them in the past. Interpreting the giggle as an expression of interest, he paused and grinned at the girls. "Hello."

There was another giggle, and then both girls sank back and pretended they had heard nothing. Deciding they were playing hard to get, Bickers drew nearer. "Hello. Do you girls speak English?"

When neither girl moved or responded, Saffron intervened. "Come on, Ken. Leave them alone."

Bickers shook off Saffron's hand. "Good-looking girls like you shouldn't be alone like this. How about letting us join you?"

Again neither girl moved or spoke. This time Saffron took Bickers' arm. "They don't want to play, Ken. Come on."

"It's not that at all," Bickers complained. "It's just they can't speak English."

"Don't be a clot. Of course they can speak English. They're just not interested. Leave them alone."

After one last effort, Bickers reluctantly obeyed. As both men moved away, neither man saw the girls lift their heads, their eyes on Saffron. As the brunette murmured something, the blonde nodded and made a moue of approval.

Unaware of their interest, Saffron was glaring at the grumbling Bickers. "What's the matter with you? Didn't you notice the clothes alongside them? They were Wrens."

Bickers gave a start. "Wrens!"

"That's right. Have you forgotten what happened the last time you tried to pick up a Wren?"

Bickers frowned. "That was a set up job. These are just two lonely girls on a beach."

"Lonely? Two girls with those faces and figures. I'll lay odds they've got a hundred Naval officers around here ready to do murder for them."

Bickers glanced uneasily around, and then relaxed. "I don't see the Navy anywhere around. Supposing you're wrong."

"I'm not wrong," Saffron said. "Wherever there are Wrens, there's the Navy keeping the girls to themselves." He waved a Sinhalese boy carrying an umbrella towards him. As the boy set up the umbrella, Saffron pulled off his shirt, revealing a muscular and well-proportioned torso. "Unless you want trouble, sit down here and forget about sex for a while."

Muttering his disappointment, Bickers sank down beside him. "At least we've got away from that draft for a while."

Saffron shrugged. "I'm surprised they're not here. They must have heard about this place."

Bickers looked dismayed. "You didn't give Cornwall and his gang liberty leave, did you? Not after what happened in Mombasa?"

Saffron shook his head. "No. I did the same as I did there. Told the Master at Arms there'd be trouble if they were allowed ashore and I wasn't in favour of it. But he pointed out we might be here for weeks if the ship was badly damaged."

Bickers' ears pricked up. "Weeks? Is that possible?"

"That's what the MA said. We'll know once those divers have taken a look at her hull."

Bickers gazed around the golden beach with its recumbent bodies and graceful palm trees and almost hugged himself. "Let's hope they find a hole big enough to sail the *Queen Mary* through."

Saffron showed his disgust. "That would suit you, wouldn't it?"

"Suit me? It would suit any sane man, mate." Then the Londoner caught sight of half a dozen servicemen plunging into the sea at the far end of the beach and his tone changed. "So Cornwall and his gang have come ashore?"

"Yes. They came out on an earlier boat."

Bickers gave an uneasy look behind him at the tree-covered ridge, then sank back. "I expect they went straight to Market Street. All they think about is nookie."

Saffron grinned. "Listen who's talking."

Bickers sniffed. "A man needs some comfort, Saffron. Particularly when he's been staring death in the face for the last week."

"Come off it. We had one rough day and night. That was all."

"All? With sharks following us and the chance of being torpedoed and thrown among them any minute? You didn't think about that, did you? Your trouble is you haven't any imagination."

"And your trouble is you can't keep yours under control. Don't you realise that by looking on the black side of everything you make it twice as hard to take?"

"It's easy for you, Saffron. You're just thick from ear to ear. But we sensitive types have to pay a hell of a price in wartime. They ought to give us double pay for what we suffer." Bickers looked pleased with his suggestion. "Come to think of it, that's not a bad idea."

"You should put it up to the War Office," Saffron said. "Double pay for all Communists and scroungers. After all, they tell me Uncle Joe gives special attention to his scroungers. Only he does it by hanging or shooting them."

Bickers showed contempt. "That's just Capitalist propaganda, Saffron. When are you going to grow up and stop believing the crap the Press dish out? Stalin doesn't need to punish scroungers. His people have something worth fighting for."

"Like salt mines and labour camps? Why don't you come clean and admit it? You wouldn't change your uniform for some Red Army solder if they offered you a free dacha after the war. Your lot are all the same. I haven't noticed any of you trying to transfer to the Red Army."

"That's only because we know they won't let us, mate. But wait until the war's over. Watch us then. We'll have the Lord Salisburys and Lord Norfolks out so fast their feet won't touch the ground. With us in power it'll be the new millenium, Saffron. The day of the common man."

The sultry heat was turning Saffron sleepy. "You mean you'll bore us all to death with your platitudes. I can't wait for it, comrade."

"Laugh if you like, Saffron, but that's how it's going to be."

Saffron yawned. "If you say so. Only will you shut up now. I want to sleep and dream about this new world of yours. Isn't it the one Huxley wrote about?"

"That's just what I'd expect from you, Saffron. Your kind can't tell Communism from Fascism. That's why people like you will have to go. You're natural enemies of the common man."

There was no reply from Saffron. Seeing he had fallen asleep, Bickers gave a grunt of disgust and took another glance across the shimmering sand to where the two girls had been lying. Finding they had gone and their umbrella had been taken away, the Londoner muttered his disappointment and laid his head on his shirt. A minute later there was no sound except for the two men's steady breathing and the rhythmical lap of the waves.

Chapter Three

"Hey. Look who's here."

The loud, raucous shout awoke Saffron. Rubbing his eyes, he sat up to see a half-naked figure standing over him. With the figure silhouetted against the sun, and with his eyes not yet accustomed to the brilliant light, Saffron took a moment to identify the man. Then, as sleep cleared from his brain, he sat up. The man was Wilkinson, one of their draft's less salubrious characters.

Wilkinson's shout came again. "It's our sergeant, Cornwall. Along with his corporal." The aircraftman grinned down at Saffron. "You enjoyin' yourself, sergeant?"

By this time Bickers was awake, although his sleep in the sun had left him muzzy. "What's happening, Saffron?"

Saffron cocked a rueful eye up at the grinning Wilkinson. "Our draft has found us. At least two of 'em have."

Bickers' first reponse was dismay. "Oh, Christ. Who is it?"

"Can't you guess?" Saffron said.

Bickers pushed his skinny torso up from the sand and peered up at Wilkinson, a ginger-headed man with a round, fleshy face and tattooed arms. The dismay in his voice grew. "It's Wilkinson, isn't it?"

The man grinned. "That's right, corporal. You enjoying yourself?"

Before the Londoner could reply, the two NCOs heard the tramp of feet in the sand. Turning, they saw a second aircraftman approaching. Cornwall, also stripped to the waist, had a torso like a Roman statue. With a shock of black hair, a square chin, and scarred, overhanging eyebrows, he resembled a light heavyweight boxer, which in fact Cornwall was.

Showing malicious humour at the encounter, Cornwall was the first to speak as he came up alongside Wilkinson. "Hello, sergeant. We thought you might be here."

Saffron was fully awake now. "I hope you didn't feel you had to come because of that?"

Grinning at his sarcasm, Cornwall glanced at Wilkinson. "We might have done, sergeant. We know you've got good taste."

"I didn't think you shared my taste, Cornwall. I'd have thought yours was more Market Street vintage."

There was a snigger from Wilkinson. "Do you think we haven't been there? First things first, sergeant."

"I wouldn't have expected anything else from you, Wilkinson. I'm just surprised the lot of you aren't spending the day there. Or are your other friends, MacMorron and Taylor, doing just that?"

Cornwall, whose rugged face wore a deceivingly genial smile, raised a scarred eyebrow. "You don't seem very friendly this morning, sergeant."

Saffron shrugged. "I wasn't aware it was my job to be friendly, Cornwall."

The pugilist cocked a glance at the grinning Wilkinson. "It must be the sun. It doesn't agree with some people. I think he's one of 'em, don't you, Ginger?"

Wilkinson let out a sycophantic laugh. As Saffron knew too well, the tattooed man was a creep and the more dangerous because of it. Nor was he one of life's ornamental people. At close quarters his fleshy face was as dotted with blackheads as a fruit cake with currents and his teeth were a dentist's despair. Indeed Wilkinson had the kind of halitosis that had once led Bickers to confide in Saffron that he could be the Allies' secret weapon. If Wilkinson ever came into contact with the Japanese, he would only have to breathe on them and the Rising Sun would wilt and sink forever beneath the South China Seas.

At the same time the tense conversation between Saffron and Cornwall was making Bickers uneasy. He knew only too well the reason behind it. While the draft had been in Kenya awaiting transportation, Cornwall had kept tormenting a youngster named Frank Merrow who, afraid of the Far Eastern posting, had consoled himself at nights by playing a violin.

Although most of the draft had shown patience with him, the youngster was no virtuoso and Cornwall and his three followers had frequently threatened to smash his violin if he continued to play it.

In turn Saffron, in charge of the draft, had warned Cornwall to leave the youngster alone. When finally the pugilist had carried out his threat and smashed the violin, Saffron, with no military infrastructure available to help him punish the offender, had accepted a challenge to a bare knuckle fight.

It had been a bloody encounter. With Saffron's boxing skills being no match for the pugilist's and with Cornwall determined to make Saffron pay for his behaviour, the Yorkshireman had won a narrow victory only by taking Bicker's advice and falling back on his unarmed combat skills.

The fight had left a feud between the two men that had lasted to this day. Aware that Cornwall linked him along with Saffron as an enemy, the Londoner was wishing Saffron would show a little more tact and sociability.

His unease grew as Cornwall turned to him. "How about you, corporal? You're very quiet. Has the sun got to you too?"

Bickers feigned a yawn. "I don't think so. It's just makes me sleepy. How do you like Ceylon?"

Cornwall winked at Wilkinson. "So far Ceylon's great. I could fight the war out here."

"Maybe you'll be able to," Bickers said. "I'm told that we could be here for a few weeks if the ship turns out to be badly damaged."

There was an obscene sound of pleasure from Wilkinson. "Let's hope so. A few weeks with that bint in Market Street and I'd be fit to take on the whole Japanese Air Force."

Cornwall grinned at Bickers. "You ought to go there, corporal. You don't know what you're missing."

Bickers was careful to avoid Saffron's look of disgust at his appeasement. "Yes, it sounds all right. All the matelots seem to recommend it."

At that moment a beach ball struck Wilkinson on the leg. Turning, all four men saw it had come from a group of small coloured children playing some thirty yards away. As one child called something to him in Sinhalese, Wilkinson kicked the ball in the opposite direction. The child stared at him in puzzlement, then ran forward and collected it.

Saffron frowned up at Wilkinson. "What did you do that for? Don't you know it's our job to make people like us, not to antagonise them."

Wilkinson shrugged. "I don't care if the bastards like us or hate us. Why should I?"

"Because when you're in uniform you're ambassadors of your country. Or aren't you capable of a thought like that?"

Wilkinson gazed at Cornwall for support. The pugilist grinned. "Isn't that a bit high-minded, sergeant? Isn't it enough we're fighting a war for them?"

"That's a joke, Cornwall. The only fighting you're likely to do here is the kind of fighting you did in Mombasa. Knocking hell out of innocent people after you get drunk."

Although the grin did not leave Cornwall's face, his eyes took on a flatness of expression that Saffron had seen before. About to reply, the pugilist turned to Wilkinson. "I don't think our sergeant likes us today, Ginger. Shall we leave him to his bad temper and get ourselves a beer?"

As Wilkinson nodded, Bickers turned to Saffron. "I wouldn't mind a beer myself. How about going up to that hotel and having one?"

Wilkinson gave his jackal laugh. "You won't have any luck up there, corp."

"Why?" Bickers asked.

Cornwall answered for his follower. "You should keep your

eyes open. Haven't you seen the Wrens and Naval officers coming and going from it?"

Bickers turned to gaze at the bluff. "What's so odd about that?"

Cornwall grinned at Wilkinson. "Only that it's a hostel for Wrens. With beds to share for every officer over the rank of lieutenant."

Bickers blinked. "You mean it's a brothel?"

"Of course it's a brothel. The Navy don't deny themselves anything. Didn't you notice that in Mombasa? They've got this place just as well organised. As an RAF NCO you've got as much chance of getting in there as getting into a nunnery."

Bickers' reaction was spontaneous. "The same old story. Them and us. The bastards!"

As Cornwall laughed, the beach ball dropped close to Wilkinson. Picking it up, he glanced at Saffron and then kicked it with all his strength in the direction of the sea. Then, before Saffron could respond, he grinned and walked towards the ridge behind the beach. As Saffron jumped to his feet, Cornwall gave a half-mocking grin and followed him.

Seeing the small boy's hurt expression, Saffron ran forward and fetched the ball from the water's edge. The boy's mother, a slim creature with long black hair and kohl darkened eyes, smiled and said something to him in Sinhalese as he presented the ball to the boy. Apologising to her, Saffron returned to his umbrella. Bicker's comment was a mixture of approval and criticism. "That was a bit over the top, wasn't it? Mind you, it's won the kid's mum over. So maybe it was smart after all."

Saffron's reply was curt. "I didn't do it for that. I don't want local people to think we're a bunch of yobbos."

"You didn't exactly treat Cornwall like a long lost friend, did you?" the Londoner grumbled. "What was the point of deliberately provoking him?"

"I wasn't provoking him. I was just making it clear I didn't want his company."

"You were provoking him," Bickers insisted. "And that's

stupid. We've got all the trouble we want without more problems with him and his gang."

Although knowing he was right, Saffron was in no mood for concessions. "Cornwall and his gang are scum. So I'm not appeasing them, now or later."

"You could think about me, couldn't you?" Bickers complained. "They take it out of me too, you know."

Knowing he was right, Saffron mellowed. "Stop worrying about it. Once we get to Bombay, the postings will come through. Then, with any luck, we'll never see them again."

For a moment Bickers brightened. Then his long face fell again. "But what if we're all posted together? By this time Records must have got us so mixed up with them they'll think we're delinquents too. Wouldn't it be terrible, Saffron, if they sent the lot of us to some ghastly place in Burma?"

Knowing the possibility existed, Saffron reacted with uncharacteristic irritation. "Stop being such a pessimist. They and the rest of them are a punishment draft. We were only put in charge of 'em until they reached Bombay. After that they'll be posted and we'll be rid of them."

"Let's hope you're right," Bickers muttered. "It's bad enough thinking we might go into the lines against the Japs. To go with those bastards would be the end. They'd probably shoot us or bayonet us in the back."

Saffron eyed him in disgust. "You really are the end, aren't you? Here we are, lying on a beach under a blue sky and a gorgeous sea to bathe in, and all you can do is moan about what might happen next month or next year. Don't you realise that millions of men would give their right arms to be in our shoes today?"

Bickers gazed along the shimmering beach, saw the slim figure of a girl entering the sea, and his tone changed. "Do you really think there's a chance we could be here a few weeks?"

"I've told you there is. You know how hard that sub hit us." Saffron settled down on his towel again. "Now will you shut up and go to sleep?"

Reassured, Bickers laid back on his own towel and

made plans on how he would spend his next few weeks in Paradise.

They returned to the harbour six hours later. The sun was a golden ball balancing on Colombo's skyline as a lighter took them over to the *City of Paris*. As they climbed a ladder to the deck, Saffron spotted the young midshipman who had monitored the liberty leave list earlier in the day. Telling Bickers to wait for him, he crossed the deck and spoke to the youngster. A couple of minutes later he returned to Bickers, who was looking curious. "What was all that about?"

"I was asking what news there was about the damage to the ship."

Bickers gave a start. "Does he know?"

"Yes. He's had a full report."

Bickers' interest was fever hot now. "Well, what is it? Are we staying here?"

Saffron shook his head. "No. The damage was only slight and it's already been repaired. We sail for Bombay tomorrow."

The Londoner's jaw dropped. "What?"

"We sail tomorrow. On the first tide."

With his dreams punctured, Bickers looked aghast. "You're joking, aren't you?"

"No. We're leaving tomorrow."

"But that's terrible, Saffron. We've only been here one day."

"It is disappointing, I agree. But that's life."

Bickers' groan would have brought tears from a wooden idol. "One day. We're given a taste of Paradise and then they snatch it from us. It's awful, Saffron."

Saffron shrugged. "It's war, mush."

Bickers' dismay turned to recrimination. "And you said we could be here for weeks. You let me believe it. Why did you do it, Saffron?"

Saffron grinned. "So now it's my fault?"

"Of course it's your fault. If you hadn't raised my hopes, it wouldn't have been such a shock. Now it feels as if someone has hit me."

Saffron took his arm. "Come on. I'll see if I can get you a beer."

"You think drink's going to help? I'm shattered, Saffron. Honestly I am."

Saffron chuckled. "Never mind. There's always the silver lining. You won't have to wait so long to go to Burma with Cornwall and his cronies."

Bickers' feelings came from the heart. "You think that's funny? You really are a bastard, Saffron. A bastard through and through!"

Chapter Four

Bickers dropped his kitbag and backpack from the Bedford truck and jumped down after them. About to speak to Saffron, who was waiting for him, he suddenly sniffed, grimaced, and held his nose. "Phew! What's the whiff? It's horrible."

Saffron, who had arrived in an earlier truck, grinned as he picked up the Londoner's backpack. "It's the town sewers. They run into the sea just below the camp."

"Sewers! You're saying the camp's built over them?"

"More or less. But don't let it worry you. They say you soon get used to it."

Bickers showed indignation. "They've done it to us again, haven't they? Who the hell wants to get used to sewers?"

Saffron gave him a shove. "Stop moaning and pick up your kitbag. I've saved a bed for you."

A minute later they entered the largest billet Bickers had ever seen, a building almost as big as an aircraft hangar. Wooden-framed beds laced with cord lined both its sides. Although over fifty men were already sitting or lying on beds, the two nearest the entrance were unoccupied. Saffron pointed at them. "Those are ours. I took them because they're nearer to the toilets and the cookhouse."

For a moment Bickers was overcome by the size of the building. "It must take a hundred men, Saffron."

"It does," Saffron told him. "In fact it takes a hundred and twenty. I counted the beds before you came. And there are more like it down the road."

"But why are they so big?"

Saffron shrugged. "They must have a big intake here. There is a war going on against the Japs, you know."

Bickers lugged his kitbag over to his bed and sank down. "You don't say. From the look of this place it's a bigger war than the one back in Europe. Was it Americans I saw down the road?"

"Probably. Their camp is attached to ours. I was told about them just before you arrived."

"Yanks, eh. Maybe we'll get some free chocolate and cigarettes."

Saffron frowned. "I hope you're not thinking of scrounging from them."

"What do you mean – scrounging? Don't they owe us something?"

"Like what?"

Bickers' shrug was all embracing. "Bringing civilisation to their country. Sorting out the Red Indians for them. Giving them a constitution. Holding off Hitler and Mussolini until the Japs kicked their backsides and pushed 'em into the war. I'd say they owe us more than chocolate and cigarettes, Saffron."

Saffron chuckled. "I hope you're not thinking of telling them all this. If you do, you'll get more than chocolate and cigarettes."

Muttering something, Bickers pulled off his shirt. "God, it's hot. I thought it was bad enough in Mombasa but I think it's worse here."

"It is. It's the humidity. They say the monsoons are due soon."

While the couple had been talking, sweating men had been pouring into the hut from the trucks queuing up outside. Among them was Cornwall and his followers. Noticing the two NCOs, Cornwall grinned at them and said something to the others that brought shouts and raucous laughter from them. As they shoved and pushed their way further into the billet it was noticeable that men were quick to move aside for them. Bickers eyed them gloomily. "I was hoping the Navy would leave 'em behind or drop 'em overboard on the way here. But no such luck."

It had been a week since the *City of Paris* has left Colombo and under the protection of coastal minefields had sailed to Bombay. There the RTO had given permission for the troops to have two hours liberty leave before transports had carried them to Worli, their transit camp.

With no time to explore the city, Saffron and Bickers had discovered a canteen near the harbour that dispensed free food and non-alcoholic drinks to disembarking troops. Expecting it to be run by local British residents, Saffron had been surprised to find it was run by Pharsees, the high caste residents of Bombay.

Saffron had found it disturbing. "If the British out here are too toffee-nosed to do anything for our troops who're coming out here to fight for them, it must mean things are worse out here than in Africa."

Bickers had frowned. "How do you mean?"

"I mean it could be even harder for you to lay your hot little hands on European women than it was in Kenya."

Bickers frowned again. "Nothing could be as bad as Kenya, Saffron."

"Don't you believe it. This is where Colonel Blimps come from. The Raj. Dinner suits, port wine, and cigars. They'd faint or call out the guard if they heard the Navy had brought a Communist into the country."

By this time Bickers had looked faint. "You're talking out of your trousers again, Saffron."

"Am I? You'd better keep quiet out here or Colonel

Blimp might call out his lancers and use your head as a turnip."

Saffron's thoughts were broken by the sight of Bickers emptying the contents of his kitbag on the bed. "I wouldn't unpack now," he said. "It'll be time to eat shortly."

Ignoring him, Bickers was rummaging through the pile of clothes and miscellaneous items his kitbag had disgorged. A moment later he gave a grunt of satisfaction and pulled out a small metal object from beneath a dirty towel. "I hadn't seen it for weeks and wanted to be sure I hadn't lost it," he explained.

Saffron leaned forward curiously. "What is it?"

Bickers glanced round cautiously to see they were not being overlooked before handing the object to Saffron. The Yorkshireman gazed down at it in disbelief. "A revolver! Where the hell did you get this?"

Bickers put a finger to his lips. "Don't tell the whole billet."

"Where did you get it?"

Bickers smirked. "In South Africa. A girl gave it to me. She said it had once belonged to her dad."

Hiding the tiny revolver with his body, Saffron examined it closer. "It's a Belgium 347. Small and as old as hell but still functional. And it's loaded. Do you realise that?"

"Of course I do. Sarah gave me the bullets with the gun."

"Why did she do it?"

Bickers shrugged. "I don't know. I suppose it was because I was posted."

Saffron nodded sarcastically. "You spun her some yarn you were going into action. Right?"

Bickers pretended innocence. "I never did. She just felt it might be more use to me than lying unused in a drawer at home."

"Why haven't you mentioned it before?"

"I thought you might get funny about it and start throwing your weight about."

"Too true I might. You know damn well there's a strict

rule about carrying firearms without permission. And it's even stricter out here. If you were caught with that, a loaded weapon, you'd be straight into the glasshouse. You'll have to get rid of it."

"Aw, c'mon, Saffron. I'm not going to use it, am I?"

"How do I know that? What if Cornwall and his gang start picking on you. You might pull it out to scare them off."

"Don't be a clot. It's just a souvenir from Sarah."

"Then why is it loaded?"

"She only gave me five bullets and as they're a special size and just about impossible to get I thought that was the safest place to keep them."

With the huge hut almost full now, the queue of perspiring men filing through the entrance was reduced to a trickle. Nevertheless Saffron hid the revolver beneath his discarded tunic as he examined it again. "Do you realise this hasn't a safety lug? That means if the hammer gets a blow it could fire the cartridge in the chamber."

Bickers frowned. "Are you sure?"

Saffron slid the revolver over to him. "Take a look yourself. You've been carrying the thing around when a sharp blow might have set it off. You aren't fit to carry a scout's knife, much less a gun."

"I've had the thing with me since we left Cape Town nearly four months ago," Bickers complained. "And nothing's happened yet. So what are you making such a fuss about?"

"You've just been lucky, mush. Take a look at it and see what I mean."

Bickers glanced behind him. All down the billet men, tired from their journey in the oppressive heat, were sinking down on their beds to get a few minutes rest before the next orders came. Deciding he was safe, Bickers was about to examine the revolver when two men in American uniform appeared in the billet entrance. As they paused and then glanced at the NCOs, Saffron gave a hiss of warning and Bickers hastily stuffed the revolver beneath his topee which was strapped to his backpack.

A few seconds later the Americans approached them. One, with a single stripe on his arm, was a tall, powerfully built man, the other, a GI, was a smaller, stockier soldier. Seeing Saffron's tunic with its three stripes lying on his bed, the taller man addressed him. "You in charge here, sergeant?"

Saffron rose from his bed. "I'm in charge of some of the men. Why?"

The lance corporal held out a big hand. "I'm Tom Hewitt and this is my buddy, Gene Clancey. We got in yesterday evening and thought we'd like to meet some of you guys. Is that OK with you?"

"Why not? There's no law against it."

"So it's OK if we wander down and talk to the guys?"

Curious himself about the Americans, Saffron shrugged. "Why wander down? Why not sit down here and talk?" As Hewitt showed pleasure at the offer, Saffron pointed at Bickers, seated on the opposite bed. "Meet Ken Bickers. He helps me to keep my draft in order."

Hewitt turned and shook hands with the Londoner. "Nice to meet you, corporal." After introducing Clancey, he pointed at the items of clothing strewn over the bed. "What gives? You guys having a kit inspection or something?"

Bickers shook his head as he made room for Clancey to sit down. "No. We've recently come from Kenya and I was just repacking my things."

"Kenya. That's in Africa, ain't it?"

"That's right. We had three months over there waiting for a ship to bring us here. We were bloody lucky to get here because —"

Before Bickers could give away news of the *Khedive* sinking, Saffron broke in hastily. "He means we'd some rough weather on the way. A bad storm."

Clancey, the smaller American, looked curious. "In the Indian ocean? There was hardly a ripple when we crossed it."

"It wasn't that bad," Saffron said, scowling at the discomforted Bickers. "But some people get sea sick easily.

Ken's one of them. So he tends to exaggerate." Before the indignant Londoner could respond, Saffron went on: "How're you finding the camp?"

Clancey shrugged. "The camp's great. We like it here."

Bickers forgot his indignation. "You like this dump?"

"Yeah, why not? It's the best camp we've been in."

Bickers grinned. "Where've you guys been? In darkest Africa?"

"No. We've come straight from the States."

"And this is the best camp you've been in? With these beds and those sewers ponging like this? You have to be kidding."

"No. We'd some goddamn awful camps back home. Mostly tents and sometimes no beds. If you guys think this camp is bad, they've been spoiling you." Clancey, who reminded Saffron of James Cagney with his jaunty appearance, turned to his buddy. "Ain't I right, Tom?"

"Sure you are, kid. Our guys are loving it here."

Bickers turned to Saffron. "I can't believe this. I always thought the Yanks had the best of everything."

Saffron grinned. "I hope you're taking notice. You've been having it soft all this time. So maybe you won't moan so much in the future."

Clancey was eyeing the contents on the bed. "There's your equipment too. It looks better than ours."

"That I can't believe," Bickers said.

Clancey was examining Bickers' backpack. "It is. Ours ain't so strong." He grinned as his fingers ran over the topee strapped to it. "And this is really something. You going to wear this, bud?"

Bickers, catching Saffron's glance, was suddenly looking uneasy. "Only if I have to."

Clancey was fascinated by the topee. "Someone told me these things are lined with silver paper." Before either NCO could check him, he lifted one side of the topee against its holding strap and saw the small revolver lying beneath it. "Say, that's a gun, ain't it? Is that a part of your equipment too?"

Bickers tried to pull the pack away but the fascinated American already had his fingers around the revolver and it came away in his hand. He glanced down at it curiously. "It's kinda small, ain't it?"

Saffron leaned forward, his voice urgent. "Get it out of sight quickly. He's not supposed to have it."

Hewitt, quicker to grasp the situation than the curious Clancey, grabbed at the smaller American's arm. "Give it back to the corporal, Gene. Right away."

Clancey was still examining the weapon. "Why? What's the problem?"

"Just do it, that's all." When Clancey still went on examining the gun, Hewitt jerked his arm to prise the gun from him. Instead the jerk broke the smaller's American grip on the weapon. Slipping from his hands it dropped with a loud clatter on the concrete floor between the paralysed Bickers' feet. A fraction of a second later there was an explosion that to the two NCOs sounded like the crack of doom itself.

Chapter Five

Although he was the culprit, Clancey was the first to recover. As all along the billet startled men rose from their beds, his shout rang out only a couple of seconds after the explosion. "Firecracker! It's OK you guys. It was just a firecracker I brought in."

After a shout here and there about crazy Yanks, men glanced at one another and then, to Saffron's immense relief, sank back on their beds. Grabbing the revolver from the floor, Saffron glanced at the sitting Bickers whose face was a sickly mixture of green and white. "Are you OK? The bullet didn't get you in the leg or foot?"

Bickers swallowed. "I don't think so."

"What do you mean – you don't think so? Take a look."

Bickers felt down at his feet and legs, then shook his head.

Stuffing the revolver into the pocket of his shorts, the sweating Saffron sank back on his bed. Clancey gave him a contrite grin. "Sorry, sergeant. But why did it go off like that?"

"Because the damn thing's old, that's why," Saffron managed.

"I'm sure sorry," Clancey said again. "But it's all OK now, ain't it?"

Hewitt took the smaller man's arm. "Let's go, kid, and leave these guys to settle in." As Clancey nodded, Hewitt glanced back at Saffron. "Sorry for what happened but it was nice meeting you guys. I hope we'll see you around before we're posted."

Saffron felt someone else was replying. "Yes. We hope so too. Good luck."

With that the two Americans left the billet. Letting out his breath, Saffron turned back to Bickers who was still sitting paralysed on his bed. "Now do you understand how dangerous that gun is?"

Bickers found his voice again. "It's all right. The bullet must have gone between my feet."

"It isn't your bloody feet I'm thinking about," Saffron hissed. "Haven't you thought that behind you are over fifty beds with men lying in them. That bullet has gone somewhere. It could be in any one of them at this moment."

Bickers' eyes went huge and his cheeks turned green and yellow again. "Oh, my God. I never thought about that."

"Of course you didn't. As always you were only thinking about yourself."

Bickers sounded faint. "But no one's cried out?"

"They wouldn't, would they, if one of them is dead?"

The Londoner groaned. "Don't say it, Saffron. Don't even think it."

Terrified himself there might be a tragedy, Saffron was in no mood to spare the Londoner's feelings. "I daren't think what the Provost people would do to you. Pobably drag you out and shoot you."

Bickers groaned again. "What are we going to do, Saffron?"

"There's nothing we can do until everyone goes to lunch. If we start walking down the billet looking at everyone they'll know something's wrong and it wasn't a firework."

"But what if someone's been hit and is bleeding?"

"Then they'll be able to tell the men around them. It's only if someone's dead that no one will know. Men will just think they're asleep."

"So we have to wait until lunch time to find out the truth?"

"That's right." Saffron was in no mood to offer comfort. "You'd better spend the time praying. Because if that gun has killed somebody we've got to tell how it happened."

The twelve minutes that followed were the longest minutes either man had known. Facing the long row of beds as Saffron was, his frantic mind was trying to estimate the trajectory of the bullet. From all he could remember, the revolver had fallen with its barrel more or less parallel to the wall of the billet. In other words the bullet ought to have taken a course that sent it in line with the upper torsos of the men who were lying in their beds. Finding this no comfort whatever, Saffron knew the critical factor was the vertical angle of the barrel at the moment of explosion. If it had been flat to the floor, there was the chance the bullet had kept low, and providing no one's legs had been the way – which, from the lack of an outcry, seemed unlikely – the bullet would have expended itself harmlessly at the far end of the billet.

But Saffron knew the chances of this were a hundred to one. Almost certainly the impact on the concrete floor would have made the revolver bounce up a few inches and this would have been more than enough to cause a rising trajectory. This would mean the men at risk were those thirty or more feet from Bickers' bed.

Bickers, seated on his bed facing Saffron, was clearly too terrified to look round. "Can you see anything, Saffron?"

Saffron nodded grimly. "Yes. A long row of motionless men."

Bickers snatched at straws. "But isn't that encouraging?

If a man had been hit, he'd have made some sound, wouldn't he?"

"Not if he'd been hit in the head or the heart. And that's the area where your bullet might have gone."

"But surely someone would have seen a man hit!"

"Not today. Everyone's too hot and tired to notice anything. Most men are asleep or dozing."

"For Christ's sake, Saffron, you're making it worse."

"If anyone's hit, it can't be worse," Saffron hissed. "I could shoot you myself for keeping quiet about the damned gun."

A distant siren was heard at last. Men sat up in their beds, shook their sleeping comrades, and began filing towards the entrance. Among them was Cornwall and his men. As they came opposite the two NCOs, Cornwall gave a derisive shout. "What's the matter, sergeant? Have the sewers spoiled your appetite?"

Neither NCO answered him. The thought of the capital Cornwall would make of the affair if he heard about it sent a shudder through Bickers. With a massive effort of will, he turned and watched the beds behind him emptying. Every now and then an occupant would be slow to rise, sending both men's hearts thumping. One man some fifteen beds away was taking no notice of the general exodus and drew both NCOs' eyes. Ten seconds of horror passed before an aircraftman ran back and shook the sleeping man. A deep sob of thanksgiving broke from Bickers as the man awoke, rolled off his bed, and took his place in the queue. "Thank God," the Londoner breathed. "I thought it was him."

It was nearly five minutes before the huge billet was empty and both men could relax. As colour returned to Bickers' cheeks, Saffron nodded grimly. "You're luckier than you deserve to be. Let's go and see where the bullet went."

Taking care they were not seen, they moved down the billet, examining each bed in turn. When they reached the sixteenth bed, Saffron gave a start and dropped on his knees alongside it. As Bickers came alongside him, Saffron pointed at a scar and depression on the upper wooden frame of the bed. He measured the hole with his little finger, then glanced up at the Londoner. "There's your bullet. In there. Four inches higher and it would have smashed the skull of the poor devil who was lying here."

Bickers went green again. "But why didn't he say anything."

"I suppose he was asleep. And it wasn't a heavy bullet so he wouldn't feel the impact. But it would still have killed him." Gazing around the empty billet, Saffron pulled out his army knife and dug out the flattened bullet. "There it is. You want to keep it to remind you what a lucky bastard you are?"

Bickers shuddered. "I don't want it. Throw it away."

Saffron, almost as relieved as the Londoner at the outcome of the incident, was still in no mood to spare his feelings. "I'm keeping the revolver until I can get rid of it safely. In the meantime have you any more little surprises for me?"

Bickers frowned. "You don't have to be sarcastic, Saffron. Any man can make a mistake."

"That's true but yours tend to be lethal. You haven't a Mills bomb or a stick of dynamite hidden in your kitbag, have you?"

The knowledge he was getting off scot free from what had seemed a disaster a few minutes ago was rapidly rejuvenating the Londoner. "You're talking as if it were my fault, Saffron. Those Yanks were to blame. So stop making so much of it."

Saffron nearly choked. "Much of it? You nearly killed a man. Of course it was your fault. You shouldn't have been carrying a loaded gun like that."

"You're forgetting about me," Bickers muttered.

"You? What about you?"

"I might have had a foot blown off. You've hardly mentioned that, have you?"

Saffron exploded. "If there was any justice you would have lost your foot. Both bloody feet, in fact."

Bickers sighed. "Can't we drop it now? If you don't we're going to miss our grub."

Not for the first time in their relationship Saffron's emotions almost overwhelmed him. "Why do I put up with you? Will someone tell me that?"

Bickers sniffed. "I could say the same thing about you, Saffron. Are you coming with me to the cookhouse or not?"

Saffron took a long, deep breath and then turned away, his teeth gritting. "I suppose I must. Yes, all right. Let's go and get it over."

Bickers looked shocked as he turned to face Saffron. "Miller? Imphal? Are you sure?"

Saffron nodded as he sank down on his bed. "That's what they've just told me. Isn't that what you expected? Nasty dangerous postings?"

The Londoner was clearly not pleased by his own prophetic pessimism. "I didn't think they'd come as quickly as this. Damn it, we've only been in the camp four days."

Saffron shrugged. "If our reputation's gone before us, they probably want to get rid of us quickly."

"But that means we might be face to face with the Japs in a week or two!"

"It's possible," Saffron admitted.

The Londoner scowled. "You'd like that, wouldn't you?"

"Not particularly. But it's what I'm in the RAF for. Not to sit on my backside drinking cups of char all day long."

"You've got a death wish, Saffron. Or something else seriously wrong with you."

Saffron grinned. "What else?"

"What do they call people who're keen on action and fighting? Psychopaths. Maybe if there wasn't a war you'd be a member of a razor gang. Or beating up old ladies. You'd never be a peaceful, harmless member of society."

"Like you?" Saffron suggested.

"That's right."

"But I thought you wanted to overthrow society and start a Communist state."

"I do. But it'll be done peacefully."

"How? Like they did it in Russia?"

Bickers scowled. "That was only because the ruling classes wouldn't give way."

"You think they will in England?"

"They'd better, mate, if they know what's good for them."

Saffron grinned. "What will you do if they don't know? Slap their wrists?"

Recognising the trap he was falling into, Bickers grew irritable. "It must be terrible to be as brainwashed as you, Saffron. Cannon fodder for the aristocrats. That's what you are, you know. A capitalistic lackey. Doesn't it ever trouble you?"

Before Saffron could reply, a fresh-faced youngster entered the billet and approached his bed. "Have you seen Taylor, sergeant?"

Saffron sat up. "Hello, Merrow. No, I haven't. Why?"

"His posting's just come through. I've been asked to tell you."

Bickers got his question in first. "Where are they sending him?"

"Somewhere in Burma, corporal."

The Londoner gave a start and then turned to Saffron. "So it's true. We are getting punishment postings. The bastards!"

Merrow looked alarmed. "Punishment postings! They wouldn't do that to us, would they, sergeant?"

Saffron frowned. "Of course not."

"But Kendricks got a bad one yesterday."

"That was just coincidence," Saffron said, throwing a dark glance at the Londoner. "The corporal was only joking."

Merrow could not hide his fear. "You're not just saying that, sergeant? You don't think they have got it against us?"

"No, Merrow. Records are too dim and stupid for that. You'll probably find the next posting goes to Delhi or Lahore. Stop worrying about it."

Merrow hesitated. Then, looking far from convinced, he nodded and moved down the billet. When he was out of earshot, Saffron rounded on Bickers. "For God's sake, Ken.

Have you forgotten how scared that kid was when he knew we were coming out here?"

For once Bickers looked ashamed. "Sorry. I'd forgotten."

"How the hell could you forget a thing like that?"

Bickers was only too aware why Saffron was angry. Merrow, whose violin Cornwall had broken in Kenya and so caused the fight between him and Saffron, had been a wireless operator manning a D/F station during the Japanese invasion of Assam. Cut off and isolated by the invasion, he and another young colleague had been forced to forage for food every night while knowing that capture would mean almost certain death. To avoid such a fate again, Merrow had volunteered for aircrew but had proved unsuitable material. Confessing his reasons for volunteering to an unsympathetic officer, Merrow had been sent on the punishment draft. Fearing all along he might suffer a similar posting, the young man was now clearly believing his fears were justified.

"Sorry," Bickers muttered again. "I was shaken by Taylor's posting. It looks as if I was right and we all are being sent to the most dangerous places."

While Saffron thought it was likely, he felt it wiser to deny it. "We've only had three postings out of forty so far. Anyway, I can't see Records holding a grudge against us. The war's too big for that."

Bickers' laugh was cynical. "They didn't forget about us after we refused to sail on that leaking old tub, the *Multan*, even although we were proven right and she did sink. The vindictive bastards don't forget a missed salute, Saffron."

In the days that followed, Saffron had to admit that Bickers seemed to be right. Posting after posting came through and every one of them sent a member of the draft to a particularly dangerous sector of the war. With each posting, Bicker's pessimism grew. "Wait until ours comes, mate. It's going to be a real humdinger. Maybe New Guinea. Or one of those Pacific islands like Okinhawa or Imo Jima."

Busy writing a letter, Saffron was preoccupied. "Never

mind. At least we'll be shut of Cornwall and his gang. Isn't that something to look forward to?"

Bickers stared. "If you mean would I prefer hordes of bloodthirsty Japs to Cornwall the answer's no." The Londoner's tone changed as Saffron continued writing. "You're not putting in another of those aircrew applications, are you?"

As Saffron nodded, Bickers made a gesture of contempt. "You're wasting your time. For one thing you've been out too long. Then you're in the Far East where nobody gets anything but a kick up the arse."

"Merrow got sent back for training. And I'm a fully qualified wireless operator/air gunner with hundreds of hours behind me."

"Yes but you were wounded, weren't you? They've got thousands of fit men back there."

"I'm fully fit again. And I don't need training."

"So what? You've put in dozens of applications and where has it got you?"

Saffron, whose burning desire was to fly on operations again, gave the Londoner a look of dislike. "You'd hate it if they accepted my applications, wouldn't you? They you'd have no one to moan to or get you out of trouble."

Bickers sniffed. "That works both ways, mate, Who's the jonah who's always dropping me into it? You've got a short memory, Saffron."

"Not that short," Saffron said grimly. "I've saved you more times than you've had hot dinners, and you know it. You'll realize how lucky you've been when you have to carry the can yourself."

Bickers looked smug. "That won't happen, Saffron. You're wasting your time with those applications."

His smugness drove Saffron into malice. "I'm not thinking about my applications. So far, because we've been on the same draft, we're kept together. But what's going to happen now that our individual postings are coming through?"

A duster could not have wiped the smugness off Bicker's

face more thouroughly. "You've never said anything about this before."

"Haven't I? I thought it was obvious."

The Londoner looked both shocked and hurt. "You could at least show some regret, couldn't you?"

Saffron returned to his letter again. "If it happens, I will. That's a promise."

"Sod," Bickers muttered.

A long silence followed while the Yorkshireman finished his letter and rose. Bicker's eyes followed him to the billet entrance. Then the Londoner could hold out no longer. "Is it really likely we'll be split up?" he muttered.

Saffron turned, hiding his amusement with an effort. "What's your problem? A self-contained character like you always gets by. So what's your worry?"

Bickers gave a scowl of resentment. "I'm not worried. I was just asking if you really believe they'll split us up, that's all."

Smiling now, Saffron returned to his bed and tossed a cigarette at the frowning Londoner. "We have to face it might happen. But we've been lucky so far. Let's hope we're lucky again."

Bickers drew deeply on his cigarette before his reluctant admission. "You're often a pain in the bum, Saffron, but I think I'd miss you."

Knowing he was never likely to receive such an accolade again, Saffron clapped him across the shoulders. "I'd miss you too, you old sod. Now forget about the war for the afternoon. Get your swimming trunks and towel out while I drop this letter into the SWO's office. Then let's go to Breach Candy for a swim."

In spite of Saffron's efforts to cheer up Morrow, the postings that came in during the following week gave the lie to his optimism. As man after man of his draft reported to the SWO's office to be given his orders and railway ticket, it became clear that Records had not forgotten their various transgressions and certainly not forgiven them. When Merrow was sent to a squadron operating near Cox's Bazaar, Bickers' belief that he and Saffron were destined for a fate worse than death became a conviction. "They're sadists, Saffron. Turning the strings tighter by keeping us until the last."

"There's some way to go yet," Saffron pointed out. "Cornwall and Wilkinson are still here even if Taylor and MacMorron have gone."

"Doesn't that prove my point?" the Londoner said. "Records know they're scum and so they're getting the same treatment as us."

Bickers' belief, bizarre though it was, seemed justified when a week later everyone from the draft but the two NCOs, Cornwall and Wilkinson had been posted. On the Monday Saffron was called into the SWO's office. When he returned to the billet, Bickers was at the entrance waiting for him. "Who is it this time, Saffron? Cornwall, Wilkinson or us?"

Saffron lit a cigarette before answering the Londoner's anxious question. Reading the signs, Bickers flinched. "It's us, isn't it?"

Saffron exhaled smoke. "It's all four of us. You and me and Cornwall and Wilkinson."

Bickers blanched. "They're going with us! That's terrible, Saffron. Terrible."

Saffron nodded. "It's not what I'd have wished, that's for sure."

Bickers' pallor grew as the implications sank in. "It must be a bad posting if those sods are going too. Where is it, Saffron?"

"Shaman," Saffron told him.

Bickers' eyes were full of fanatical Japanese and Samurai swordsmen screaming for his life. "What part of Burma is that?"

"It isn't in Burma."

"Then where is it? Japan?"

"Don't be a clot. It's up on the North West frontier."

Some news is too unexpected to register immediately.

37

Bickers blinked. "North West frontier? Of what country?"

"India, you idiot."

Bickers' mouth dropped open. "But that's miles and miles from the Japanese front."

"That's right. A thousand miles."

"A thousand miles," Bickers repeated. There was still disbelief in his eyes. "But why are we going there, Saffron?"

Saffron waved him to sit down. "If you stop asking questions, I'll tell you."

Still looking astonished, the Londoner sank down on the edge of his bed. "I can't believe this, Saffron. I was sure it was going to be Burma or worse."

"Don't get too happy," Saffron told him. "It's not going to be a bed of roses. You did take a short course on gas warfare after your armourer's course, didn't you?"

"Yes. Why?"

"That's the reason you're going up to Shaman with me. It seems that a few weeks ago three British swaddies were found dead in a fox hole near the Jap lines and after examination it was found they'd been killed by a grenade filled with hydrocyanic acid gas. It's started a panic right through SEAC that the Japs will soon be using poison gas on a big scale, which means all our armourers, RAF and Army, need urgent training in its use. So, because I'm a senior armament instructor and because we've both had courses on gas warfare, we're being sent up to Shaman to open a gas school." Seeing Bickers' expression, Saffron turned caustic. "I suppose this'll make you happy? A thousand miles from where the action is."

Bickers' relief was there for all to see. "Too true I'm happy. I'm no bloody hero, mate. But why are Cornwall and Wilkinson going with us?"

"God knows. Maybe they're short of drivers up there. Maybe they're going to drive our poison gas around. I don't know."

Bickers frowned. "Poison gas?"

"Of course. We're not just going to talk about gas up there.

They're going to send us the real stuff, mustard gas, phosgene, the lot. Some of it in bombs."

"You're not serious? You can't be."

"That's what the SWO said. I told you it isn't going to be all beer and skittles."

"Live gas," Bickers muttered. "I've never handled live gas before. Have you?"

Saffron nodded. "Yes. Mustard gas. But don't worry. It's safe enough if you take the right precautions."

Bickers was trying to assess the pros and cons of the situation. "I suppose in the main it is good news?"

Saffron pulled a face. "Providing you can take Cornwall, Wilkinson, and live poison gas, you ought to be happy. But it's not what I wanted."

With fanatical Japanese warriors fading from his eyes, Bickers decided the dice had not fallen too badly for him after all. "Never mind, mate. You can earn your medals fighting Cornwall and Wilkinson. They ought to be worth a gong or two."

Seeing the Yorkshireman's irritation, Bickers tried to smooth ruffled feathers. "We are still together, mate. That's no small thing, is it?"

Saffron stubbed out his cigarette. "No, I suppose not." He motioned at Bickers' untidy bed space. "You'd better start packing your things. We're off at 07.00 hours tomorrow and I don't want you moaning you're not ready."

Growing more convinced by the moment that fate had been kind to him, Bickers took no offence. Humming, totally unaware and unprepared of what lay ahead, he joined Saffron in preparing for their departure on the morrow.

Chapter Six

Bickers' sigh of relief came from the heart as he heaved his kit into the carriage. "Thank God for inefficiency,

Saffron. Another two days with those sods would have seen me off."

Saffron grinned as he picked up his own kit from the platform. "You take it too seriously."

"Seriously? There wasn't a minute when I didn't think you and Cornwall were going to start knocking hell out of one another again. Apart from that, what about Wilkinson's breath? If he'd breathed on me just once more I'd have died."

Saffron threw his own kit into the compartment. "Well, it's over now. You can relax and read those lurid paperbacks of yours in peace."

Bickers, ever the pessimist, was not fully convinced of his good fortune. "Don't forget we still have to change at Hyderabad and Rohri. What if they stick us back in the same compartment again?"

Saffron shrugged. "At least we'll have had one quiet day." Then, seeing Bickers' expression, he clapped the Londoner's shoulder. "Stop worrying about it. If they try to put us back together, I'll spin them some yarn that the RAF doesn't allow NCOs and men to travel together. I don't say they'll believe it but I'll try."

Half an hour later the journey began again. Soon the fertile plains of India were left behind and the train plunged into the Sind desert. With dust getting into the carriages the heat was intense. Bickers fanned himself. "Let's hope it isn't this hot in Shaman or I'll melt away."

Saffron shook his head. "It won't be too bad at this time of the year. Shaman's 6000 feet up. But it gets blazing hot in the summer."

Bickers eyed him suspiciously. "How do you know this?"

"Because I've bothered to find out." Saffron fished in his pack and pulled out a thin book. "Here you are. All about Shaman."

Bickers gave it a cursory look, then gave a start. "It mentions earthquakes. What sort of earthquakes?"

Saffron grinned. "Just ordinary earthquakes. Like the

one in 1935 that killed over 20,000 people and diverted an entire river."

Bickers looked shaken. "20,000 people!"

"That's right. Shaman's on a fault in the earth's crust that runs down from the Himalayas. Apparently they have earthquakes every spring and autumn."

Bickers looked even more shaken. "Isn't it going to be dangerous having a gas school there?"

Saffron shrugged. "It won't be as dangerous as slogging it out with the Japs in Imphal or Burma."

The comparison brought little comfort to the Londoner. "It's plain stupid sending live poison gas to a place that has earthquakes. Doesn't anyone in the Services ever put two and two together?"

Saffron laughed. "How long have you been in the RAF?"

The long journey wore on. The Sind Desert was crossed at last and a curious section of mountains appeared. Reddish in colour, without a vestige of vegetation, they looked for all the world like a row of massive dominoes pushed over by some giant hand. Here and there tiny red buildings could be seen on their summits. "Old forts," Saffron told Bickers. "Once manned by the British Army."

Bickers peered up at them and shuddered. "What the hell did the poor bastards do with themselves?"

"Just sweat it out, I suppose, until they were relieved."

The train was climbing now, the pounding of its pistons more laboured. A second engine was added, and then a third. Tunnels began to block out the sunlight, some for a few seconds, others for minutes. As the train swept from them, huge arid valleys were seen below, some shimmering white from the salt that ancient seas had deposited before their retreat. The sight of one valley, so huge it took the train over two hours to circumnavigate it, brought a rueful comment from Bickers. "Where the hell are they sending us, Saffron? To the end of the world?"

They reached Shaman the following day. For three hours the train, reduced to a centipede by the vastness of the terrain around it, had been crawling along the fringe of a barren valley flanked by high mountains. Then the northern mountains made a sharp right angle turn and Saffron noticed a white smear on the distant surface of the valley. He pointed it out to Bickers. "That must be Shaman."

Bickers' long face mirrored his dismay. "If you're right, it is the end of the world."

Saffron was proven right two hours later when the train finally came to a halt in Shaman station. With a choice between horse drawn tongas and old taxis, Saffron turned to Bickers. "What do you think? Can we afford a taxi?"

Bickers was staring up and down the street outside the station. "I don't see Cornwall and Wilkinson anywhere."

"Good. Maybe they missed a connection." As a rickety old taxi drew up before them, Saffron gave Bickers a push. "Come on. Let's do it the easy way for a change."

The driver, a character of indeterminate age, gave them a toothless grin. "Where to, sahibs?. The college?"

Bickers glanced at Saffron. "College?"

The Yorkshireman nodded. "Didn't I tell you? There's a military college here?"

"Here? You must be kidding."

"No, it's true. Or so the book says."

Bickers gave a groan. "That means the place will be full of pukka sahibs."

Saffron turned back to the driver. "No. We want the camp, please."

Thirty seconds later the ancient taxi shot out into the narrow streets like a Ferrari commencing the Monaco Grand Prix. As pedestrians leapt for their lives Saffron leaned forward and tapped the driver's shoulder. "Take it easy. We don't want to kill anyone on our first day here."

The toothless one clearly thought it was a great joke because if anything he stepped on the gas. As cursing Indians leapt left and right, he glanced back. "You will like it here, sahibs. Many things can be done in Shaman."

Saffron had no time to answer as the taxi roared past a

cluster of bicycles, only to stop as a khaki-clad policeman shout out a hand to allow a bullock and cart to cross the road. As the taxi shot forward again, the driver chuckled. "My brakes are very good, yes?"

Bickers, who had let out a howl, was now rubbing a grazed knee. "We've got a bloody lunatic here, Saffron."

A chuckle floated back, then another question. "Which camp, sahibs? The airmen's or the Ghurkas?"

"The airmen's," Saffron told him.

Instantly the taxi swung to the right, forcing a pedestrian to jump for his life. Unperturbed, the toothless one glanced back. "The airmen's camp is called Long Barracks, sahibs. It is built on the old river bed."

By this time both NCOs had resigned themselves to injury or death. "What do you mean – old river bed," Saffron shouted over the asthmatic roar of the engine.

"It was the big earthquake, sahib. It sent the river far away. Once we grew fruit here. Now there is only you, the military people."

With the old town left behind, the taxi was roaring past a square of small bungalows set out in geometrical symmetry. Bickers leaned forward. "Who lives in these bungalows?"

"Those are Army quarters, sahib. For memsahibs and old officers who do not fight wars any more."

Bickers turned to Saffron. "You hear that, Saffron? A cantonment full of old retired majors and colonels."

Saffron laughed at the Londoner's expression. "So what?"

"So what? It was you who warned me about Colonel Blimps. Think what'll be like here if the place is full of the bastards."

Rows of dilapidated shacks followed, then a sun-burned football field flashed past, and finally the taxi screamed to a halt in front of a huge steel meshed gate. "Long Barracks, sahibs. All present and correct."

Saffron heaved out his kit, then turned to the grinning driver. "How much?"

"Ten rupees, sahib."

"What?"

"Ten rupees, sahib, for getting you here safe and sound."

"Safe and sound? You damn nearly killed us. And you haven't come more than two miles. Three rupees."

If anything the driver's smile grew. "Seven rupees, sahib."

"Four rupees."

"Six rupees."

"Five rupees and not a penny more."

The toothless one's shoulders rose. "My three wives and children will starve, sahib. How can you be so unkind?"

"Three wives? You shouldn't be so greedy," Saffron told him. "Here's five rupees."

The driver took them, then lifted a hand in salute. "May Allah bless you, young sir."

"He still conned you," Bickers said as the taxi shot off in a cloud of blue smoke.

Saffron, who felt it was true, gave the Londoner a glare. "I notice you didn't offer to handle him."

"You didn't give me a chance, did you? I'd have done a better job than that. Five rupees was bloody ridiculous for a journey that length."

At that moment a grinning sentry positioned at the other side of the huge gate, swung it open. "Are you two coming in or staying out all day arguing?"

The two NCOs glared at one another and then, somewhat shamefacedly, picked up their kit and entered Long Barracks.

Chapter Seven

The small, ginger-haired Warrant Officer opened the office door and nodded at the two NCOs waiting on the parade ground outside. "All right. You can come inside now and meet Squadron Leader Prentice."

The two men entered the small office. A plump, florid-faced

officer with a balding head was seated at a desk with two sets of documents lying before him. A cheery-faced young corporal was standing behind him. As the Warrant Officer led the two NCOs inside, Prentice's somewhat protruding eyes gazed at the two men curiously as their names were called out. "Sergeant Saffron and Corporal Bickers, sir."

Prentice nodded. "Thank you, Warrant Officer McGrew." He acknowledged the salutes the two men gave him with a flip of a pudgy hand. "So you're our two new postings. I understand you're both from Worli, the transit camp."

When both men nodded, McGrew's sharp voice rose a full tone. "Say 'yes sir' when you answer an officer!"

Saffron gave him a look before turning back to the squadron leader. "Yes, sir. We left there four days ago."

Prentice looked both curious and quizzical. "Your documents say you were both sent out here on a delinquent draft. Yet there's no mention of any charge brought up against you. Can you explain that?"

Seeing Bickers give a start of alarm, Saffron spoke for him. "There wasn't any charge, sir. As we were being posted to SEAC we were simply sent out with the draft. There was no other connection."

Prentice looked amused now. "You mean you hadn't put up a black yourselves, like sinking the *Royal Oak* or bumping off an air marshal?"

Saffron smiled. "No, sir. Nothing like that."

Prentice nodded at the brevet on Saffron's tunic. "Why are you wearing that wireless operator/air gunner badge. Were you once a gunner?"

Saffron told him the reason, not failing to seize the opportunity offered him. "I want to get back on flying operations as soon as possible, sir. So if you don't mind I'd like to . . ."

Realising where the conversation was leading, McGrew interrupted sharply. "Answer the officer's questions, sergeant, and no more. He doesn't want to know what you'd like to do."

You are an officious little twit, Saffron was thinking. Ignoring the rebuke, he addressed Prentice again. "I'm very keen to fly again, sir. Flying is why I joined the RAF."

There was a choking sound from McGrew but Prentice looked only amused. "I'm sure it was, sergeant, but at the moment we need you for other things." He glanced down at the documents again. "I see you are also a Senior Armament Instructor. And you gained that qualification when you were only a corporal. How did that happen? I thought it was only officers who were given that course."

"I took the SAI course in South Africa," Saffron told him. "There wasn't any promotion over there."

"I also see that your marks were over 90%. Those are very high marks. It's very commendable, sergeant."

While Prentice had been announcing these qualifications, Saffron had noticed him give an amused, almost mocking glance at McGrew, giving the Yorkshireman the feeling his SAI course was being used as a weapon against the grim-faced McGrew. "Thank you, sir."

Prentice nodded and turned his attention to Bickers. "I see you are a junior armament instructor, corporal. I didn't think gas warfare was included on that course. So when did you take it?"

Bickers glanced at Saffron. "I took it along with Sergeant Saffron in South Africa, sir. We were stationed at the same airfield."

Prentice's eyes ran down the Londoner's gangling frame. "And you were also included in the same draft. What was your crime, corporal? Did you clip a warrant officer's ears or just steal a Spitfire?"

Bickers gave a weak smile. "I didn't do anything either, sir. We were just put in charge of the draft."

"It must have been quite a task, corporal. How did they react when you had that trouble in the Indian Ocean?"

Seeing Bickers was about the answer, Saffron stepped in quickly. "We can't talk about that, sir. I'm sorry but we can't."

It was all too much for the simmering McGrew. "Keep quiet, sergeant. The squadron leader wasn't talking to you."

Saffron swung round. "We're both on oath to say nothing about that affair. So we can't answer any questions about it."

McGrew had small hairless eyes which the hot sun had done nothing to improve. They narrowed at Saffron's protest. "You'd better watch that tongue of yours, sergeant. It's too loose for my liking."

Saffron's old dislike of mindless authority that had caused him so much trouble in the past was in spate again. "It's not loose enough to break an oath, sir. I don't think you should encourage us to break it."

From the deep breath and the shudder McGrew gave, Saffron knew he was a man with a violent temper. "Are you criticising the squadron leader for asking the question, sergeant?"

"I'm not criticising anybody, sir I'm simply pointing out that Corporal Bickers and I took an oath and we intend keeping it."

Before McGrew could reply, Prentice, who seemed to be enjoying the altercation, waved an amused hand. "He's right, McGrew. He's just obeying orders. I shouldn't have asked the question in the first place."

The cartilaginous sound of McGrew's swallow could be heard right across the office. His reply sounded as if it had come out of a meat grinder. "If you say so, sir."

Prentice turned back to Saffron. "As you know, your job will be to teach the mysteries of gas warfare to Army and RAF armourers. As we can't keep live gas in Long Barracks, your quarters will be up on Hill camp. However, as we're not ready for you yet, you'll billet down here for the time being. You can also have the rest of the day off to sort yourselves out."

As both NCOs thanked him, Prentice turned and waved forward the cheery-faced corporal. "Show them their billet, Jackson, and where the facilities are. All right, both of you, you can dismiss now."

Both NCOs saluted and then followed the young corporal outside. As he passed McGrew Saffron felt as if two red hot pokers were boring into his back. Outside on the dusty parade ground, Bickers could hold himself in check no longer. "You've done it again, haven't you? Hell and damnation, you've done it again."

Saffron frowned. "Done what?"

Bickers was almost choking himself with rage. "Don't tell me you don't know. You did it in South Africa and had that bastard Kruger on our backs for the next three months. And now you've done it here. On our first day, just as you did in South Africa. What's the matter with you? Do you hate warrant officers? Or isn't there any way you can keep out of trouble?"

Saffron frowned. "I only pointed out that we had to keep our oath."

"Only! You as good as told McGrew to get stuffed, and right in front of Prentice. Didn't you see what it did to him? He wanted to tear you apart."

Saffron shrugged. "Don't blame me. He was picking on me from the beginning. I don't know why but he was."

"I know why." The words came from the young corporal who both men had almost forgotten in their argument. Saffron turned to him. "Go on. Why?"

Jackson was grinning. "McGrew wasn't happy earlier on when your documents came through and he saw you were an SAI. I know it because I heard Prentice teasing him about it."

"Why should Prentice do that?" Saffron asked.

Jackson glanced back at the receding office block before replying. "Because McGrew, like Prentice, hasn't had an SAI course. They've never got on too well because Prentice took his armament course nearly twenty years ago and so McGrew has lorded it over Prentice when decisions have had to be made. But you'll change all that. You'll have the technical edge over McGrew and I think Prentice is tickled pink about it."

Saffron looked dismayed. "So that's it."

Bickers, whose attack on Saffron had been checked by the corporal's revelation, was looking puzzled. "What's the matter? Won't it help if you have the edge on McGrew?"

"Help? You don't know much about men, do you? He'll feel it's an insult to his rank if I have to take decisions he can't make. He'll hate it."

Nothing more was needed to fire Bickers' resentment again. "So I was right. He will be down on you like a ton of bricks. And down on me too because I'm stuck with you."

"Oh, shut up," Saffron muttered.

But there was no stopping Bickers now. "It's always the same. I get it in the neck because of you. You're a jonah, Saffron. I've said it before and I was right. You draw trouble like a bloody light draws insects. They ought to put away people like you."

"Will you shut up?" Saffron hissed.

"No, I won't shut up. I keep my nose clean but still get dropped in it because of you. It's all so bloody unfair."

Saffron gave him a glare, then went trudging on across the parade ground. Left alone with Jackson, Bickers cast an uneasy glance back at the office block and then at the grinning corporal. "Do you really think McGrew will pick on us?"

Jackson nodded. "From the way he acted I think it's likely."

Bickers winced then gave the youngster a shove. "Then get us to our billet and out of sight before the bastard decides to start things up right away."

Bickers raised an arm and brushed his face. The fly rose a few inches and then settled on the Londoner's nose again. Bickers swung his arm once more. This time the fly buzzed loudly and landed on his ear. Cursing, the Londoner lifted his head. "Don't they use DDT in this place?"

Saffron, half asleep on the bed alongside him, gave a grunt. "What did you say?"

"I asked if they used DDT here. The bastard flies are driving me half crazy."

"Go to sleep," Saffron muttered.

There was silence but only for a minute. "I thought you said it would be cooler here. I'm as hot as I was down in Bombay."

When there was no reply Bickers tried again. "What's happened to Cornwall and Wilkinson? There hasn't been a sign of 'em since we got here. Do you think they're beating up the town?"

Saffron's reply was short and to the point. "Probably."

Bickers took another swing at the fly. "Thank God we weren't put in charge of 'em." Lifting his head, the Londoner gazed down the billet at the two empty beds positioned along it. "You don't think McGrew will put 'em in here, do you? Christ, that would be the end."

Saffron's drowsy reply was irritable. "Stop talking a load of crap. This is an NCOs' billet."

"Let's hope McGrew keeps it that way," Bickers muttered. As the drone of the fly was heard again, his tone changed. "Why is it so quiet in this camp? I noticed it when we left Prentice's office. Do you think everyone's at lectures?"

There was the sudden creak of wooden bed supports as Saffron sat upright. "Of course they're at lectures. I told you armament isn't the only thing taught here. What the hell's the matter with you? You said you wanted a sleep. So why don't you go to sleep?"

"I can't sleep. I keep on thinking about McGrew. Do you really think he'll have it in for us?"

"I don't know. And right now I don't care. Tomorrow's another day."

"It's all right for you, Saffron. But I can't put things out of my mind like you can. If Jackson is right, McGrew's going to be in charge of us. So, if he really is bloody-minded, he could make our lives a misery."

"Stop feeling so sorry for yourself. If he puts his knife in anyone, it'll be me. I'm the SAI, not you."

Bickers' mutter suggested he drew little comfort from that reminder. As a silence fell, Saffron dropped back on his bed. But a minute later the Londoner's voice came again. "Do you ever get lonely, Saffron?"

"What?"

"Do you ever get lonely? You know, miss your family and friends."

Saffron stared at him. "I suppose we all do sometimes. Why?"

"I know I do. That's why I was so glad when they posted us together again."

"I thought I was a jonah and you were tired of being stuck with me?"

"I was just upset, Saffron. I didn't want the same sort of time we had under Kruger back in South Africa."

Although Saffron felt Bickers' fears were justified, he felt it kinder not to press the point home at that moment. "I knew that. So you're forgiven."

There was a sniff, another silence, and then a deep sigh. "There's another thing. I miss women."

Saffron grinned. "That sounds more like you."

"No, I don't just mean that. I miss looking at them and talking to them. I'm sick of spending my life just with men. Haven't you ever had that feeling?"

"Most of the time. So what?"

"This isn't a natural life for young men, Saffron. We're like bloody hermits who've sworn the oath. If the war lasts much longer we'll be too old to do anything but kiss 'em on the cheek or pat 'em on the head. We're being cheated of our birthright, mate."

Saffron laughed. "I think you're exaggerating a little, but I know what you mean."

"It's not funny, Saffron. I'm up to the crop with this bloody war."

Making a quick decision, Saffron swung his legs to the floor. "You're in a bad way, mush. Climb out of your pit and put your shorts on."

Bickers groaned. "What for?"

"Lying there isn't doing you any good. You need a tonic."

Bickers blinked at him. "What kind of tonic?"

"You'll see in a minute. Come on."

Chapter Eight

Up on the rocky hilltop there was a slight breeze. Bickers accepted it gratefully. "That's better. I thought I was going to die climbing up here."

"Don't you feel better?" Saffron asked. "It's no use lying in your pit and moaning when you get the blues. Good healthy exercise is the answer."

"You never told me we were going to do something as daft as this," the Londoner grumbled. "These hills are nearly as high as bloody mountains."

Saffron grinned. "Never mind. Look at the view you get."

The two men, stripped to the waist, were standing on top of one of the hills that surrounded the RAF base and the view was vast and spectacular. To their left Shaman was a white smear in the dun brown spread of the valley. Beyond it a huge range of mountains towered into the dazzling sky. Ahead, more distant mountains rose up from the convoluted valley. Saffron pointed at them. "According to our book, that's Afghanistan. You can't go in there without special permission or they shoot you."

Bickers gave a grunt. "Friendly types. Who are they? Pathans?"

"I think some are although the book says Pathans are a number of nomadic tribes who live in this area. You saw some as we drove in from the station. They were the ones with the turbans and fierce eyes. The book says they have a reputation for cruelty."

Bickers grunted again. "They've sent us to a happy place. Is anyone pleasant around here?"

Saffron made no reply. His eyes had moved to a huge range of mountains that barred passage to the east. He pointed them out. "If I'm reading the map right, those are the Hindu Kush mountains. They run on to the Himalayas and eventually to China." Saffron took in the entire scene again, awesome in its vastness, and took a deep breath of pleasure. "Isn't it marvellous? Doesn't it do something to you?"

Bickers shook his head. "All it does is make me feel I'm at the end of the world. Look at it. As barren as the moon." He pointed down the rocky hillside. "The camp looks out of place here. Too small and scared among all these mountains."

Gazing down Saffron had to agree with the Londoner. The camp's workshops, offices, and billets looked smaller than matchboxes against the hills and mountains and almost as fragile. As his eyes explored it, both men heard the sound of a far off hooter. A moment later they saw tiny antlike figures pouring out of the workshops. Saffron glanced at Bickers. "There are your camp trainees. Taking their afternoon break and having their char."

While Bickers was watching the distant scene, Saffron's eyes moved along a thread of road that ran from Long Barracks up a plateau to the east where a a few, dun-coloured huts could be seen. Miles beyond the huts was a sprawl of tiny tents. He pointed both establishments out to Bickers. "It must be Hill Camp on the plateau. The tents to the north must be the Ghurkas' training camp."

Bickers gave a start. "Hill Camp? Isn't that where Prentice is sending us?"

Saffron nodded. "That's what he said."

The Londoner was showing disbelief. "They can't billet us there, Saffron. It must be three or four miles from the main camp. And it isn't used. You can see it isn't. What the hell would we do there?"

Saffron gave a mocking smile. "Teach gas warfare, I suppose."

Bickers was looking aghast now. "What would we do at nights? Without transport we couldn't go anywhere. They can't stick us out there, Saffron. It would be like burying us alive."

"There you go again. Looking on the black side. Perhaps they'll give us transport."

"What? McGrew? He'll probably take our boots from us so we can't walk away from the bloody place."

Saffron glanced behind him. Huge sun-bleached rocks littered the hill crest. Moving towards one that retained his view of the awesome valley, he drew a packet of cigarettes from his shorts. "I'm not going to worry what might happen. I'm just going to enjoy being on top of the world." He held out the packet to Bickers. "Why don't you do the same?"

Shaking his head, Bickers slumped down beside him. "It's such a wild and empty place, Saffron. You forget I'm used to London and millions of people round me."

Saffron searched in his pocket for his lighter. "I'd have thought you'd find it a relief to get away from them."

"Relief! Crowds are company. A man feels lost without them."

Finding his lighter, Saffron pulled it out, only for his elbow to snag against the rock alongside him. As the lighter fell, it hit a stone on the ground and shot sideways. Bending down to pick it up, the Yorkshireman heard a faint metallic click and saw the dull glint of sunlight on metal some twenty paces to his left. The glint, coming from a gap between two rocks, disappeared almost immediately but the Yorkshireman needed no more warning. As he turned back to Bickers, he saw the Londoner was gazing at him curiously. "What's the matter?"

Saffron took a deep breath to steady himself, then lit his cigarette. "Don't look around and don't move. Just do everything I say."

Inevitably Bickers glanced over the Yorkshireman's shoulder. "Why? What's going on?"

Saffron hissed the words through his clenched teeth. "I said don't look round, you bloody fool. Someone's got a rifle trained on us. So look as normal as you can."

Bickers went very pale. "What do we do, Saffron?"

"You follow me and act as if you hadn't a care in the world. Got it?"

Bickers swallowed. "I'll try."

"Good man. Here we go." With a loud laugh Saffron rose from the rock and gazed down at the frightened Londoner. "I want to look at the view from the other side. You coming?"

Nodding, Bickers rose on shaking legs. "Yes, why not?"

Expecting a bullet at any moment and certain he would receive one if he gave the hidden rifleman the slightest idea he was detected, Saffron drew on his cigarette and began wandering across the crown of the hill, his intention being to interpose the huge rocks between himself and the hidden marksman. As he walked, he spoke to Bickers from the corner of his mouth. "Get ready to run downhill when I give the word."

Bickers opened his mouth to reply, and then closed it again. For both men the next twenty yards seemed like half a mile as their backs cringed in anticipation of a fatal bullet. Praying the rifleman had not shifted his position to keep them covered, Saffron waited until he judged there was enough cover behind him and then gave a shout. "That's it! Make for that hill shoulder!"

Throwing all dissemblance aside, both men went down the hillside like mountain goats, making for a ridge that should effectively cover them from rifle fire no matter where the rifleman positioned himself. Slipping, sliding, colliding with boulders, it took them forty endless seconds before they reached it and began scrabbling down its far side. Although Bickers was already in physical distress, Saffron kept him running for another half minute before signalling him to halt. "That'll do," he panted. "We're well clear now."

Drenched in sweat, Bickers could hardly get the words out. "Are you sure?"

"Yes. He can't get a sight on us now without following us down. And we're nearly out of range."

Although Bickers was bruised and winded, fear was urging him on. As he lurched forward again, Saffron grabbed his arm. "It's all right. We're safe now. You can take a rest."

With a last glance up the steep hill, Bickers collapsed in a heap and gasped for air. "God, Saffron, that was awful. Who was it?"

"I don't know. One of the local tribesman, I suppose."

"But why would he want to shoot us?"

"How do I know? Maybe he just doesn't like the British."

With the worst of the shock over but still shaking, Bickers was badly in need of someone to blame. "An hour ago I was lying comfortably in my bed. And then you drag me up here. Why did I come, Saffron? I should have known it could only lead to trouble."

Saffron, fully recovered now, gave a sarcastic laugh. "Comfortable? You were the original laughing boy back there. Moaning about everything. I brought you up here to take your mind off things. At least it's done that, hasn't it?"

"You mean it nearly got me killed? In the future just leave me with my problems, Saffron. At least they don't shoot at me."

Saffron threw him a cigarette. "Why don't you admit that rifleman has put everything in perspective? You weren't worrying about McGrew or about not having a woman when you were running for your life, were you?"

Bickers suddenly looked suspicious. "Just a minute. I never saw that rifleman back there."

"So what? You never see anything unless it's pushed right under your nose."

"Was he really there, Saffron? You weren't just kidding me? Because if you were I'll kill you. Look at me. I'm cut and bruised from head to foot."

Saffron gave an impatient frown. "Don't be a fool. There was a rifle pointing right at us. It's a miracle he didn't open fire and kill us both."

"But why would some tribesman want to shoot us? And if he did, why didn't he open fire before those rocks came between us?"

It was Saffron who was angry now. "I probably saved your life back there. Is this all the thanks I get?"

"Maybe you want me in your debt," Bickers said darkly. "I wouldn't put it past you."

Saffron climbed to his feet and pointed back up the hill. "All right, if you don't believe me, climb back up there and prove me wrong."

Bickers scowled. "You know damn well I'm too tired to do that."

"You mean you're too scared. You don't like being grateful to me, do you? So now you're safe you try to make out it didn't happen." Before the Londoner could reply, Saffron glanced back up the hill and then gave a violent start. "My God, I was wrong. He *is* coming after us."

Bickers gave a yelp and, ignoring his bruises, leapt to his feet and began running hell for leather down the hillside again. He had covered at least twenty yards before he heard Saffron laughing. Grabbing hold of a rock to steady himself, the Londoner glared back and gave a yell that came echoing back from the surrounding foothills. "You're a sod, Saffron. I always said it. You're a rotten cheating sod."

Jackson was sitting on one of the empty beds when the two NCOs entered their billet. He looked relieved as he jumped to his feet. "Where've you two been? I've looked everywhere for you."

Bickers jerked a thumb at Saffron as he sank wearily on his bed. "Ask him. It was his bloody idea."

"We climbed the hill behind the camp," Saffron explained. "Why? Does someone want us?"

"Yes. McGrew wants you in his office. He told me to look for you half an hour ago." The young corporal's eyes moved over the Yorkshireman's scratched body and earth-stained shorts. "What did you do? Roll all the way down?"

Saffron grinned. "Just about. Do you know what McGrew wants?"

"No, he didn't say. But he'll be bouncing up and down in his chair at having to wait so long."

Saffron glanced down at his stained shorts. "He'll have to bounce a few times more while we clean up. Otherwise he'll have something to moan about."

"Don't tell him you climbed that hill," Jackson said hurriedly. "Or you will be in trouble."

"Why? Hill climbing isn't a crime here, is it? And Prentice did tell us we had the rest of the day off."

"Haven't you read Station Orders?" the youngster asked.

"Give us a chance. We've only been in the camp a few hours." Then Saffron frowned. "What's on STOs about hill climbing."

"It's forbidden. The hills are too dangerous. They say there are hundreds of tribesmen up there."

Saffron cast a glance at Bickers who had stopped mopping his sweating torso with a towel and was listening. "You mean they live up there?"

Jackson shrugged. "I don't know whether they live there or just come and go. The story we're told is that they get particularly active when earthquakes are due so if a big one comes they can swarm down and loot the town. As the quakes are due twice a year, the camp has to stand by every spring and autumn."

Saffron glanced at Bickers again. "So the book was right." He turned back to Jackson. "Has there been a quake while you've been here?"

"Yes. There was one last autumn but it was only small."

"Tell me more about these tribesmen," Saffron said. "What happens if any of the camp personnel gets up among them?"

"It depends what he's carrying. It's said they'll kill a man for an empty cartridge case. Certainly they will if he is carrying a gun or wearing a cartridge belt. If they aren't sure they'll shoot him anyway."

Bickers looked shaken as Saffron indicated his own bare

torso. "So our lives were saved because we weren't wearing a tunic or shirt?"

Jackson gave a start. "You didn't run into any, did you?"

Saffron gave the shaken Bickers a triumphant grin. "We were practically looking down a tribesman's rifle barrel. But he didn't think we were worth a spent cartridge."

The youngster looked impressed. "You were lucky. But you won't be if McGrew hears about it. Did anyone see you going out there or coming back?"

"I don't know. But when we returned everyone was back in their workshops, so perhaps not."

Jackson nodded, then gave another anxious look at his watch. "You'd better hurry up and get over to McGrew. He'll give me a hell of a bollicking if you don't appear soon."

Saffron walked towards his bed and picked up a towel. "Don't worry. We'll tell him we've been looking round the camp and you couldn't find us. That should take care of things."

Left alone with Bickers, Saffron turned to him. "So I was only kidding, was I? I probably saved your life and all I got was abuse. Don't you think an apology is due?"

Bickers gave a snort of disgust. "Apology? When it was you who got me into it?" As Saffron flicked him playfully with the towel, the Londoner gave a yell. "Don't do that. I'm black and blue all over."

"Don't exaggerate. You've only got a few bumps and scratches."

Bickers looked apprehensive as he picked up his soap and towel again. "What do you think McGrew wants?"

Saffron had been wondering the same thing. "Perhaps the gas has arrived and he wants us to take care of it."

"I've got the feeling he's found a dirty job for us. Or why would he want to see us today?"

Saffron pushed him towards the washroom. "Stop being such a pessimist and mind you get those knobbily knees and elbows washed. Otherwise McGrew's going to guess you've been up the hills hunting down tribesmen."

Chapter Nine

With his ginger hair and sun-scorched face, McGrew looked as fiery as a hot ember as the two NCOs entered his office. "Where the hell have you two been?"

"We've been making ourselves familiar with the camp, sir," Saffron said. "Squadron Leader Prentice did say we could have the rest of the day off."

The reminder did nothing to improve McGrew's temper. "That didn't mean you had to vanish off the face of the earth. You haven't been in town without a pass, have you?"

"No, sir."

"Then where have you been?" McGrew's eyes moved from Saffron's scratched arms to Bickers' equally scratched knees and shot his question at the Londoner. "What have you been up to, corporal? You didn't have those scratches when I saw you earlier."

Bickers' large Adams' apple did a double roll. Then, about to glance at Saffron for help, he remembered the football pitch he had noticed just outside the camp. "We borrowed a football and had a kick about, sir."

McGrew's eyes moved up and down the Londoner's gangling frame. "You played football! In the afternoon heat! What are you, corporal? Nat Lofthouse in disguise?"

Bickers managed a weak smile. "No, sir. But I do enjoy kicking a football about now and then."

Although clearly unable to think what else the two NCOs could have been doing, McGrew was still showing disbelief. "You could have fooled me, corporal. But I'll remember it the next time we pick a team to play the Gurkhas." After making the promise sound like a threat, he turned his gaze on Saffron. "Are you a football fanatic too, sergeant?"

Saffron, who was thinking Bickers' lie was inspirational,

gave an enthusiastic nod. "Oh, yes, sir. I never missed a Leeds game before the war."

McGrew's lips curled. "Leeds? You could have had better taste, sergeant."

It was only then that Saffron realised that the man's appearance and accent suggested a Liverpool pedigree. Bickers however, less swift to make the tribal distinction, thought he saw a way to ingratiate himself. "I've told him that, sir. He ought to have followed real teams like Arsenal or Chelsea."

The effect was not what Bickers hoped. McGrew gave him a scowl. "I didn't call you two in here to talk about the merits of football teams, corporal. I've got an important job for you both tomorrow morning." His eyes turned back to Saffron. "It's something that should be right up your street, sergeant, with those high qualifications of yours."

"Really, sir," Saffron said.

"Yes, really. I don't know whether you know it yet but at one time there was a small airfield here. Its purpose was to keep the local tribesmen in order by bombing their villages if they stepped out of line. For that reason bombs had to be stored here. Only they couldn't be stored outside the camp because the same tribesmen might have stolen them to use against us in all kinds of unpleasant ways. So the bomb dump had to be sited within the camp."

Saffron gave a start. "A bomb dump inside the camp?"

McGrew grinned maliciously. "Does it disturb you, sergeant?"

Saffron was never one to hide his thoughts when asked for them. "With earthquakes around, it didn't sound a wise move to me. I'd have thought it much more sense to site it outside the camp and put guards on it."

"Is that what those qualifications of yours would have advised, sergeant?"

Saffron's dislike of the man was growing by the moment. "I'd say it's what common sense would have advised, sir."

McGrew looked amused. "So you don't have a high opinion of our predecessors, sergeant? Although you've only been here a few hours you feel you know more about local conditions than they did?"

The Warrant Officer's sarcasm was fast bringing out Saffron's Northern bloody-mindedness. "I suppose you're going to tell me a few guards wouldn't have stopped the tribesmen if they'd wanted the bombs."

"That's quite right, sergeant. They wouldn't."

"Then the dump should have been given as many guards as it needed. However many, it would still have been a better bet than siting it within the camp."

McGraw made a tut of regret. "It's a pity you weren't here all those years ago when the decision was made, sergeant. But as the RAF wasn't lucky enough to have your advice, the bomb dump was built in here and it's been here ever since."

Bickers made a tentative foray into the minefields of the conversation. "But the squadron took their bombs with them, didn't they, sir? They wouldn't leave them here."

"Wouldn't they, corporal?"

Bickers's eyes opened wide. "They're still here, sir?"

McGrew turned back to Saffron. "Somewhere along the line there was a lash up. Although most of the bombs were removed, a few were forgotten and left behind."

Saffron looked astonished. "Then why haven't they been removed or destroyed?"

"We only found this out a few days ago, sergeant. Don't forget we haven't been here that long ourselves."

"But surely the bomb dump should have been one of the first things to be examined. Particularly because of the danger of earthquakes."

Although his eyes were throwing red hot spears at Saffron, McGrew kept his temper well. "No one dreamed the squadron would have been so careless as to leave bombs behind. Had they been stored in the same store room as our ammunition and pyrotechnics they would have been found. As it is, the bombs have remained undetected until a few days ago."

Saffron was not going to let him off as lightly as this.

"The bomb dump should still have been checked, sir. Old bombs can exude and become highly sensitive."

McGrew took a deep steadying breath. "I'm fully aware of that, sergeant. And the culprits have been punished, so recrimination is just water under the bridge. Our job now is to check if these bombs are safe enough to be transported away. As you are the expert on such matters, I want you and Corporal Bickers to do this tomorrow morning."

By this time Saffron had expected nothing less. "Where do we get the key?"

"You can pick it up in the guardroom in the morning."

"I'd like it today, sir."

As Bickers gave a start, McGrew gazed at Saffron curiously. "Why today?"

Suspicion of McGrew's story brought out all of Saffron's Yorkshire bluntness. "If these bombs have been here as long as you say, they should have been processed the day they were found. So I don't think we should waste a minute in assessing their condition."

Watching McGrew's face, the breathless Bickers was expecting an explosion to equal the detonation of the bombs themselves. Instead the fiery warrant officer kept himself under control although his eyes promised the price of Saffron's insolence would be paid later. "It's your choice, sergeant. I'll phone the guardroom right away and tell them to have the keys ready for you."

Bickers' voice was bitter as the two men walked away from the office. "It's always the same, isn't it. You antagonise the bastards and drop me into the frying pan alongside you."

Saffron gave a grunt of disgust. "He was lying all along the line. I'll lay odds he's known about the bombs for months and neither he nor Prentice have had the guts to move them. So we get the job"

"You didn't exactly try to dodge it, did you? This was supposed to be our day off."

Saffron gave him a sharp glance. "This isn't something that

can be left for another day. Not when there are earthquakes about."

"They've left 'em all this time and nothing's happened," Bickers grumbled. "I can't see another day would make all that difference."

As they approached the guardroom, two figures carrying packs and kit bags were seen leaving it and making towards them. Saffron nodded in their direction. "Here are two friends of yours. Remember them?"

"Pity," Bickers grunted. "I was hoping they'd run into trouble and got themselves knifed or shot."

Saffron was noticing the two men's unsteady gait. "They've got themselves tanked up. I'm surprised the guardroom hasn't kept them inside."

Cornwall's loud shout as the two pairs of men drew nearer confirmed his assertion. "Look who's here! It's our favourite sergeant. Hello, sergeant. Why didn't you come into town with us?"

"What did you steal this time?" Saffron asked. "A cartload of booze?"

Cornwall's laugh boomed across the parade ground. "He's a funny man, is our sergeant." A huge hand, slapping Wilkinson's pack, nearly sent the half-drunken aircraftman on his face. "Isn't he, Ginger? A funny, funny man."

Saffron saw the noise had not gone unnoticed by the guardroom. An SP corporal had emerged from it and was gazing at them. Saffron pointed him out to Bickers. "Come on. Let the drunks find their own way to their billets."

Leaving Cornwall and Wilkinson jeering after them, the two NCOs approached the SP, a tall Canadian with a flattened nose. He nodded at the drunken couple. "You know those guys, sergeant?"

"Sadly, yes," Saffron said. "They were on the same train as us."

The SP grinned. "I ought to book 'em for being tanked up like that. But we don't like droppin' on guys too hard on their first day here."

Saffron was thinking it was a pity the same sentiment did not run through the Armament section. "We've come for the keys to the bomb dump. Have you got them?"

"So you're the guys? Yeah, I'll fetch 'em. Only you'll have to sign the books."

"What books?"

"One for the ammo store and the other for the bomb dump."

"Does that mean you have a record when you give the keys out? The date and who takes them?"

"Yeah. It's all in the books."

The Canadian returned a couple of minutes later with two large keys, two tattered exercise books, and a large torch, all of which he handed over to Saffron. "You'll need the torch. McGrew says the light's gone." He pointed to the older of the two books. "This one's for the bomb dump. As you see, it ain't used much."

Saffron opened it and saw it contained McGrew's signature with a date only five days old. Prior to that the last signature went back for years. Disappointed, he was about to sign the book when he gave a start. "There's a page torn out of here. Who did that?"

The SP took a closer look, then shrugged. "I dunno. Maybe it was done by someone from the old squadron."

Saffron gave Bickers a triumphant glance before signing the book and handing it back to the SP. "Where is the bomb dump?"

The Canadian pointed at the ten foot lane that ran round the perimeter of the camp. "Follow that past the recreation hall and the transport pool and you'll see it right ahead."

"Recreation hall?" Bickers enquired.

"Yeah, the old hangar. The guys have dances in there every few weeks."

Bickers' ears suddenly pricked up. "Dances? Who with?"

"Local dames. Why? You like shaking a leg?"

"Can anyone go to them?" the Londoner asked eagerly.

"Yeah, as far as I know." The SP cast a glance down Bicker's gangling body and grinned. "Mind you, you gotta have plenty of muscle to get a dance. There's usually a dozen guys to every dame."

Impervious to warnings where women were concerned, Bickers followed Saffron down the perimeter track. He jerked a thumb at the wooden hangar that loomed up alongside them. "It doesn't sound as bad as we thought, Saffron. Who'd have thought they'd have dances here?"

"I shouldn't get too excited," Saffron told him. "You haven't seen the women yet. They could all be memsahibs of the local Colonel Blimps."

Bickers refused to be discouraged. "At least they'll be women, Saffron. I'm starting to forget what a woman looks like."

They passed a small transport pool and then saw an earthen mound topped by two ventilators rising ahead of them. Saffron pointed to an entrance facing the lane. "That looks clean, so I'll bet that leads into the ammunition store. Let take a look round the back."

Bickers followed him to the other side of the mound. Here steps led down to an entrance covered in dust and pebbles. "This'll be it," Saffron said, trying one key and then the next. "Let's see what surprises McGrew has got for us."

The lock was stiff and required an effort by Saffron to turn it. The thick, wooden door was equally stiff and groaned loudly as the two men pushed it open. Faced by a rectangular patch of darkness, Saffron fumbled for an electric switch, only to discover the SP was right and the circuit was dead. Switching on the torch, he motioned Bickers to follow him inside.

It was like entering a long sealed tomb, Saffron thought. The air was musty with a slightly acid content that he could not identify. Shining the torch from side to side he tried to examine the vault but with his eyes accustomed to the brilliant sunlight outside, he found the torch beam too pale to penetrate the darkness. Bickers' complaint told he was having the same problem. "What's wrong with the torch, Saffron? Has the battery gone?"

"No, I think the torch is OK. It's just our eyes that have to adjust."

Saffron was proven right a few seconds later. First the floor appeared, a dusty surface of hard-packed earth. Then empty wooden racks could be seen on either side of the two men. Finally Saffron caught a glimpse of a low half-circular dome above. Lifting the torch, he saw the roof was made of small, irregular red bricks. As he moved forward Bickers gave a grunt of disgust. "It's bloody claustrophobic, Saffron. But I can't see any bombs."

As Saffron moved forward his torch picked up dark prints on the dust-covered floor. "McGrew's footprints," he told Bickers. Before the Londoner could make a comment, Saffron saw something glinting dully beneath one of the gallery shelves. Picking it up, he saw it was a spanner of unusual shape. He passed it on to Bickers. "Recognise that?"

The Londoner turned it over in his hand. "No. What is it?"

"You should know. It's the type of spanner used on bombs with central tubes. So at least some of the bombs they used must have been old types. Perhaps even last war bombs."

Bickers sounded sceptical. "The squadron wasn't here that long ago, was it?"

"I didn't say that. There were plenty of old type, central tube bombs left over when the war broke out in 1939. We dropped some of them ourselves when I was on operations."

Bickers motioned at the empty racks on either side. "Anyway, there don't seem to be any in here now. So what was McGrew getting on about?"

"He didn't send us in here for nothing," Saffron told him. "There must be a few around somewhere."

They found nothing in the four galleries on the right side of the store, making Saffron begin to wonder himself if McGrew had sent them on a fool's errand. It was only when he was examining the last gallery on the eastern side of the vault that his torch beam detected something black at its far end. A moment later his shout echoed back to Bickers who had given up the search and was waiting near the entrance. "Here they are! Six of the brutes."

Bickers moved along the gallery and saw Saffron shining his torch on a row of black, streamlined bodies. "112 pounders," the Yorkshireman told him. "And every one of them possibly dangerous."

Bickers approached cautiously. "Why were they left here?"

Saffron shone his torch on the nose of the nearest bomb. Around the orifice designed to take an exploder tube and a bomb pistol, there was a circular, multi-coloured crust. The effect was that of a huge fish with an open, diseased mouth. "Crystals," Saffron told the Londoner whose face had gone pale. "Sensitivity 17. That's why they weren't moved at the time. And why McGrew didn't move them when he and Prentice moved into the camp."

"But McGrew said he didn't know there were any bombs left until he found them this week."

"He's a bloody liar," Saffron said. "You saw there was a page torn out of the book. That was when he first found them. And he's kept quiet about it until we were posted here and he saw a way of getting himself off the hook."

"But why didn't Prentice do anything?"

"Perhaps McGrew has never told him. Or perhaps he's involved too. Who can say?"

The enormity of the discovery was coming home to Bickers now. "We can't move these ourselves, Saffron. The slightest scratch could set off those crystals and the entire dump would blow up. It's a job for bomb disposal experts."

"Don't be stupid. It comes in our brief." Saffron bent down and pointed at the wooden rack supporting the bombs. "Anyway, the job can't wait. Look at this frame."

Bending down, Bickers saw that two of the cross members that supported the frame were fractured. "That must have happened during one of the earthquakes," Saffron told him. "If there's another, it only needs those stays to give way and any or all six bombs could slide or fall down. You know what that would mean. Half the camp would be blown sky high."

Bickers was looking pale in the torchlight. "So what can we do?"

"What do you think? We have to make them harmless and then destroy them."

"But how? We can't move them or we could still blow the camp up."

Saffron took his arm. "The first thing is to see McGrew. I've things I want to say to him."

Chapter Ten

"It's disgraceful, sir. The person who allowed those bombs to stay in that dump ought to be court-martialled."

McGrew lit himself a cigarette. "You think so, sergeant?"

Saffron had no intention of sparing him. "Don't you, sir? Don't you think that anyone who's cowardly enough to risk the lives of every man on the camp deserves it?"

McGrew's cheeks went very pale. Watching the scene with trepidation in McGrew's office, Bickers could feel the man's fury at being unable to respond to Saffron's attack without betraying himself. "Perhaps he didn't realise how dangerous the bombs are, sergeant. Have you thought of that?"

"No, sir, I haven't. Because I'm assuming you, a responsible officer, would only send someone into the dump who was qualified to know a dangerous bomb when he saw it. Isn't that true?"

A subtle change in the man's voice indicated an awareness he was dealing with no rank and file interrogator. "Of course it's true."

"Then who was he, sir? I couldn't find his name myself because the page in the record book where his signature should be has been torn out."

McGrew lifted a sun-bleached eyebrow. "I wonder how that could have happened?"

Saffron was in no mood to pick and choose his words.

"I'm wondering too, sir. Because it suggests there's a cover up somewhere."

McGrew's voice was dangerously calm. "I don't know what you mean by a cover up, sergeant. No one's covered anyone up. As I've already told you, the culprit has been adequately punished."

Saffron had no intention of sparing him anything. "From the way you've been defending him, it doesn't sound like it to me. Was he court-martialled? Because if he wasn't it's a disgrace."

It was Saffron's first mistake. The change of attack from McGrew's earlier indefensible position to his disciplinary behaviour gave the warrant officer the chance at last to vent his frustration. "Don't be so bloody impertinent. How Squadron Leader Prentice and I punish our men has nothing to do with you. Whatever your qualifications, you're only a sergeant and you'd better not forget it. Instead of shooting off your mouth, your job is to make those bombs safe. So get on with it instead of being so damned insolent?"

Saffron ignored his anger. "I think there are a few things you don't know, sir."

"What things?"

"Firstly, if we are to work on those bombs, I'll need the entire camp evacuating."

McGrew's pale eyebrows came together. "All of it?"

"Yes. If there was an accident no one can say what casualties there might be. But that isn't all. I'll need a fire tender and a long hose that'll reach right down to the bombs."

Mcgrew shook his head. "We don't have a firetender on the station. And I doubt if we'll have a hose that'll reach to the nearest water pipe. But I'll see what I can do. What else do you need?"

Taking a deep breath, Saffron played his trump card. "I shall need you or Squadron Leader Prentice, sir. Air Ministry Regulations insist that an officer must be present when defective bombs are moved and/or destroyed. So you or Mr Prentice will have to be in the bomb dump with us when we begin our work."

Surprised himself at Saffron's demand, Bickers was expecting McGrew to show some kind of emotion, whether it was defiance, anger or dismay. Instead he heard only a sigh. "I'm fully aware of AMO regulations, sergeant. But unfortunately the two of us are expected up at the Military College tomorrow. With this new gas scare affecting everyone, the staff up there want all details of the school we are setting up and the chemicals we'll be getting. So I'm afraid you'll have to do without us."

All of which had been carefully arranged since his documents had given notice of his SAI qualifications, Saffron thought. "In that case we'll have to wait until you get back, sir. I don't suppose another day will make all that difference."

McGrew lifted his shoulders in regret. "I'm afraid the Staff College doesn't work that way, sergeant. They want us there for a minimum of three days."

"We'll still have no choice but to wait, sir. We can't go against AMOs, can we?"

McGrew's reply told both NCOs that every move of the chess game had been carefully planned. It also told Saffron that McGrew had the initiative now. "You've just told me the matter is urgent, sergeant: that the camp could be in danger if another earthquake comes. I think you'll find that AMOs say that if such a dangerous situation arises, the rule about officers in attendance can be waived."

Saffron knew it was true and that he was defeated. The triumph in McGrew's expression led him to yet another indiscretion. "You could ask the commanding officer of the station to stand in for you and Squadron Leader Prentice, sir. I'm sure he would appreciate the situation."

The glint in McGrew's eyes told Saffron yet another cross was being added to his list of sins. "Don't be a fool. The CO has no armament qualifications and in any case it isn't his job to take risks of this kind. It's our pigeon and we have to take care of it ourselves."

The man's hypocrisy was too much for Saffron. "Have you thought of it another way? The CO might think the safety of his station is more important than you and Prentice spending a few days at the staff college. He might arrange for one of you to stay here and face the mess this cock up has caused."

McGrew's face had gone very pale again. "Are you suggesting we are afraid to handle those bombs, sergeant?"

Saffron did not back away an inch. "I'm suggesting you and Prentice ought to be putting the safety of the camp before your own interests. And at the moment that's the last thing you're doing."

As McGrew jumped to his feet, the breathless Bickers saw he was trembling with rage. "You're asking to be arrested, Saffron? Do you know that?"

Saffron shrugged. "It's up to you, sir. Only then you might have a problem in finding someone to do the dirty job for you."

The sudden hush in the office was like an explosion. It was broken by McGrew's hoarse whisper. "Get out, both of you. And mind you get that job done tomorrow or you'll wish you'd never been born."

"We can't do it until the camp's evacuated," Saffron said.

McGrew's eyes were feral as they stared at him. "That'll be done by 12.00. And you'll get whatever equipment the station can provide. Now get out of my office before I have you arrested."

Bickers looked at Saffron with awe as the office door closed behind them. "You're mad, Saffron. Raving, screaming mad to say those things. He'll punish us now for the rest of our time here. Don't you realise that?"

Although fully aware he had gone too far, Saffron was not going to admit it to Bickers. "He's a lying bastard who deserves everything he gets."

"Yes, but he's the man in charge. He can make our lives hell if he wants to."

Saffron stared at him. "Who's side are you on? He's the bastard who fixed it so you have six highly dangerous bombs to handle tomorrow. You ought to hate the sod like I do."

It was the last reminder Bickers needed. "I'm not going to get a wink of sleep tonight, Saffron. And I thought Shaman was going to be a cushy posting. Why didn't they send me to Burma instead?"

Saffron lowered his pail of water to the earthen floor then turned to Bickers alongside him. "Now remember. You soak the crystals well before you try to remove them. At all costs they mustn't still be brittle when you start work on them. I don't need to tell you why, do I?"

Bickers, who was looking very pale in the light of four storm lanterns set on the floor beneath the bombs, shook his head. "What if the crystals don't dissolve?"

"They should eventually. Remember there's no hurry."

Bickers glanced round the vault, black except for the yellow circle of the storm lanterns, and gave a shudder. "There is for me. This place is like a tomb."

Saffron tried to make a joke of it but realised afterwards it was not the most tactful thing to say. "Make sure you don't turn it into one."

It was 14.00 hours the following day. All that morning servicemen had been vacating their billets and workshops and moving to the far side of the station. The order had come from the station commander, a middle-aged, benign Scot named Fraser who had called Saffron to his office after McGrew had notified him of the sergeant's request. "So you're the laddie who wants to send all my personnel into Shaman for the day."

Liking the look and style of the man, Saffron returned his smile. "Not into Shaman, sir. A quarter of a mile from the bomb dump should be enough."

Fraser rubbed a somewhat prominent chin. "A quarter of a mile, eh. You think we need go that far?"

"There are six bombs, sir. And it's better to be safe than sorry."

"Do you think it'll be far enough if the men wait over at the far side of the station?

Saffron hesitated only a moment. "Yes, I think so. Providing no one strays back."

"My SPs will see to that." Fraser's blue eyes examined Saffron with some approval. "How do you feel about doing this job, laddie?"

Saffron shrugged. "It's my job, sir."

"I understand you've got some help?"

"Yes, sir. Corporal Bickers is going in with me."

"You've got all the equipment you need?"

"We've got all that's available, but in any case we don't need much. Providing things go well, that is."

"What if things don't go well, laddie?"

Saffron left out the obvious. "Then we might have to ask for more equipment. But that can wait until later."

To his surprise the Scot lifted his tall, bony frame from his desk and held out his hand. "Good luck, sergeant. I appreciate what you are doing."

Saffron left the Administrative Block to find Bickers waiting for him outside. "Did he ask why the bombs had been left there all this time?" the Londoner enquired.

When Saffron shook his head, Bickers gave a relieved grunt. "It's just as well. If he had I suppose you'd have blown the gaff and put us into more trouble."

Saffron had wondered himself what his answer might have been and finally decided Bickers was probably right and the matter was better left there. He had seen nothing of McGrew that morning and assumed he and Prentice had already left for the Staff College. Aware Bickers was nervous, he had done his best to calm the Londoner down. "There shouldn't be any danger as long as we're careful. But I want you to wear these," and he had tossed Bickers a pair of overalls.

The Londoner had examined them suspiciously. "What do I want these for? It'll be hot in there."

"I've had the buttons removed and strings put in their place.

We mustn't wear anything that'll scratch those crystals. So don't carry anything in your pockets."

The reminder had done nothing to ease Bickers' state of mind. "I never volunteered for this job, Saffron. Have you considered that?"

Saffron had grinned. "I never thought of asking you. I knew beforehand you wouldn't let me down."

Although Bickers had muttered something, he had made no further complaint or effort to escape the task: something Saffron had noticed and appreciated. But now, standing in the tomblike vault, facing six bombs that could blow them to bloody fragments, Bickers was looking anything but a willing assistant. "We must be crazy, Saffron. While everyone else on the station is taking cover, here we are like two kitchen maids with mops and buckets of water."

Saffron had to laugh at the simile. Without a hose pipe long enough to reach into the vault and hose down the bombs, buckets of water, two sponges, and a roll of gun barrel cotton waste had been all Saffron could muster. "Never mind. There'll be plenty of free pints for us in the Mess tonight."

"Not from McGrew," Bickers muttered. "I'll bet he's already working on the next filthy job he can give us."

Saffron dipped a sponge in his pail of water. "Forget McGrew. The CO is behind us. He'll probably kiss us on both cheeks when the job's over." Before Bickers could reply, he moved to the bomb at the far end of the rack. "I'll start on this one. You take the one at the other end. Take it easy and don't use the cotton waste until the crystals are fully dissolved."

With that Saffron lifted the filled sponge and carefully squeezed it over the bomb's gaping mouth. Water trickled through the jagged crystals and dripped down to the earthen floor. Saffron squeezed his sponge again and again until it was dry. As he bent down to the pail to fill it again, a grumble came from Bickers. "You sure this is the right treatment. Mine aren't dissolving at all."

"It's takes time," Saffron told him. "Remember they've been here for years."

Bickers was not convinced. "There must be some chemical we ought to use and you've forgotten what it is."

"Even if there is, we wouldn't have it in this station, would we? So shut up bleating and go on with the treatment."

It was ten minutes before Saffron noticed a discoloration in the water dripping from the bomb. Heartened, he examined the crystals closer and saw they were shrinking in size. "It's working," he told Bickers. "Mine are starting to dissolve. What about yours?"

Bickers nodded. "Yes, I think they are. But bloody slowly."

"Be patient. Whatever you do, don't try to wipe them off until they've almost disappeared."

It was another twenty minutes before the tubes in the bombs were clear of crystals and only a stain remained. Examining Bickers' bomb, Saffron nodded and handed him a length of soft cotton waste. "All right. You can wipe it clean now."

Bickers hesitated. "You're sure?"

"Yes. It's safe now." When the Londoner still hesitated, Saffron took a length of cotton waste and ran it round the nose of his own bomb. "Don't you remember? It's only the crystals that are dangerous."

Although relaxing, Bickers was still cautious as he gingerly wiped his own bomb clean. His sigh was heartfelt as he finished. "Thank the Lord for that. Let's have a smoke. We can, can't we?"

Saffron nodded and drew him away from the four remaining bombs. "That wasn't so bad, was it?"

Bickers' hands were trembling as he accepted a light from the Yorkshireman. "I suppose not. But we're still got four more of them, Saffron."

"That's all right. They shouldn't prove any more of a problem than the others."

Bickers gave him a look. "Don't you know you should never say things like that? Don't you ever learn?"

Saffron, who was delighted at the outcome so far, clapped

him across the shoulders. "Come on, you old pessimist. Let's get the job done in time for dinner."

They filled their pails from the nearest water tap and began working on the bombs again. The first two were cleaned relatively quickly, giving Saffron hope that the job would be wrapped up within the next hour.

It was a grumble from Bickers as they worked on the last two bombs that gave the warning all was not well. "These crystals aren't dissolving at all, Saffron. Are yours?"

To that moment Saffron had paid little attention to the delay. Now he realised the Londoner was right. "No. They are taking longer." Lowering the sponge, he picked up one of the storm lanterns and peered at the bombs' serial numbers. He was frowning as he turned to Bickers. "These two are from a different batch to the others. I wonder if that accounts for it."

"In what way?"

"The bomb fillings or the component tubes might have been made of different materials to the others. In which case different main fillings or alloys might form different crystals."

Bickers looked alarmed. "What does that mean? We won't be able to soak them away?"

"It's too early to say yet. They might just take longer to dissolve. So keep on trying."

They tried for another half-hour, using two more pails of water in the process. At the end the crystals looked as jagged and glintingly dangerous as when the soaking process had begun. Groaning, Bickers leaned against the wooden gallery. "It's hopeless, Saffron. The buggers are waterproof. We're just wasting our time."

Saffron reached out to touch the crystals on his bomb. "Let's see if they're softening at all."

Bickers gave a yelp. "You can't touch 'em. You might set 'em off."

"Don't panic. I'm not going to scratch or jar them."

Hypnotised, Bickers watched Saffron's fingers carefully

touch and feel the crystals. As the Yorkshireman drew back, he shook his head. "No. They're still hard and brittle."

"Then what are we going to do, Saffron?"

"There's only one thing we can do. Take them away from the camp with the rest and blow them up."

Bickers' jaw sagged. "Carry them in that state. It'd be suicide."

Saffron picked up one of the storm lanterns. "Tell me what choice we've got. I'm going to tell the CO he'll have to quarantine the camp again tomorrow."

Bickers checked him. "You said yourself the slightest jar could explode them. We'll have to call in a bomb disposal squad, Saffron. There's no other way."

With Saffron fully aware himself of the risks involved, his temper was short-fused. "Where the hell are you going to find one of those in an outpost like this. The nearest one is probably in Burma. And who's going to ask for one when I'm supposed to be the expert. McGrew? Stop whining and help me clean up in here."

Unable to give a plausible solution, Bickers could only fall back on his old complaint. "I might have known something would go wrong if you were involved. I suppose it was written in the stars."

Saffron glared at him. "What's that supposed to mean?"

"It's that jonah thing again. I know you can't help it but it never fails, does it?"

Saffron's hand tightened round the handle of the storm lantern. "If you call me that once more I'll smash your skull in. I will, so help me."

Bickers was beyond threats. "I shouldn't bother, Saffron. The bombs will do it for you tomorrow."

"God, what a pessimist you are. How the hell did I ever get saddled with you?"

The Londoner gave Saffron a hurt glance. Then, with a resigned sigh, he picked up two of the storm lanterns and without another word began trudging towards the vault entrance.

Chapter Eleven

Fraser gazed at the twelve transport drivers lined up before him with considerable disdain. "Are you telling me that not one of you is going to volunteer? Not for the sake of the camp and your fellow airmen?"

No one answered unless the shuffling of feet and the avoidance of eye contact were replies in themselves. The only man who did neither was Cornwall. Although he made no audible comment, his eyes, fixed on Saffron and Bickers who were standing alongside the CO's desk, were giving his view of the situation in the most emphatic terms.

Seeing he was getting nowhere by calling on camp fraternity, Fraser tried another tack. "Think about these two NCOs standing alongside me. It is they who've discovered these six bombs must be destroyed and it is they who have to do it. Don't you feel you want to help them? I know I would in your shoes?"

Although again nobody spoke, in another dimension Saffron could hear the derisive shout. "So what's stopping you, mate?"

When a full ten seconds passed without a man stepping forward, Fraser decided the time of cajoling was over. "All right. If you won't volunteer you've given me no option. I'll have to choose two of you." He turned to Saffron. "Have you anyone in mind, sergeant?"

Alongside Cornwall, Wilkinson had been trying to look as inconspicuous as possible. Now, hearing the CO's question, he looked horrified as Saffron's eyes dropped momentarily on him and Cornwall.

There was no denying that Saffron was tempted. Alongside him, Bickers sensed it and gave him a warning nudge. The Yorkshireman pulled himself together. "No, sir. If you don't mind I'd rather you made the choice."

Fraser frowned. "Everyone's a bit coy today, aren't they? We're not going to win the war this way, you know." Seeing him glance back at them, every man but Cornwall tried to look obtuse, incompetent, and inconspicuous. Although it was hardly Cornwall's intention, the man's refusal to diminish himself drew Fraser's attention. "You and that man alongside you, aircraftman. Aren't you new here? Didn't you arrive with Sergeant Saffron and Corporal Bickers?"

As Wilkinson blanched at being noticed, Cornwall nodded. "Yes, sir."

Fraser's gaze ran over the pugilist's muscled body. "You don't look the type who's afraid of a bomb or two. So how about helping the sergeant and his corporal?"

Although Cornwall's face tightened his voice remained steady. "If that's what you want, sir."

Fraser moved on to Wilkinson. "What's your name, aircraftman?"

The sound Wilkinson made was little more than a squeak. "Wilkinson, sir."

Fraser did his best to sound jolly. "Then as you all came together, why not do the job together? One for all and all for one, what? Don't you agree?"

Wilkinson's face had turned white enough for his blackheads to be seen from the desk. "Me, sir?"

"Yes, lad. You. There's nothing to it. You'll just help the sergeant to carry the bombs to your truck and then drive him to a spot where they can be detonated. Then you'll sit back and watch a firework display. You'll probably enjoy it."

Before the hapless Wilkinson could express his grave doubts, the CO turned to Saffron. "When do you want the trucks, sergeant?"

Saffron was trying to decide whether he was pleased or dismayed at the outcome. "At 14.00 hours, sir. At the bomb dump."

Fraser swung back to Cornwall. "You got that, aircraftman?"

"Yes, sir."

"Good. Then it's all settled. The rest of you can get back to your duties. Dismiss."

As the men saluted and filed out, Fraser turned to Saffron. "Have you planned your route, sergeant?"

"No, sir. I haven't had a chance yet."

"Then I want you to do that right away. The guardroom will provide you with a truck and driver and Sergeant Barlow will go with you. He knows the terrain around here better than anyone and he'll find a safe spot for you to detonate the bombs. Have you decided what safety precautions to take during the journey?"

"I'd like half a dozen mattresses to line the floor of the truck, sir. Hopefully they'll absorb any jolting on the way."

Fraser nodded. "The Orderly Room will arrange for you to get them from the store. But I don't want you driving those bombs through the camp. By this afternoon there'll be a hole made in the perimeter fence opposite the bomb dump and that's the way you'll go out. Any questions?"

"I don't think so, sir."

"Then get on with it and let's get the damn things blown up and out of the way. After today I don't want the camp disrupting again. All right?"

Saffron nodded, saluted, and led Bickers from the office. "Bastard," the Londoner muttered as they made for the guardroom. "Did you hear him? It doesn't matter whether we blow ourselves up or not. In fact I get the feeling he's expecting us to. All he's worried about is getting the bombs off the camp so he can meet his schedules."

"Forget it," Saffron said. "Let's get hold of Barlow and get our route planned out. It'll be too late once those bombs are on board."

"Why had he to pick on Cornwall and Wilkinson to help us?" Bickers complained. "I don't know about Cornwall but you could see Wilkinson is scared to death."

Saffron gave him a grin. "Are you saying he's the only one?"

For once Bickers did not take umbrage. "What if I am? I

don't want to be blown to pieces just because someone was too lazy to do the job themselves. Do you?"

Saffron showed contrition. "I wasn't getting at you, mush. If the truth's known, I'm just as scared as you are. But not quite as scared as Wilkinson."

Mollified, Bickers gave a malicious chuckle. "Did you see his face when Fraser chose him? I thought he was going to pee himself."

"Maybe he still will when he sees those bombs leering at him."

Sobered by the reminder of what was awaiting them that afternoon, Bickers' tone changed. "Do you think this is going to work, Saffron? The thought of those bombs bouncing up and down in a truck gives me the willies."

"They'll be all right when we've got them resting on mattresses. We'll just have to take it slowly, that's all."

"Let's hope they're softer than the one I've got on my charpoy," the Londoner grunted. "Or we'll all be playing harps this afternoon."

Saffron grinned. "Don't flatter yourself. Old Nick's got a great big pitchfork waiting for you."

"Funny, funny," Bickers muttered.

Saffron slapped his shoulders. "Come on. Let's get over to the guardroom and get that truck and driver. We've a lot to do before Cornwall and Wilkinson visit us this afternoon."

A large shadow at the entrance of the bomb dump announced Cornwall's arrival. "You in there, sergeant?"

Saffron, inspecting the bombs and their shaky supports, nudged Bickers' arm. "Here they are. You ready?"

Bickers, looking pale in the gloom of the dump, swallowed. "As ready as I'll ever be, I suppose."

"Good man." Saffron gave a shout. "Yes, we're here. Have you got the trucks?"

"They're waiting outside. Shall we come down?"

"Yes."

Footsteps sounded and a few seconds later Cornwall and

Wilkinson rounded the corner of the bomb dump. Like Saffron and Bickers, both men were wearing overalls. Saffron eyed them critically. "You've done as I told you and got rid of any buttons?"

Cornwall sounded sullen. "Yes."

"What about underneath your overalls? You're not carrying anything that could jar or scratch the bombs?"

"No. Nothing."

Saffron glanced at Wilkinson who was looking even paler than Bickers. "What about you?"

Cornwall gave a gesture of impatience. "He's all right. I've checked him myself."

With his own nerves tightly stretched, Saffron was not taking well to Cornwall's sulleness. "He'd better be," he said. "You both know what could happen otherwise, don't you?"

"For Christ's sake, we're both clean. What else can we tell you?"

Saffron nodded. "All right. What about the mattresses?"

"They're in the trucks."

"Are the tail gates down?"

"Yes."

Saffron turned to Bickers. "Go and check everything's OK. We don't want to waste time up there staggering around with bombs in our arms."

Cornwall scowled at Saffron as Bickers hurried away. "You don't trust anyone, do you?"

Saffron shook his head. "Not when old bombs are concerned. And you haven't exactly given me cause to trust you in the past, have you?"

"I'm not a fool, Saffron. I don't want to go up in smoke any more than you do."

"I'm glad to hear it," Saffron said dryly. He turned to Wilkinson. "How are you feeling?"

Wilkinson glared at him vindictively. "How the hell do you think I feel? You'd no right to give us this job. We're not bomb disposal experts."

"I didn't give you this job," Saffron told him. "The CO did."

"Are you sayin' you didn't put him up to it?"

"Do you think I'd have chosen you if I'd had any choice? I've got more sense, Wilkinson."

As Wilkinson vented his feelings with a string of obscenities, Bickers returned and gave Saffron a nervous nod. "Yes. Everything's all right."

Saffron motioned all three men nearer to the bombs. "Then let's get on with it." He pointed to the four bombs without exudations. "We're going to take these four first. That way we'll be able to check the route we picked this morning. If we find it too rough, we can try another before we go out with the last two."

"If we're going to take 'em that way, why do we need two trucks?" The question came from Wilkinson. "Why can't we put the last two bastards on one truck? If we do that we won't all need to go."

With his dislike of the filthy-tongued Wilkinson even greater than his dislike of Cornwall, Saffron was tempted for a moment to give him the straight graphic answer. He was checked only by the thought that the truth might unnerve the man so much he would prove useless or even dangerous. "We don't want the bombs rolling about and crashing into one another. So it's safer to use two trucks."

Before Wilkinson could reply, Cornwall gave a loud, sarcastic laugh. "That's a load of crap, Saffron, and you know it." He turned to Wilkinson. "I'll tell you why they're using two trucks and two drivers. It's in case one of the bombs blows up on the way out. That way they only lose a couple of us instead of all four. Isn't that the truth, sergeant?"

Seeing the effect on Wilkinson, Saffron was inwardly cursing Cornwall's insensitivity. At the same time he knew it reflected the pugilist's secret contempt of Wilkinson's cowardice. Concerned it might affect the man's behaviour, he tried to minimise the trucks' significance. "It's always done in cases like this, Wilkinson. It's common prudence, and doesn't mean anything more dangerous than that."

Cornwall blew a sarcastic raspberry. "You're full of crap, sergeant. Don't you think we've a right to know how dangerous the job is?"

Saffron decided he had taken more than enough from Cornwall. "From the eager way you both rushed to volunteer this morning, I thought you knew it wasn't going to be a picnic."

Cornwall's expression told Saffron his sarcasm had struck home. "Only fools volunteer, sergeant. Haven't you been in the service long enough to know that?"

Saffron took a deep breath. "I've been in the services long enough to know arguing with people like you is a waste of time. So belt up and listen what I have to tell you. Remember your lives might depend on it."

His last sentence ensured silence while he described the essential differences between the two types of bomb. "There shouldn't be any danger moving these first four, although obviously because they're old the less they get knocked about the better. We'll discuss the other two later. At the moment we need to split up into pairs, to carry the bombs to the trucks and to drive them to the demolition site." His eyes moved to Cornwall and the pale-faced Wilkinson. "Do you two want to keep together or split up?"

"How much do the bombs weigh?" Cornwall asked.

"112 lbs each," Saffron told him.

Cornwall gave a contemptuous grunt. "We can carry one apiece, can't we?"

Saffron shook his head. "No. It would be too dangerous with the exuding bombs. So I want you to practise with the safer ones first. One man at the nose, the other at the tail, and heave 'em gently up on the mattresses. How do you want to pair up?" His eyes moved to Cornwall. "I'll take Wilkinson if you like."

Cornwall's glance at Bickers was full of contempt. "No, I'll take the devil I know." He grinned at Wilkinson. "Don't let the brutes drop on my toes or I'll kill you."

With that he moved towards the first of the inert bombs. With Saffron lending a hand, the bomb was slid forward until Cornwall's cupped hands were beneath its nose. Sliding it further forward, Saffron motioned the reluctant Wilkinson towards him. "All right. Get your hands beneath it. Steady. That's right. Can you hold it?"

With Wilkinson looking as if nervousness would make him drop his end at any moment, Saffron lost patience and nodded at Cornwall. "Let's do this ourselves. It'll save time."

With both of them powerful men, the bomb was carried up the bomb dump steps and to the nearer truck within a minute. Sliding his arms towards the belly of the bomb, Cornwall nodded at Saffron. "Jump up and I'll pass it up to you."

Hesitating a moment, Saffron saw the pugilist could support the bomb easily and jumped up into the truck. Seeing Bickers and Wilkinson had followed them, Saffron shouted at them to help Cornwall but the man shook his head and lifted the bomb effortlessly over the tailgate. Jumping up, he then helped Saffron to lift it on to one of the mattresses. He jerked a derisive thumb at Bickers and Wilkinson below. "Let's do the others ourselves, Saffron. Or one of them's going to break a foot or a toe."

Saffron shrugged. "If you're willing it's all right with me. But remember if the others don't get any practice we'll have to handle the last two bombs ourselves as well."

Cornwall's gaze was challenging. "Wouldn't you rather do it yourself than risk them blowing us up?"

Disliking the man as he did, Saffron could not fault his logic. "I suppose you're right. OK. Let's go and get the rest."

It took them another fifteen minutes before all four bombs were loaded on to the mattresses and by that time both men were sweating freely. Noticing Bickers' satisfaction at avoiding the hard work, Saffron took the smile off his face as he struggled past him with the fourth bomb. "Don't look so pleased with yourself. You're going to carry them when we get to the detonation site!"

With all the four inert bombs loaded on to one truck, Saffron told Cornwall to take the wheel. "I'll come in the cab with you to show you the way." He turned to Bickers. "I want you to ride in the back with Wilkinson to see how the bombs behave when we hit the track up the mountainside."

Bickers looked none too pleased at his role. "What if they start rolling about? Won't it be dangerous?"

Saffron grinned, his quip aimed as much at Wilkinson as the Londoner. "No more dangerous for you than for us. Maybe they'll let us share the same cloud up there."

Wilkinson's eyes looked glassy. "I thought you said these four bombs weren't dangerous?"

Saffron relented. "They're only dangerous if they roll on you. So if they start bouncing about too much, bang on the cab and we'll slow down."

With the four men in position, the truck pulled away. Ten metres down the track a gap had been made in the perimeter fence. As the truck approached it, Saffron saw the tall figure of Barlow, the Canadian MP, standing outside. When the truck drove through the gap, he motioned it to halt and came up to Saffron's window. "Hiya! You got the bombs on board?"

"Four of them," Saffron told him. "We'll come back for the other two."

Barlow, who had taken Saffron and Bickers up to a likely demolition site that morning, took a look in the back of the truck and then returned to Saffron. "Shall I come with you? Or do you think you can remember the way?"

"I think we'll be OK. You say it doesn't matter what spot use as long as it's not far from the old rifle range?"

"Yeah, that's right," Barlow grinned. "Anywhere as long as there aren't any tribesmen about. If you blow any of them up, you could start another World War. I don't think the old man would like that."

"Where is the old rifle range?" Cornwall asked.

Barlow pointed at the rock-strewn hillside that rose to the left of the macadamised road. "It's that grey smudge up there. But your sergeant knows where it is."

Saffron thanked him, nodded at Cornwall, and the truck

rolled forward again. At the far side of the football pitch a pile of stones was heaped at the roadside. Saffron pointed to it. "That's the track. Take it easy once we turn."

The Bedford slowed down and turned up a dusty path. Within minutes it began to rock and roll like a ship in a storm. No longer maintained, the track was ridged by erosion and strewn with wind-blown stones. As a wheel sank into a pothole, there was a yell and a thump from the rear. Cornwall gave Saffron a malicious grin. "It sounds as if they're having a load of fun back there."

Telling him to halt, Saffron jumped from the cab. Bickers stared down at him indignantly. "You've got to find another way, Saffron. The bloody things are rolling all over us."

Saffron gazed at the rugged mountainside around them. "There isn't any other way. Can't you pack the mattresses around the stores?"

"You come and try it yourself. These bombs are heavy, Saffron."

"They're not that heavy," Saffron said impatiently. "You'll have to manage until we reach the butts."

"But what if the brutes hit the side of the truck?"

"It won't matter if they do. I've told you. Those bombs aren't dangerous now."

"But what about those other two? You can't bring 'em this way. It'll be suicide."

At that moment Saffron felt he was right. Then his ability to put future problems into the future where they belonged came to his aid. "We'll meet that problem when it comes. Now stop bellyaching and hang on a few minutes longer. We're nearly there."

Chapter Twelve

Bickers collapsed beside Saffron with a groan. "I'm clapped, Saffron. Bushed."

Saffron, who was attaching a cable to an electric detonator, gave him a sympathetic grin. "Never mind. Just think how fit all this exercise is making you."

Bickers jabbed an indignant finger at the Bedford which was being backed away from the rifle butts. "You should've given all the work to those two. What's the point of being an NCO if a man does all the work?"

Saffron, who was as sweat-stained as Bickers, finished attaching the cable. "They've done their whack. I've seen to that."

Bickers eyed the retreating Bedford. "I wouldn't put it past 'em to drive back to camp and leave us stranded. That little prick Wilkinson never stopped moaning all the way here."

Saffron grinned. "And you didn't?" When Bickers scowled but made no reply, Saffron rose to his feet. "I want you to go back to the other side of the rifle butts and made certain there's no one on that side of the mountain."

Bickers glanced round the massive hillside. "Who the hell would be up here?"

"Tribesman, Pathans," Saffron suggested.

Bickers, who had not forgotten his fright of two days earlier, scowled. "I hope some of 'em are."

"Don't be stupid. If we were to kill anyone there'd be hell to pay. Go and make sure before we blow up the bombs."

Grumbling, Bickers started towards the high wall of the rifle butts. Below, the Bedford had halted and Cornwall and Wilkinson could be seen walking back up the mountainside. "You haven't seen anybody around here, have you?" Saffron asked as they approached.

To his surprise Cornwall nodded and pointed in the direction of Shaman. "I saw two guys and a motorbike down there. You can't see 'em from here because of that hill shoulder."

"How far away are they?"

Cornwall shrugged. "A quarter of a mile. Maybe a bit more."

"We'll have to move them. We can't risk a rock dropping on them."

Cornwall glanced at Wilkinson. "The world isn't going to miss two wogs, is it?"

As Wilkinson, who had recovered from his trip, gave a sycophantic laugh, Saffron frowned. "Don't be a fool." At that moment he saw Bickers returning from the far side of the rifle butt wall and called him over. "Cornwall says there are two men just beyond that hill shoulder. Go and tell them what we're doing and that they must keep away for the rest of the afternoon. OK?"

Bickers showed unease. "You think they might be tribesmen?"

"I don't know what they are. But they must be told they're in danger."

"But what if they get stroppy?"

Before Saffron could answer that, Cornwall grinned aggressively and slapped Bickers across the shoulders. "Let 'em try. I'll come with you. Come on."

With Saffron offering no objection, the two men started for the hill shoulder. The Yorkshireman turned to Wilkinson. "I want to set up the electric detonator in the shelter of the rifle butt wall. So help me to ease the cable over."

Saffron had the electric detonator planted in the sand and ready for use when Bickers and Cornwall returned. "Well," he asked Bickers. "Did you tell them what we're doing?"

"I'm sorry we did," Bickers muttered. "One was a big, black-bearded bastard and as surly as hell."

"Did he understand you? Did you tell him we were coming back later to explode two more bombs."

"Yes. We told 'em everything. And the big bastard didn't even thank us. He just looked at the other man, then they climbed on the motorbike and drove off."

"Are you sure he could speak English?"

Cornwall gave the answer. "He could speak English all right. But one thing's for sure. He doesn't like us."

Saffron shrugged and pointed at the electric detonator. "We're ready to explode those bombs now. Lie down in the sand under the wall and you should be all right."

Wilkinson was looking uneasily at the high brick wall which

had once served to stun bullets when fired at target practice. "You don't think it'll blow back on us, do you?"

"No. It's strong and thick. It'll shield you from any rocks that might get thrown this way." When Wilkinson still looked doubtful, Saffron became sarcastic. "But if you want your skull smashed with a rock, it's all right with me. Only make up your mind. I'll be blowing those bombs up any moment."

Cornwall, grinning at Saffron's impatience, caught Wilkinson's arm. "There's nothing our sergeant would like better than for the two of us to go up with his bombs. So let's get our heads down and disappoint him."

Saffron turned to Bickers. "You too."

Bickers was looking as dubious as Wilkinson. "If the wall goes we could be showered with hundreds of bricks. How can you be sure it'll hold?"

Saffron was fast losing his temper. "Because the bombs are three hundred yards further up the mountain. And they aren't 4000 lb block busters."

"Maybe not but there are four of them," Bickers muttered.

Breathing hard, Saffron bent over the detonator and began counting. "Ten, nine, eight . . ."

Realising he meant business, Bickers gave a yelp and flung himself alongside Cornwall and Wilkinson. Seven seconds later Saffron drove down the dynamo plunger and dropped into the sand himself. A tense second passed and then a huge multiple explosion rocked the mountainside and a shower of earth and rocks rose high into the air.

Keeping their heads covered with their arms as rocks kept thudding back to earth, the four men heard the explosions reverberating back and forth across the wide valley. When the last echo died away, Saffron climbed to his feet. "That's it. A piece of cake. All four of them gone. Now we've just the other two to bring up and the job's done."

There was a long pause as the men looked at one another. Then Wilkinson made his appeal. "As there's only two bombs and you and Cornwall are handling 'em, do we need to come with you, sarge? If we wait here we could make sure no wogs get back into the danger zone."

Finding it a shrewd excuse, Bickers opened his mouth to concur when he caught Saffron's glance. "A good try, Wilkinson," the Yorkshireman said sarcastically. "But you've forgotten we're bringing two trucks this time. So get back into that Bedford on the double. I want the job done well before sundown."

The sweat was pouring down Saffron's face as he crouched over the large bundle of mattresses in the back of the leading Bedford. As a rear wheel sank into a pothole and the bundle began to roll, he threw himself forward and interposed his body between the bundle and the metal side of the truck. A second later the Bedford halted. Cursing, Saffron climbed to his feet and addressed the white-faced driver. "What the hell is it this time?"

To say that Wilkinson was looking scared would be a understatement. "When the wheel went down I thought you'd want me to stop, sarge."

"You've been saying that ever since we left the main road," Saffron raged. "And you've been crawling along at a snail's pace. I want to get up there and get this job finished. Can't you understand that?"

"But the bomb, sarge. You've said how dangerous it is."

"It is dangerous," Saffron hissed. "But that doesn't mean you have to stop every time we hit a pothole or a bump. What the hell do you think I'm doing back here? Twiddling my thumbs?"

"But I can't see what's happening from the cab. I don't know if you're able to hold the bomb."

"You'll know soon enough if I can't hold it, Wilkinson. There'll be a bloody big bang and a moment later old Nick'll be sticking a pitchfork up your arse."

It wasn't, Saffron realised a moment later, the most tactful comfort to offer the frightened aircraftman. "I'm sorry, Wilkinson. But we must get the job done before it gets dark. And you're holding up the other truck by crawling along like this."

The other truck Saffron referred to, driven by Cornwall, was half a mile back along the dirt track. Ordered by the sergeant to keep that distance apart, it too had stopped moving. Wilkinson eyed Saffron dubiously. "But is it safe to go any faster?"

"Just a little faster," Saffron urged. "And you don't stop unless I let out a yell. Then you stop on the double. All right?"

Wilkinson moved reluctantly back to the cab. "All right. But tell me if I'm going too fast."

It was hardly likely, Saffron thought as he positioned himself beside the bundle of mattresses again. As the engine revved and the Bedford lurched out of the pothole he wondered how Bickers was coping at the back of the other truck.

Bickers would be scared, of that there was no doubt whatever. For that matter he, Saffron, was scared. Loading the two bombs on to the trucks had been a perilous enough act, their transport up to the demolition site was even more dangerous. Although Saffron had tried to minimise the risks incurred during the journey by binding mattresses around the two bombs, he had no way of knowing what shocks the exuding bombs could take without exploding. Moreover, providing they reached the demolition site safely, the bombs still had to be off-loaded and manhandled, and even although four pairs of hands were available, Saffron was only too aware that at least two pairs would be shaking so much they could not be trusted.

Another pothole took Saffron's mind off his future problems. As the track became rougher and the Bedford grunted and rocked and the bundle rolled this way and that, the Yorkshireman kept having the gravest doubts he would be left alive to face them.

With time extended like a drawn out tooth, Saffron was almost surprised when the butts appeared alongside him and the Bedford drew to a halt. A moment later Wilkinson, looking like a man just reprieved from the electric chair, appeared below. "We made it, sarge."

Rising to stretch his legs, Saffron felt a word of encouragement wouldn't come amiss. "Well done, Wilkinson. It wasn't so bad after all, was it?"

Wilkinson's failure to reply was a statement in itself. He stared back at the second Bedford that was still far down the mountainside. "Shouldn't they wait until we've unloaded this one?"

Saffron jumped down to the ground. "No. We'll all be needed to handle the bombs."

With the second Bedford forced to drive at the same slow pace, it was nearly ten minutes before it drew up alongside. Cornwall was the first to emerge. Although clearly relieved the journey was over, he managed a malicious grin as he jerked his head at the rear of the truck. "You'd better help your oppo to get down, Saffron. I don't think his legs'll make it otherwise."

Saffron peered over the raised tailgate. Bickers was slumped on the floor of the truck alongside the bundle of mattresses. Seeing Saffron, he gave a groan. "Are we there, Saffron?"

"Not quite," Saffron told him. "We still have to drive up to the demolition site. But I thought we'd take a short rest here and have the tea and grub the cookhouse gave us. How did you get on?"

"Gawd, it was hell, Saffron. I thought my time was up every time we hit a bump." Peering over the side of the truck and seeing Cornwall talking to Wilkinson, the Londoner turned back to Saffron. "Why did you give me Cornwall? I'm sure he hit every bump he could just to scare me."

Saffron grinned. "He'd as much to lose as you had. Stop bellyaching and act like an NCO. You don't want Wilkinson laughing at you, do you?"

Bickers groaned again. "You know your trouble, Saffron? It's all right for you because you've no imagination. But for people like me that was a terrible experience."

"Stop exaggerating and get down. Otherwise those two characters will eat all the grub."

Edging gingerly past the bomb, Bickers swung his legs over the tailgate. "You'll have to give me a hand. My legs don't belong to me."

Saffron steadied him as he dropped to the ground. "The worse's nearly over. We've just got to get the bombs on the site and then you and the others can get your heads down while I set the charges. You'll be telling jokes about it in the Mess tonight."

Bickers gazed at the rugged terrain beyond the rifle butts. "Some jokes, Saffron. How are we going to get them up there?"

"How do you think? The same way we did with the other bombs."

"But the track ends here. The trucks'll be all over the place."

Saffron clapped him across the shoulders. "One thing at a time. Let's go and eat now."

Standing by the second truck, Cornwall and Wilkinson were opening a packet of sandwiches. Saffron and Bickers had almost reached them when it happened. A loud, harsh voice made all four men spin round. A second later the packet of sandwiches fell from Wilkinson's hands.

A party of six tribesmen, led by a tall figure with a black beard, was emerging from behind the rifle butt wall. All the men were carrying rifles which were pointed menacingly at the four airmen. Cornwall's low curse reached Saffron. "That's the bastard we warned off the range!"

The party of tribesmen lined up before the airmen. Saffron found his voice. "What do you want?"

The tall, bearded man answered him in surprisingly good English. "I am Razim Khan. You are in charge, sergeant?"

"Yes. Why are you pointing those rifles at us? What do you want?"

The man said something to his followers. A loud laugh

followed his joke. The tribesman turned back to Saffron. "What do we want, sergeant? We want those bombs you have so kindly brought. We want them so that we can kill more of you British soldiers."

The situation was so bizarre and unexpected that Saffron had difficulty in knowing what line to take. "Those bombs are no use to you. They're aircraft bombs. There's no way you could use them."

The bearded man made another aside to his men, which brought an even louder laugh from them. He turned back to Saffron and thrust his rifle forward. "You see this, sergeant. This was not made by you British. We made it ourselves, copied from your own guns. We are not fools, Englishman, as some of your people already know."

The man's own words seemed to inflame him and make his black eyes burn like coals. Recognising a fanatic when he saw one, and wondering what the man intended to do with his party, Saffron tried to make his reply as conciliatory as possible. "I never suggested you were. But these two bombs are too dangerous. You could kill yourself if you tampered with them."

Before he finished speaking Saffron felt a foot tap his own and from the corner of his eye saw Cornwall had moved alongside him. But the move had not gone unnoticed by Razim Khan. Moving forward, he jabbed his rifle against the pugilist's stomach. "Why did you do that?"

"Do what?"

"Why did you tap the sergeant's foot? What were you telling him?"

Although pale, Cornwall met the man's fierce eyes. "I was telling him not to argue with you. If you want the bombs, he should give them to you."

For a long moment Razim Khan studied Cornwall's face. Then he nodded and stood back. "You show some sense." He turned to a tall, black-bearded tribesman who could have been a twin brother in his likeness and said something to him. Nodding, the man indicted three of the party to follow him. As they started towards the trucks, Saffron took a step forward. "What are you doing?"

Khan turned to him. "We are moving the bombs into one of your trucks, Englishman. Then we are going to drive the truck away."

Saffron could feel the sweat pouring down his back. "You mustn't do that. You could kill us all. You must believe me. Those bombs will explode unless they're properly handled."

Khan turned to the armed tribesman alongside him. "The Englishman thinks we are fools. Are we fools, Rashid?"

The tribesman, whose face was pock-marked from smallpox, grinned back and spat betal nut juice to the ground. He made some caustic reply but Saffron's eyes were on the four tribesmen who had reached the trucks and were preparing to lower their tailgates. Saffron made a last desperate appeal. "If you won't listen to me, then at least let us transfer the bomb. Please."

Khan said something to the pock-marked tribesman that brought another laugh from him. Then Khan shrugged and turned back to Saffron. "Why not? We like to see Englishmen work. Go and move the bomb yourselves."

Led by the relieved Yorkshireman, all four airmen ran towards the second truck. Beside him Saffron heard Cornwall's harsh whisper. "Do you think all the bastards will ride away in the truck?"

"I hope so," Saffron muttered back. "But we'll soon find out."

By the time they reached the Bedford, the tribesmen had lowered its tailgate. Grinning among themselves, they stood back and watched the airmen gingerly lower the bundle of mattresses down and carry it to the first truck. As they hoisted it up, Saffron heard Cornwall's whisper. "Get the ropes off the bloody thing."

Before Saffron could argue, Cornwall had jerked on a couple of knots and the mattresses fell away. Pushing him aside, both Bickers and Saffron tried to re-set the mattresses but as they were fumbling with them, Khan came to the tailgate. "You take care of your bombs well, sergeant. But we know all about them and do not need them wrapped up in cotton wool."

Saffron tried one last time. "These bombs are dangerous. You must believe me."

"You insult my intelligence, sergeant. I do not like that." Before Saffron could reply, Khan turned to the man who resembled him so closely. "Take Zalom and go, my brother. We will see you tonight."

The man nodded and accompanied by a second tribesman clambered into the cab. Cornwall glanced at Khan. "Aren't you all going?"

Khan showed his white teeth. "No, Englishman. We shall soon be walking back through Shaman like the innocent traders that we are."

The inference that Khan and his followers would go unrecognised after the incident had implications that dismayed Saffron. But then the sound of the Bedford engine starting up drove all other speculations from his mind. As the truck began swinging round and a wheel lifted over a protruding rock, all four airmen dropped to the ground.

Above him Saffron heard Khan's half amused, half suspicious voice, "What are these antics? What are you doing?."

The Bedford's engine revved again as its driver changed gear. Peering over his folded arms, Saffron saw it swinging in a circle to regain the track. As it lurched he heard the clang of metal and knew the sound came from the released bomb colliding with the metal side of the truck. As his spine cringed he heard Bicker's horrified voice. "Can't we stop him, Saffron? Can't you do anything?"

The Bedford was on the track now and moving faster. With every nerve in his body stretched to breaking point, Saffron watched it over his folded arms. Every second or two it jolted and brought the clang of metal. Guessing the bomb had rolled right off the mattresses by this time, he could see it in his mind's eye rolling all over the metal floor. By a miracle it had survived the impacts so far but Saffron knew that the moment it pivoted round and its crystals came in line with the metal sides, hell would break loose. Holding his breath, he waited for the explosion.

It came when the Bedford was fewer than a hundred yards down the track. A massive dual explosion that kicked the mountainside beneath Saffron's body and drove the air out of his lungs. Tortured pieces of metal were hurled in all directions, a wheel went spinning across the hillside, and half a body soared in the sir. Seconds later clods of earth and stones came thudding down like freak hailstones. As the reverberations came echoing back, Saffron heard horrified cries from the tribesmen behind him.

He rolled over, to see Razim Khan lying on the ground. Blown down by the explosion the man had a large contusion on his face. Like the other three tribesmen, he was looking dazed and bewildered. Then, as Saffron tried to see if his men were safe, Khan rose to his knees and gave a cry of anguish. Staggering to his feet, ignoring Saffron and his party, he began running down the mountainside to the blazing wreck. As the remaining tribesmen picked themselves up and followed him, Cornwall's satisfied voice broke the sudden silence. "That's the end of the bastard's brother. Pity he didn't go with him."

Saffron sat up. "Is everyone all right?" Receiving affirmative replies, he glanced back at the blazing Bedford where Khan and his men could be seen picking through the debris. "We've got to get out of here. God knows what Khan will do now."

A tap on his arm made him spin round. Bickers was standing alongside him with a rifle in his hand. "Khan must have dropped it when he went running after his brother," he muttered.

Saffron grabbed it, jerked off the ammunition clip and saw it was full. Glancing back at the four tribesmen searching through the rubble, he saw that three of them still retained their rifles. Cornwall came up alongside him. "What are you going to do?"

Glancing round, Saffron pointed at the high wall of the rifle butts that was less than forty feet away. "I'll cover them from there. The rest of you act normally when they come back."

"You could pick the bastards off from here," Cornwall argued.

"No. They'll be experts at taking cover in this terrain. Better to wait until they're nearer."

Cornwall caught his arm. "You do realise they'll want our blood after what's happened?"

Saffron pulled away. "I know that. Don't worry. I'll open fire if they threaten you."

Before Cornwall could argue further, he ran for the wall and hid behind it. Down the mountainside the tribesmen had realised the futility of their search and been called to Razim Khan's side. A tall, impassioned figure, his desire to avenge his brother could be felt as well as seen as he ranted at them and gazed up the slope at the airmen. "Let's hope the sod doesn't realise we've got his rifle," Cornwall muttered.

Bickers flung a frightened glance back at the hidden Yorkshireman. "Saffron! What if they open fire before they reach us? I think we ought to try to get away."

Wilkinson, no less scared, made the same appeal. "So do I. The bastards have got knives. They'll cut us up if we stay here."

Saffron's warning hiss was full of urgency. "They'll catch or shoot you if you run and I won't be able to help. Stay where you are, for God's sake."

Cornwall glared at the two frightened men. "He's right. Our only chance is to get 'em close. So don't move and don't panic."

For a moment it was touch and go whether the two airmen would obey. With his black beard jutting forward, with his eyes blazing hatred, and his body language crying out for vengeance, Razim Khan was a sight enough to terrify the strongest of men as he led his small party back up the mountainside. Beside him, their swarthy faces bitter with anger and their rifles at the ready, his three tribesmen looked as menacing.

Cornwall's comment came from the corner of his mouth. "He's so heated up he doesn't seem to realise Saffron's missing." Then: "I hope Saffron's a good shot. Is he?"

Bickers could feel his knees knocking together. "He says he is."

"Let's hope he's not shooting a line," Cornwall grunted.

The three tribesmen were a dozen paces away when Khan halted them. His vengeful eyes surveyed them, then he gave a start. "Where is the other one? Where is your sergeant?"

"He's gone off for help," Cornwall told him. "It'll be here any minute now."

Khan snatched a rifle from the tribesman nearest to him and pointed it at Cornwall. "You lie, Englishman. Your sergeant. Where is he?"

Before Cornwall could reply, there was a shout from Saffron. "Drop your rifles or I'll shoot! Go on! Drop them!"

Khan's response had the speed of a striking snake. Spinning round he fired at the sheltering wall in one lighting movement. As his bullet made a puff of red dust, a second shot sounded and dust kicked up at Khan's feet. "Drop it, Khan, or I'll kill you. I mean it."

For a long moment it seemed that Khan's hatred would overcome his sanity. Then, with a curse, he threw the rifle to the ground and ordered the other tribesmen to do the same.

It was the signal for Saffron to emerge from behind the wall, his rifle at the ready. He nodded at Cornwall. "Get those rifles and any other weapons they're carrying."

The exultant Cornwall was only too ready to oblige. Dropping two rifles and three wicked-looking knives at Bickers' feet, he aimed the other rifle at Khan. "Now, you bastard. How would you like a bullet in the belly?"

With black eyes burning with hatred, Khan drew himself upright. "You are nothing but the droppings of a pig, Englishman. I have no fear of you."

Cornwall lifted the rifle and aimed it. "Then let's give you some fear. I'm sending you to Allah, you bastard."

Saffron gave an urgent shout. "Drop it, Cornwall! Drop it! Do you hear me?"

For a moment it seemed Cornwall would disobey. Then he

cursed and lowered the rifle. "What's the matter with you, Saffron? This swine was going to kill us all."

"He's unarmed," Saffron said. "We don't kill unarmed men."

"These bastards would. They'd have chopped us up."

Ignoring him, Saffron turned to Khan. "I'm sorry about your brother. But I did warn you how dangerous those bombs were."

The tribesman was showing no gratitude to Saffron for saving his life. Instead his face was a mask of hatred as he stared at the sergeant and then at Bickers. "You lie, Englishman. You and your corporal here set those bombs to explode. I saw you do it with my own eyes."

The memory how he and Bickers had been bending over the bomb when trying to replace the mattresses took some sting from Saffron's reply. "We didn't touch the bombs, Khan. They were dangerous when we brought them up here. That was why they were wrapped in mattresses."

"You lie! You and your corporal set those bombs to kill my brother. As Allah is my witness, you will both pay for it. I swear it on my brother's grave."

"Shoot the bastard," Cornwall said. "Shoot him and the other three or you'll never feel safe here."

Saffron could not help stealing a glance at Bickers. The Londoner's face was covered in sweat, making Saffron wonder at his thoughts. He turned back to the four tribesmen. "You can go now. Jildi!"

Cornwall looked aghast. "You're not taking them in?"

Saffron shook his head. "No. This man's just lost his brother."

"So what? Who's bloody fault was that? You're crazy, Saffron. He's just threatened to kill you."

There was a bitter laugh from Khan. "Your sergeant is much clever than you, Englishman. He knows that if Razim Khan was made a prisoner by the British, these very mountains would burst into flames." His fierce eyes moved back to Saffron. "But don't think I shall spare you for this, sergeant. I have sworn it to Allah and on my brother's death. You and your corporal will die and your death will not be pleasant."

"Shoot the sod," Cornwall said again. "If you don't you deserve all you get."

Saffron suddenly felt very tired. "Pick up the rifles and those knives and let's get back to camp. Otherwise they'll be sending men up here to see if we've blown ourselves to pieces."

With a last stare at the tribesmen, Cornwall ignored the order and walked angrily to the remaining Bedford. Carrying the weapons between them, the other three airmen followed him. A minute later they were driving past the still blazing remains of the other truck and heading down the mountainside, with Khan and his tribesmen gazing vengefully after them.

Chapter Thirteen

Fraser was reading some requisition orders when he heard a tap on his door. Switching off his desk light, he sat back. "Come in!"

A young sergeant entered and saluted. "Warrant Officer McGrew and those two new NCOs are here, sir."

"All right, sergeant. Send them in."

McGrew came in first, followed by Saffron and Bickers. Fraser answered their salutes, then took in details of the two NCOs whose shirts and shorts were still soiled from their escapade up the mountain. "I understand you lads have had a nasty encounter with our old friend, Razim Khan. Tell me all that happened."

McGrew, clearly agitated, broke in quickly. "They lost one of our trucks, sir. And two tribesmen have been killed."

Fraser's initial reaction was concern. "Killed?"

"Yes, sir. Blown to pieces."

The CO winced, then nodded at Saffron. "Tell me about it, sergeant,"

Saffron did his best to explain all that happened. When he finished there was quizzical amusement mixed in with Fraser's concern. "You lads don't do things by halves, do you? Only here a couple of days and you clash with Khan, the most powerful tribesman in the territory. It must be a record."

McGrew was quick to put matters into perspective. "It's certain to bring us more trouble from him, sir."

"Maybe, but you can hardly blame these lads for that. It wasn't their fault Khan tried to steal the bombs, was it?"

McGrew's reply could hardly have been more grudging. "No, I suppose not."

"At least they had the good sense not to bring Khan into custody." Fraser turned to Saffron. "That was smart of you, laddie. Had you heard about the Razim Khan directive?"

Saffron shook his head. "No, sir. I didn't know one existed."

"Well, there is and it's explicit. Under no circumstances has Razim Khan to be made a target of revenge or retribution. So you did the right thing by letting him go."

The Yorkshireman was showing surprise. "I don't understand, sir. His intention was to steal the bombs so he could use them against us. So why is he given immunity?"

"It's the game that's played up here, sergeant. Tribesmen are allowed to take pot shots at our men and we're allowed to shoot back in self-defence. That way we keep the status quo and everyone's happy. Unless there's an earthquake, of course. Then it's a free for all. But that hasn't happened since I've been here."

"But bombs, sir. He didn't mean any pot shots with them."

Fraser shrugged. "That's true. But thanks to you and a bit of luck, he didn't get them, did he? So that's something we don't have to worry about."

McGrew was not sharing the CO's sang-froid. "What I want to know is how he got wind of those bombs." His glance at Saffron was full of dislike. "Did you talk about the disposal of those bombs in front of any of the Indian waiters?"

"No, sir, I didn't. But everyone must have known about them after we evacuated half the camp."

Although it was a point McGrew could hardly dispute, Bickers found his tongue and cleared Saffron even further. "In any case, Khan found out before we blew up the first four bombs, sir."

Fraser turned to him. "How do you know that, corporal?"

"He and another man were on the mountainside within blast range of the bombs, sir. Sergeant Saffron sent me to move them."

Fraser's eyes moved down Bickers' lanky figure to his skinny legs. "You went to move Razim Khan! What did he say, corporal?"

"Nothing really, sir. He just acted sullen and moved away with the other man."

Glancing again at Bickers's unmilitary figure, Fraser raised a quizzical eyebrow. "You've either got a way with you, corporal, or you were born under the right stars." Keeping his face straight with an effort, he turned back to Saffron. "Is that the full story, sergeant?"

"Yes, sir. You've heard everything."

"Then I consider you behaved very well indeed. Bravely, in fact. Your corporal and the two aircraftmen did well too. All this will go into my report and into your documents."

Before Saffron could speak, McGrew interrupted again. "What about the truck they lost, sir? Surely it would never have happened if the sergeant had planted a look-out on the rifle butts before they came down for the second bombs."

The unfair criticism was too much for the Yorkshireman. "We had no way of knowing Khan would try to steal a bomb, sir. I'd never heard about him until today. And if we'd left someone up there, wouldn't the tribesmen have just cut his throat and still ambushed us?"

Fraser eyed the two men's antagonistic faces before giving his reply. "I think the sergeant has a good point there, Warrant

Officer. Two points in fact. I really can't fault his conduct in any way." Before McGrew could reply, Fraser rose from his desk. "That's all. I want to get my dinner and I suggest you all do the same. So you can dismiss now."

Saffron could almost feel the resentment emanating from McGrew when he and Bickers followed him outside. They were on the darkened parade ground, lit only by a couple of lamps and a crescent moon, when McGrew addressed them. "I've got some good news for you two. Your gas equipment arrived this afternoon while you were playing heroes up the mountainside. Report to me at 08.30 and I'll arrange for the transfer to be made." His last words carried back to them as he turned away and made for his quarters. "I hope you're going to like what they've sent you."

Bickers dropped on his bed with a groan. "What a hell of a day!"

Resilient as ever, Saffron shrugged. "It's turned out all right, hasn't it?"

"You mean we're still alive? Do you realise what happened, Saffron? We were nearly blown to bits by our own bombs; we nearly had our throats cut by some Mad Mullah; and we got a death threat in the name of Allah. On top of all that, McGrew would have put us on a charge for losing one of his trucks."

"And instead we got a commendation from the CO. That's what I'm saying. It hasn't been a bad day after all."

Bickers showed his disgust. "You're a head case, Saffron. You think it'd be lucky if a chimney pot fell and only broke your foot. I suppose it has something to do with that jinx you have."

Saffron's grin faded. "Don't start that again."

"But it's true, Saffron. Who but you would have been unlucky enough to have that Mad Mullah on the mountainside the very afternoon we're destroying those bombs. It must have been a chance in a thousand."

Saffron lit a cigarette. "Rubbish."

"You can't deny it. A thing like that could only happen to

a man with a jinx. Mind you, I'm not blaming you, Saffron. It can't be a lot of fun to be jinxed."

"You're all heart," Saffron said.

Bickers shrugged. "A man tries to feel sympathy. The trouble is it doesn't stop with you, does it?"

"I thought that would be coming next," the Yorkshireman grunted.

"Well, it's true, isn't it? Who released those mattresses around that bomb today? Cornwall. And yet who did the Mad Mullah blame? Not just you. Me!"

"That's only because you were helping me."

"That's what I mean. Your jinx always drags me in too. Why didn't you tell Khan I'd nothing to do with it?"

"How could I do that?"

"Why not?"

"An NCO can't put the blame on his men. Don't you see that?"

"No, I don't. Because you kept quiet I'm going to have my throat cut instead of that bastard Cornwall. You think that's fair?"

"You're not going to have your throat cut," Saffron said impatiently. "That was all wind and water."

"Wind and water? Did you see that Mad Mullah's eyes? He meant it all right."

"What if he did? You couldn't be in a safer place than a military camp."

"With all those Indian bearers and waiters about? Anyone of 'em could sneak into our billet during the night or get us when we're walking about the camp. You've done it to me again, Saffron. You won't admit it but you have."

Saffron wondered if it were guilt that gave him a twinge of sympathy. "You're making too much of it. The man was half crazed because he'd just seen his brother killed. Anyone would make threats at a time like that."

"You should have done what Cornwall said and shot him. That's what they do to mad dogs."

"Could you have shot him in cold blood?" Saffron asked.

"I'd have had a damned good try," Bickers muttered. "Bugger principles if they're likely to get your throat cut."

"You're not going to get your throat cut. So stop talking about it."

There was a moment of silence, then Bickers rolled over to face Saffron again. "What did McGrew mean about the gas equipment?"

"Come again."

"He said he hoped we liked what they'd sent. Didn't you hear him?"

Saffron inhaled smoke. "I heard him."

"Then what did he mean? He's another one who's out to get us. I thought he sounded as pleased as hell about something."

Before Saffron could answer there was a tap on the door. A second later Jackson appeared, his cheery face showing excitement. "I hear you guys had a ding dong with Razim Khan today."

"A real knees up," Saffron said sarcastically. "And we don't want to talk about it. What do you want?"

Jackson looked disappointed. "But they say two tribesmen were killed."

"There were. But we still don't want to talk about it. What have you come for?"

The good-natured Jackson shrugged. "OK. Tell me later. What about the dance in the camp tomorrow night. Do you want to talk about that?"

Bickers sat up. "Women?"

Jackson grinned. "What else?"

"What sort of women?"

"Big, small, fat, thin. All kinds."

Bickers showed impatience. "No. I mean will there be any white ones?"

"There are usually a few. Officer's wives from the cantonment who take pity on us."

"Can we go?"

Jackson nodded. "You can now you're on the staff. But

you must have your name down in the Orderly Room before 10.00 tomorrow. I'll do it for you if you like."

Bickers glanced at Saffron. "You hear that? You'll go too, won't you?"

"I thought you were bushed," Saffron said. "And too scared to go anywhere. Maybe one of the women will carry a knife and stick it in your gizzard when you're shooting that line of yours. Have you thought of that?"

Bickers frowned. "Don't talk like a prat. Will you go or won't you?"

"Yes, I'll go. I want to see your face when those memsahibs look down their noses at you. I'm told they use NCOs as errand boys in these parts."

The prospect of women entering his life again was reviving Bickers. "Speak for yourself, Saffron. Some men know how to handle women. Keep your eyes open tomorrow night and you might learn a thing or two."

Saffron, with his temper recovered, gave Jackson a wink. "You didn't know his second name is Casanova, did you? Or that he's known from London to Timbuktu as The Stud."

Jackson grinned back. "Then he's picked a hell of a place to come. You're dead right about those memsahibs. They do it in the line of duty but treat us like cases of cholera."

"You still want to go?" Saffron asked Bickers.

"Of course I do. I haven't got an inferiority complex like you, Saffron. Women don't play the Lady Bountiful with me."

"So speaks the big Communist," Saffron said. "All right, Jackson. Stick our names down and let's see what it feels like having cholera."

Chapter Fourteen

McGrew nodded at the armed SP standing outside the door of the store room. "All right, corporal. You can let us in. These two men are our new gas instructors."

The SP glanced at Saffron and Bickers and then nodded. "Yes, sir.

As he drew aside, McGrew produced a bunch of keys and opened the heavy door of the windowless room. Sniffing the air cautiously, he then stepped inside and clicked on a light switch. "Come and look what SEAC has sent you," he said to Saffron.

Saffron followed him inside, followed more cautiously by Bickers. The far wall was covered by wooden crates of all shapes and sizes. McGrew nodded at them. "As you see, they've sent you plenty of stuff to play with."

By this time Saffron had noticed that most of the crates had been opened. "What kind of gas have they sent?"

McGrew waved him forward. "Take a look."

Saffron began pulling back loosened lids. The first three crates he examined contained carboys heavily labelled as containing dangerous chemicals. He glanced at McGrew. "These'll be the mustard gas containers."

McGrew nodded. "They must think you're going to swill it all over the camp. There are another three behind them."

Saffron was peering into another smaller crate. Giving a start, he bent forward and began lifting out a fish-shaped bomb. Behind him McGrew made an involuntary step back to the door as Saffron laid the small bomb across his knee and studied the markings round its nose. A moment later he turned to McGrew in disbelief. "This is a filled bomb. A 25 pounder filled with phosgene. What the hell have they sent us filled bombs for?"

There was a startled yelp from Bickers. "That can't be right. Maybe they've just left the markings on."

Saffron shook the bomb cautiously, then glanced at McGrew again. "It's full all right. What's going on? Have they gone mad back in Cawnpore."

McGrew indicated the padded crate. "Put it back safely before you moan about it."

Saffron slid the bomb back and straightened. "How many more are there? Do you know?"

"Eight," McGrew said.

"Eight? But that's crazy. What can we do with eight filled phosgene bombs?"

McGrew smiled maliciously. "You can show your armourers what they look like."

"But we don't need filled bombs to do that. Empty ones will do just as well. These'll have to go back."

McGrew shook his head. "Squadron Leader Preston has already been on with Cawnpore. They say the threat is so serious that your armourers have to get used to handling filled bombs. In other words it's important they get accustomed to battle conditions."

"But these things are lethal. If one was to get cracked in an accident we could have half the camp coughing its lungs up. They can't remain here."

McGrew shrugged. "That's obvious. Just as it's obvious the mustard gas can't remain here either. As soon as a secure store is ready for them, they'll be taken to it."

Saffron was beginning to understand the malice in the man's hairless eyes. "And where's that going to be? Hill Camp?"

McGrew smiled again. "I see you remember. Yes. Far enough from Long Barracks to prevent a disaster should a gas tank or a bomb leak."

There was a strangled cry from Bickers. "Does that mean we have to instruct up at Hill Camp?"

Showing mock surprise, McGrew turned to him. "Who else? You're the gas instructors, aren't you? The courses will be brought up to you every day."

"But Razim Khan has threatened to kill us. We'll be sitting ducks up there."

"You don't take notice of a stupid threat like that, corporal. In any case Mr Prentice is arranging for you to have Ghurka guards day and night. You won't be in any danger."

With Bickers looking shattered, Saffron took over. "I suppose this means we have to sleep up there as well?"

"Naturally. You have the gas to look after. But you'll have comfortable enough billets. It's true they haven't been used for some time but bearers will clean them up for you. You won't be alone either. Mr Preston is arranging for two young armourers to billet with you. Once you've trained them, they'll be able to share some of your work load."

Saffron took a deep breath. "When do you want us to move?"

"I'm told the store for the bombs should be ready in a couple of days. Naturally you'll supervise the transportation of the gas. Any other questions?"

Seeing the dazed Bickers opening his mouth, Saffron got in first. "No. I take it you'll let us know when we're needed?"

McGrew's smile was that of a very satisfied man. "I'll let you know, sergeant. In the meantime you're free of duties to enjoy the facilities of the camp."

With that he locked the storeroom, smiled again at the two NCOs, and walked away like a triumphant cockerel. Ignoring the look of the SP, Bickers sagged against the brick wall of the storeroom. "I don't believe all this, Saffron. What's the world doing to us? When does it stop?"

For once Saffron was lost for words himself. "We're not having all the luck that's going, are we?"

"Luck? All we need now is a bloody big earthquake and that's it."

Saffron took his arm and led him away. "Never mind. You've still got the dance tonight. Maybe you'll find a nice voluptuous memsahib who'll forget you've got cholera and take you to bed."

For once the prospect of sex failed to comfort Bickers. His groan came from the heart. "There's only one thing I can think of at the moment, Saffron. And that's the Mad Mullah smacking his lips and sharpening his knife while he waits for us at Hill Camp."

The five piece band paused and then broke into a tinny but enthusiastic version of 'Besame Mucho'. Couples rejoined and began dancing a fox trot. Although the majority of the women were Anglo-Indians and the men belonged to other ranks, here and there white women and officers could be seen. Alongside Saffron, Jackson was grinning. "You didn't expect this, did you?"

Saffron shook his head. "You're right. I didn't. Mad tribesmen, gas bombs, snipers, and now this. It's like Alice in Wonderland. Where do the girls come from?"

"The Anglo-Indians and a few of the European women come mostly from Shaman hospital. The posher ones are the memsahibs we talked about." Jackson pointed across the floor. "Your oppo's dancing with one of 'em. See him?"

Saffron spotted Bickers as he was doing a nifty pirouette. Resplendent in newly pressed khaki shirt and slacks, the Londoner was dancing with one of the younger European wives, a woman in her early forties with a well-kept buxom figure. Although her face was not unattractive, she looked as if she had a peg in her nose as she answered Bickers' comments. At the same time she appeared to be enjoying the complicated dance steps Bickers was providing.

"That's Mrs Lavinia Oldroyd," Jackson told Saffron. "A hell of a snob but they say she likes a bit of rough with the lads."

"You know her then?"

Jackson grinned. "Only by sight. Her old man's a Colonel up at the college. He's twenty years older than her, a red-faced old bastard who'd shoot anyone who tries to get their hands up her dress."

The dance ended and a sweating but happy Bickers found his way back to Saffron. "This isn't bad, kid. Who'd have thought they've have had anything like this in such a crummy place."

"I notice you've been making a beeline for the memsahibs," Saffron said.

Bickers' shrug was almost apologetic. "I can't help it, Saffron. Only white women seem to appeal to me."

"The last one was very white. So white she kept looking at you as if you had leprosy."

Bickers' indignation was short-lived. "What do you know

about women, Saffron? That woman likes dancing with me. So much she's promised me more dances before the night's over."

"That's only because of your poncy footwork. I'm talking about her snooty looks. Do you know who she is?"

To Saffron's surprise, Bickers nodded. "Yes. Mrs Lavinia Oldroyd. Her old man lectures at the college."

"According to Jackson here, he's also as jealous as hell. So watch yourself. We're in enough trouble as it is."

"Women aren't trouble, Saffron. They help to file away the sharp edges."

Saffron glanced at the grinning Jackson. "This guy has got us into more trouble over women than you've had hot dinners. And now he's telling me they file away the edges."

Bickers smirked. "They do, Saffron. I think this one could." He glanced across the floor where Lavinia Oldroyd was seated on a bench with three older white women. "She's got a great figure, hasn't she?"

Not for the first time Saffron was reminded the Londoner was attracted by large bosomed women. "Jackson says she likes other ranks but only for a bit of rough. So you watch it, lover boy. Or you could have her old man as well as the Mad Mullah chasing your tail."

Bickers had only heard his first sentence. He turned to Jackson. "Is that right? Does she mix it with the other ranks?"

Jackson nodded. "That's the story that goes around."

Bickers' eyes were beginning to glow. "That's the feeling I got out there. But it helps to be sure."

"Leave her alone," Saffron said. "You aren't in England or South Africa now. They've got it all sewn up out here. If you start mucking about with colonels' wives you'll end up in an Indian glasshouse."

With adrenalin and testosterone swamping his natural caution, Bickers was not listening. "She might be the first good thing that's happened since I set foot in India, Saffron. So don't be such a spoilsport."

Before the Yorkshireman could answer him, the band struck up again and like a sprinter from his blocks, Bickers shot off across the floor. Saffron gave a groan. "Why did I tell him that? He'll be after her now like a dog after a big juicy bone."

They watched Bickers talking to the haughty Lavinia. For a moment it seemed she was going to refuse the Londoner. Then, acting as if her sacrifice was purely for King and Country, she shrugged, rose, and walked on to the dance floor with him.

Jackson was clearly impressed. "You've got to hand it to him. He must shoot a hell of a line."

If the truth were told, Saffron was impressed himself. "He does. Where women are concerned, he's the best line shooter in the business."

They stood watching the couple as they circled round the floor towards them. Bickers was chatting volubly and although Lavinia was gazing at him as if she still had a peg on her nose, she was obviously listening. As they disappeared among the other dancers, Jackson turned to Saffron. "What's he saying to her?"

"If I told you, you wouldn't believe it," Saffron said.

"Try me," Jackson grinned.

"According to him, he softens them up for a few minutes and then comes straight out with it. Will they go to bed with him?"

"You're kidding!"

Saffron shrugged. "That's what he says. He reckons women like the direct approach. When we were in South Africa he said he had a ninety per cent success rate."

"Do you believe him?"

"He didn't do too badly," Saffron admitted.

Jackson sounded almost awed as he turned his eyes back on the dance floor. "Do you think he's saying that to Lavinia Oldroyd? Christ, he deserves a medal if he does."

Saffron nodded across the floor. "She's still dancing with him."

At that moment two Anglo-Indian girls in their late teens approached Jackson. Their familiarity made it clear they were friends of the young corporal. After he was introduced to them, Saffron found his evening pleasantly occupied and it was only after The King was played and the guests began to disperse that Bickers joined him again. The Londoner was grinning from ear to ear. "Hiya, kid? You enjoyed yourself?"

Saffron nodded. "What about you?"

Bickers made a circle with his forefinger and thumb. "Great, kid. First class."

Saffron nodded at a taxi parked among the tongas outside the camp gates. "From your antics I thought you'd be taking the memsahib home."

Bickers winked as he fell in step alongside Saffron. "All in good time, kid. Poppa's home tonight. But it won't be long."

Saffron stared at him. "You're not thinking of going to her bungalow? Not seriously? If you're seen, her old man will skin you alive."

Bickers laid a finger alonside his nose. "We've got it all worked out. That Lavinia's quite a woman."

"What sort of a line have you been shooting her? That you're the greatest stud since Casanova."

Bickers smirked. "Some men don't need to say it, Saffron. Women can sense it."

"Don't give me that. You heard she likes a bit of rough and you've worked on it. That means she'll spit you out like a piece of chewed string when her mood changes. Don't you realise that?"

Bickers only grinned as he threw open the billet door. "Jealousy'll get you nowhere, Saffron. I've got a date with a white woman in this godforsaken place and no fat old colonel's going to spoil it for me."

"Not even with a gun?" Saffron asked, dragging off his shirt.

Bickers frowned. "Who said anything about a gun?"

"Jackson did. You're playing with fire, buster. Don't say I didn't warn you."

Bickers' frown faded as a picture of Lavinia's voluptuous

figure came to him. "She's knows what she's doing. She wants me as much as I want her."

"Let's hope you're right," Saffron said. "Because, in case you've forgotten, half of Baluchistan is after us already. Now get your head down. We could have a hard day tomorrow."

Chapter Fifteen

The two Bedfords, driven by Cornwall and Wilkinson, were rumbling up the long hill that led from Long Barracks to Hill Camp. Bickers, squashed in the cab of the first transport with Saffron and Cornwall, glanced back in dismay. "It's a hell of a way, Saffron."

"Three miles give a hundred yards or two," Saffron said.

"Who told you that?"

"McGrew."

"That bastard couldn't tell the truth if he tried."

Cornwall at the wheel was grinning. "What the matter, corporal? You got your mind on Razim Khan?"

He received a look of indignation from Bickers. "You're the one who should have that death threat, Cornwall. I was yards away when you untied those ropes."

Cornwall's grin spread. "The penalty of office. You should be like me. No authority, no pack drill."

Bickers scowled at the unfairness of it. "Not only that but McGrew has detailed two armourers to work with us up here. It's you and Wilkinson he should be sending. Not two innocent erks."

"We've got to bring your students up here in the mornings and take 'em back at night. And bring up your grub three times a day. What more do you want?"

With Saffron seated between him and the pugilist, Bickers felt safe in his bellicosity. "If I'd my way the two of you would be on guard duty outside the gas store every night."

Cornwall cast an amused glance at Saffron. "Your corporal's in a friendly mood this morning. You think it's his liver?"

The shortness of Saffron's reply gave evidence he had not forgiven Cornwall for his past transgressions in spite of his behaviour the previous day. "He's got a point. Don't you think so?"

Cornwall's laugh was full of malice. "I think it's damn funny, Saffron. And so does Wilkinson now he's got over his fright."

"That creep would," Bickers grunted. "Let's hope Razim Khan ambushes you both when you're coming up here. Come to think of it, he might when he finds out you're bringing us food. I'd recommend him for a gong if he did."

Cornwall grinned again. "I'll pass that on to Wilkinson. Then he'll be so scared you'll never get fed."

They reached Hill Camp a couple of minutes later. At first sight it was a dozen or so mutti huts standing in the middle of a barren plateau. A hundred yards from the huts was another disused rifle butt. Otherwise there was nothing but arid hills and valleys sweeping away to vast horizons. "Gawd, what a place," Bickers muttered.

As they jumped down from the Bedford, McGrew and two aircraftmen emerged from the nearest hut. The SWO waved the two NCOs over. "Here are the two armourers who're going to work with you. Barron and Malcolm."

Barron turned out to be a stockily built young man with a mop of fair hair and a cheerful, freckled face. Malcolm, an inch or two taller, was slimmer in build with sensitive, good-looking features.

After the introduction, McGrew led the NCOs into the nearby hut which Saffron saw was larger than the rest. Six long benches stood across it laterally and a large desk and chair faced them. "This will be for your courses," McGrew told the two men. "The men will be driven up here at 08.30 hours prompt. A char wallah will sell them mid-morning tea and their food will arrive at 13.00 hours. The gharry will take them back to Long Barracks at 17.00 hours and your meal will be sent up at 18.30. Any questions?"

"Where are we going to store the gas?" Saffron asked. "I'd like to get it out of the sun as soon as possible."

He received a look of dislike. "Give me time. Any questions about your routine so far?"

Bickers had one. "When do we get down to Long Barracks or into Shaman, sir?"

"I haven't worked out your duty roster yet," McGrew snapped. "As soon as I have I'll let your sergeant have it. Now let's get over to the gas store."

He led the four men to a mutti hut in the centre of the rectangle of huts. It was surrounded by an angle iron fence laced with barbed wire. Unlocking a gate also strung with barbed wire, McGrew turned to Saffron. "You'll keep your gas equipment as well as your gas in here. As you see, it doesn't have a window and the roof has an earth lining, so it keeps fairly cool throughout the day."

The hut had a low, narrow entrance. With an earthen floor, it was empty except for a pile of old sacking, a coil of rope, and a few empty wooden crates stacked in one corner. "What was kept here before?" Saffron asked.

"I understand the Army used it for weapons and ammunition. There used to be a small garrison here that serviced the rifle butts and a grenade range beyond it."

The hut's position had not escaped Saffron's notice. "Why was it sited in the centre of the billets? As a protection against tribesmen?"

McGrew's displeased glance made it clear he did not want emphasis laid on the dangers of the isolated post. "It's common practice in India to site weapon stores inside compounds. That's why the bomb dump is inside Long Barracks."

Although he had no wish to alarm the two armourers by discussing the potential threat from tribesmen, Saffron had no option but to criticise the defences of the hut. "This barbed wire fence is useless. It wouldn't keep a determined thief out for thirty seconds."

"Do you think I don't know that?" McGrew snapped. "But with the equipment we've got, what else can we do? Don't forget you're going to have Ghurka guards every night."

"How many, sir?"

"Two in four hour shifts. That's all the regiment can spare. But you'll have to stand guard yourselves tonight until I get things organised."

Saffron was showing concern. Seeing Bickers and the two young armourers were listening, he drew McGrew away. "Two guards aren't going to be enough, sir. What happens if the tribesmen make an attack?"

McGrew frowned. "They're not going to attack. That's all hogwash."

"But they could create havoc with these chemicals. Particularly the mustard gas."

McGrew waved the suggestion scornfully away. "Tribesmen wouldn't have a clue what to do with it. They'd only poison themselves."

In his mind's eye Saffron was seeing Razim Khan's fanatical but intelligent face again. "I wouldn't be so sure about that, sir. If they can make rifles, they can learn about poison gas. I think for the safety of the camp you need better security here."

McGrew's dislike of Saffron was on the surface again. "Well, I can't give you better security. I've no materials and I've no time. The first batch of RAF armourers are arriving at Long Barracks tomorrow."

Saffron gave a start. "Tomorrow?"

"That's right. And they have to be trained and sent back to their units in fourteen days. So you have to get your finger out. I want you and your corporal to start lectures the day after tomorrow."

Saffron jerked a thumb at the two silent aircraftmen. "I thought I was supposed to train these two men first."

"They'll have to go into your first class," McGrew told him. "Anything else they need to learn you can teach them in your spare time." He turned and pointed at the two waiting transports. "I want you to get them unpacked now. I have to be back in camp within an hour."

As he was about to walk away, McGrew turned back. "There's one other thing. Your billets." He pointed at the rectangle of empty mutti huts. "There are ten of them, so you can take your pick. They've all got charpoys inside and I've a couple of bearers sweeping 'em out at the moment. The bearers will be here every day to clean up for you. But remember one thing. You each billet in a separate hut. I don't want anyone sharing billets."

"Why not?" Saffron asked as the warrant officer paused.

McGrew gave a warning glance at Bickers and the two aircraftmen. "Do I have to spell it out? You don't put all your eggs in one basket in this country. No matter what, you sleep in different huts. If I find out you disobey this order, there'll be hell to pay. Do you understand?"

Saffron understood only too well. "Then you do think a raid is possible. What do we do if it happens? Are you going to give us guns?"

"Good God, no. No one's allowed to carry guns in this country unless they've got special permission. You'd just have to use your initiative."

Saffron decided it was a moment to dig his heels in. "What initiative am I supposed to use if a dozen armed tribesmen come howling for blood? Am I supposed to wave a phosgene bomb at them?"

His sarcasm brought a scowl from McGrew. "Don't try to be funny, Saffron. What do you think you've got guards for?"

"All two of them? We're entitled to weapons, sir. You know that as well as I do."

McGrew's scowl spread. "What I know or don't know has nothing to do with it, Saffron. As a protection for civilians, there's a directive right from the top that airmen and soldiers mustn't carry weapons inside India except in extreme circumstances."

"Don't you think these are extreme circumstances, sir?"

"No, I don't," McGrew snapped. "Now if you've finished

with your questions, let's get that gas into the store. I'm late as it is."

"The bastard." Bickers was watching the two Bedfords rumbling down the long hill towards Long barracks. "He couldn't get rid of us and the gas fast enough, could he?"

Saffron gave a rueful laugh. "I suppose in one way you can't blame him. It's a hell of a responsibility, particularly as they've sent so much of it."

Bickers cast a glance around the barren plateau. "So he dumps us up here. Look at it, Saffron. Not a tree, not even a bush. It's like being on the bloody moon."

Saffron sighed. "I suppose if poison gas has to be anywhere, this is the best place for it."

"But we're sitting ducks, Saffron. If that Mad Mullah finds out about us, he'll have our guts for garters. And he will, sooner or later."

Although Saffron knew it was highly unlikely their presence could be kept a secret for long, he did his best to allay the Londoner's fears. "That doesn't mean he'll attack us. He might have made that threat in the heat of the moment. If our own brother had been killed like that, we might have reacted in the same way."

"He meant it all right, Saffron, and you know it. For that matter, so does McGrew. Or why wouldn't he let us all share the same billet?"

Saffron shook his head. "No. Even McGrew wouldn't do that. I think that's standard procedure in these remote hill stations. If you noticed it, the huts are quite small, so even under normal conditions they couldn't take more than two men. It's nothing more than a sensible precaution."

"You mean if one or two of us get our throats cut in the night, it gives the others a chance to escape? I don't find that very comforting, Saffron."

Giving him a warning look, Saffron glanced round. To his relief Barron and Malcolm were standing talking outside the lecture hut and well out of earshot. "Stop looking on the black side of everything. I don't want those two kids terrified to go to bed at nights."

"But you don't mind if I do," Bickers muttered. "Because I'm going to be. And so are you if the truth's known."

Seeing an Indian bearer complete with mop and bucket emerging from one of the mutti billets, Saffron glanced back at the Londoner. "Have you chosen a hut yet?"

"No. Of course I haven't."

"Then go and talk to that bearer. He'll find you a nice clean one. Go on. It'll give you something to think about and keep you from being so pessimistic."

Bickers hesitated. "What about you?"

Saffron indicated the two armourers. "I want a word with those two first. Then I'll come over."

Bickers hesitated, then drifted reluctantly away. Seeing him address one of the bearers, Saffron approached the two armourers. "Have you two chosen a hut apiece yet?"

Barron answered him. "Yes, sarge, but we wonder if we can share one. It's going to be lonely here at nights."

Saffron nodded. "I know that but I want you to do as the SWO asks for at least a week or two. I've a suspicion he'll check on us. After that we might make a few changes."

Seeing the questions on both the armourers' faces, the Yorkshireman quickly changed the subject. "I don't know if you overheard the SWO but he wants you to attend the class I'm going to give during the next fortnight. After that I hope you'll be fit to help us with other intakes."

"What's gas like to handle, sergeant? Is it dangerous?" The question came from Malcolm.

"No more than live bombs which you must have fused often enough."

"But why has the mustard gas come in tanks?"

"One of our jobs is to show armourers how to fill their Smoke Curtain Installations if the Japs start using poison gas. But don't worry. You'll be fully protected when you demonstrate. I'll make sure of that."

A yell from the billet block drew all three men's attention. A moment later Bickers and one of the Indian bearers appeared. Seeing Bickers was arguing furiously with the Indian, Saffron moved towards them. "What's the matter now?"

Bickers turned a hot and aghast face towards the Yorkshireman. "You're not going to believe this, Saffron. Come and look in the billet this character has chosen for me."

The Indian bearer, an old man with a wrinkled face and betal-stained teeth, gave Saffron a puzzled grin. Led by the Londoner, Saffron followed them both to a hut that had been recently swept out. Halting in the doorway, Bickers waved Saffron inside. "Go on. Take a look!"

Seeing nothing at first but a single charpoy bed covered with a mosquito net, a paraffin lamp, and Bicker's possessions, the puzzled Saffron glanced back at the Londoner. "What's wrong with this? Did you expect a bathroom and toilet thrown in?"

Bickers almost choked. "Wrong with it? Look behind the mosquito net."

Stepping forward, Saffron drew aside the net and then recoiled. "My God!"

"You see." Bickers glared at the ancient bearer. "Get it out! Do you hear? Jildi, jildi!"

The Indian threw out his arms in protest. "*Ne*, sahib. He is your friend. He will protect you."

Bickers nearly choked again. "Protect me? It'll eat me." He appealed to the startled Yorkshireman. "Tell him to get it out, Saffron."

Recovering, Saffron took another look at the thing on the wall. At least as large as a tea cup saucer, it had the body and legs of a spider with the pincers of a crab. A pair of eyes on stalks shone suspiciously as they gazed at him.

Saffron turned to the bearer. "What is your name?"

"Moin, sahib."

"Why have you left this thing in the corporal sahib's billet, Moin?"

"Sahib, it is good. The corporal sahib is lucky. He will not be bitten. I will try to get one for you and the other sahibs. But they are not easy to find."

Saffron frowned. "What do you mean – the corporal sahib will not be bitten? Bitten by what?"

"By scorpions, sahib. This spider kills scorpions. If one enters the corporal sahib's billet, he will be eaten and die. Do you understand, sahib?"

Saffron glanced at the shaken Bickers. "I think the corporal sahib is more afraid of being bitten by the spider than by scorpions. Is it dangerous to people?"

The bearer' wrinkled hands made another gesture of protest. "*Ne*, sahib. He likes people. He will make friends with the corporal sahib if the corporal sahib feeds him every day."

Saffron grinned at the Londoner. "You hear that? Feed him and you're his friend for life."

Bickers shuddered. "You think I could go to sleep at nights with that things crawling all over me? Tell him I want it out."

Saffron turned back to the bearer. "You'll have to move it or my friend will get the heebie jeebies."

"The heebie jeebies, sahib? What are the heebie jeebies?"

Saffron grinned. "Just take it out."

Sighing, the bearer leaned over the bed and held out two wrinkled hands. To the airmen's astonishment, the creature sprang into them. "He knows you," Saffron said.

"Yes, sahib. I have often fed him when I have been sent up here." One of the old bearer's hands tickled the creature's back. "You see. He is quite harmless."

"What will you do with him now?" the Yorkshireman asked.

"I do not know, sahib. If you gentlemen do not want him, perhaps I will put him in one of the empty huts. But he might come back to you if you bring food into your billets. If he does not find any scorpions, he will go hungry."

The prospect of a social visit brought another shudder from Bickers. Saffron grinned. "So you'd better not have any midnight feasts while we're here." He turned back to the bearer. "If you're sure he's safe, you can put him in my hut. I'm no lover of scorpions."

The old man's wrinkled face lit up. "You will feed him, sahib?"

"If you tell me what he eats, yes."

"He eats anything, sahib. Bread, biscuits, meat, anything. Just leave food on the floor and he will find it."

"All right, Moin. Put him in the billet next door."

As the delighted old man hurried out with the creature, Bickers relaxed. "You're mad, Saffron. I always knew it but now it's on the record. Stark, raving mad."

"What? For giving a home to a scorpion spider?"

"Don't you realise what it means? I won't be able to visit you for a chat in the evenings."

Saffron's eyes twinkled. "What better reason for giving a home to a spider."

Bickers sounded hurt. "It's all right your talking, Saffron, but it's going to get hellishly lonely here at nights."

"Perhaps that's what the old man was thinking. It'd be company for you."

Bickers frowned. "Be serious for a minute. This is a hell of a posting. We're right in the middle of nowhere and we've no protection. It's not funny, Saffron."

"I know that, kid. But we'll get used to it as we've got used to things before." Then the Yorkshireman's tone changed. "Why are you wriggling about like that?"

"It's that bloody spider," Bickers muttered. "It's made me want to pee. Where are the toilets round here?"

Laughing, Saffron went out looking for the bearer. When he returned he had difficulty in hiding his amusement. "You want the toilets? Come on. I'll show you where to go."

He led the Londoner to a hut at the far end of the block and waved Bickers inside. "Here you are. Help yourself."

Bickers peered inside, then gave a gasp of horror. "That's it?"

"That's it. When it gets full, the bearers empty it. You should feel lucky we haven't got the job to do ourselves."

Bickers was staring at a large metal pail sunk into the earthen floor. "Is that for all of us?"

"All of us," Saffron told him. "Bearers and all."

Bicker's voice quivered in disbelief. "I've got to bare my backside in front of these Indian bearers? This is the end, Saffron. We've been going down all the time but now we've struck rock bottom. They hate us up there. They must do."

Grinning, Saffron clapped him across the shoulders. "Get your pee over and let's have a talk with those two armourers. We have to work out a roster for guard duty tonight."

Chapter Sixteen

It was the creaking of the door that awoke Saffron. With his heart suddenly pounding, he sat upright and threw back the mosquito net. "Who's that?"

A familiar voice made him relax. "It's me, Bickers. Can I come in?"

Saffron sighed. "I suppose so." Fumbling for the paraffin lamp at his bedside he found a box of matches. Striking one he held it up and saw Bickers standing in the doorway. A moment later he gave a start. "What's that on your head?"

Before Bickers could reply, the match burned Saffron's fingers. Cursing, he let it fall and darkness flooded back. Striking another match, he lit his oil lamp. As yellow light began spreading round the hut, Bickers came into sight again and Saffron gaped at him. "That's a tin helmet you've got on, isn't it?"

Bickers sounded both ashamed and defiant. "What's wrong with a tin helmet? They tried to shoot us once before in these bloody hills, didn't they?"

The helmet was huge, hiding most of Bicker's lugubrious face. Saffron felt hysterical laughter sweeping over him. "Where the hell did you get it from?"

Gazing around, Bickers saw a crate Saffron had brought in

from the gas store. He dragged it towards the bed and sank down on it. "I've just come off guard duty."

"I know," Saffron said. "I made out the roster." Leaning forward, he tapped Bicker's helmet. "The tin hat. Where did you get it?"

"I got it on the ship coming over," the Londoner admitted. "Someone must have left it lying around. I thought it might come in useful out here."

"You mean you've had it in your kit bag all this time?"

"Yes," Bickers said defiantly. "Why not?"

Saffron could contain his mirth no longer. "He must have been a big bastard. It's like a jerry pot on your head."

Bickers gave a grunt. "The bigger the better as far as I'm concerned."

"You don't exactly take chances, do you? Didn't you think they'd issue us with helmets if they were necessary?"

"Do they ever do anything right in the bloody Services?" the Londoner demanded. "If they did, we'd be issued with rifles already. A thought struck me when I was out there tonight. Have you still got that revolver you took from me?"

Saffron, who had forgotten the gun, gave a start. "Yes, I have. Why?"

"I'd like it back, Saffron. A man's entitled to some protection in a place like this."

Saffron's voice brooked no argument. "Oh, no. You nearly killed one of our own men in Bombay. Don't you realise what would happen if McGrew found out you were carrying a gun? You'd be straight into the glass-house."

"But you asked for rifles yourself."

"Officially, yes. But no private weapons."

"You've got a nerve, Saffron. You've got the revolver so you're all right if someone tries to cut your throat. But what about me?"

"I'd forgotten about it," Saffron admitted. "I'll have to get rid of it."

"Don't be a fool. It's the only protection we've got."

Saffron realised there was truth in the remark. "All right. I'll hang on to it for a while."

"Hanging on to it isn't any use. You have to carry the bloody thing in case we're attacked during the day."

Saffron relented. "All right then. I'll keep it in my pocket. It's small enough to go unnoticed anyway. Does that make you happy?"

Bickers sniffed. "I'd rather have it myself but I suppose it's the next best thing."

Saffron changed the subject. "Was Malcolm at the gas store when you left?"

Bickers gave a gloomy nod. "Yes. I woke him up. He didn't look too happy doing his turn round the huts. In fact I thought he looked scared."

"How did your two hours go?"

Bickers muttered something but made no reply. Fishing in a pocket he drew out his pipe and with it a packet of cigarettes. "Want a smoke?"

Saffron nodded, then indicated the Londoner's pipe. "You don't seem to be smoking that thing so much these days. Why is that?"

"A man needs a contented mind to smoke a pipe, Saffron. We don't seem to have had a moment of it since we left South Africa."

"What about Ceylon? That wasn't bad, was it?"

"And how long did that last?" Bickers grumbled. "One bloody day."

A long pause followed before the Londoner waved his unlit pipe at the open door. "It's hellishly quiet out there, Saffron."

"I know. It was quiet in here until you arrived."

Bickers ignored the quip. "I've never known silence like it. It's so quiet it's full of noise, if you know what I mean. You can hear the blood pumping in your ears."

"Isn't that the way we want it?"

Bickers frowned. "I suppose we do. But it's creepy. It's going to take some getting used to."

"That's because you're a big city man. There's always noise in cities. You're not used to wide open spaces."

For a moment Bickers took umbrage. "Listen to the Lone Star Cowboy talking. Since when was Yorkshire the Wild West?"

"That's more like it. I thought for a moment you'd come to tell me you're resigning."

"Can't you be serious for a moment, Saffron? Don't you find it weird out here? All this space and emptiness and the stars so low you feel you ought to duck your head. Didn't it get you thinking when you were on duty?"

"Yes. I kept thinking how bored I was and whether you'd remember to relieve me on the next shift."

Bickers gave a resigned shrug of his shoulders. "I don't know why I ever teamed up with you, Saffron. No two men could be more different."

Saffron grinned. "I'll tell you why you teamed up with me, buster. Because you needed someone to yank you out of those moods of yours and to get you out of trouble. Which I've been doing since God knows when."

For once Bickers ignored the Yorkshireman's sarcasm. "How long are they going to keep us up here, Saffron? It's the kind of place you read about, where men become unbalanced. We could grow into hermits. We might even go mad."

Saffron shook his head. "And you've been here less than twenty-four hours!"

"That's just the point. If it can do this to a man in one day, what will it do to him in a week or a month or a year?"

Examining him in the yellow light of the oil lamp, Saffron decided a little mercy would not go amiss. "You won't be here a year. We're both due for repatriation before the year's out."

"Yes, but what if they decide this Jap gas threat is so serious we have to stay on? They seem to be in a bad panic about it. What happens then?"

Saffron knew it was possible but felt it wasn't the time to admit it. "Don't let's meet problems before they happen.

What about that date you've got with Lavinia Oldroyd? Isn't bed with her something to look forward to?"

Bickers' refusal to perk up at the thought of sex was an pointed indicator of his mood. "That was before we were sent up here. How am I going to see her now?"

"McGrew has to give us some time off. I'll try to get that evening for you."

For a moment Bickers' face brightened, only for his shoulders to sag again. "McGrew's not going to do us any favours. He's got his knife in us and he'll keep on twisting it. You'll see."

Saffron grinned. "You've really got the blues tonight, haven't you? Mind you don't talk this way to those two kids. I don't want them getting broody too."

Bickers looked hurt. "As if I would. But I can talk things over with you, can't I?"

Saffron yawned. "That's what you've been doing for the last fifteen minutes. Don't you think you ought to get to bed now?"

Ignoring the suggestion, Bickers glanced around the billet. "You haven't got a drink, have you?"

"I have but you're not having one in the middle of the night. Wrap it up and go to bed."

"You're a miserable sod, Saffron. If you felt like talking, I wouldn't throw you out of my billet."

Saffron's eyes suddenly twinkled. "It's not just me you're keeping awake. It's Horace."

The Londoner frowned. "Horace?"

"The spider. I don't think he likes being disturbed in his beauty sleep."

With a yelp Bickers shot to his feet. "Christ, I'd forgotten all about him. Where is he?"

"I don't know. Take a look."

Grabbing up the lamp, Bickers shone it around and saw two pinpricks of light on the wall above Saffron's mosquito net. "My God! He's right above you, Saffron! On the wall!"

"He is? What's he doing?"

"He's staring straight at me!" His voice almost hysterical, Bickers lowered the lamp and ran to the door. "How can you lie there like that?"

Grinning, Saffron stubbed out his cigarette. "As you're in a chatty mood, why don't we talk about the course we're taking tomorrow? Do you want to do the talk on mustard gas and SCIs or would you like me to handle it?"

There was no reply. The doorway was empty and Bickers had gone.

Chapter Seventeen

Saffron peered at the brilliant blue sky through slitted eyes. High above the mountain that overshadowed the plateau he could see a tiny hovering speck. Moving his eyes he thought he caught sight of another far to the south but it vanished as his eyes tried to focus on it. Using a trick he had learned in his air combat days, Saffron moved his eyes a fraction to one side and the speck appeared again. It was there. And there was yet another, far to the east.

He closed his eyes again and forced his limbs to relax and remain motionless. After five minutes he cautiously opened his eyes again but the specks were still riding the air currents high in the limitless sky. He was just deciding to give it another five minutes more when a curious voice disturbed his concentration. "What the hell are you doing, Saffron?"

The Yorkshireman sighed and sat up. "I was playing dead until you mucked it up."

"Playing dead? You gone doolally or something?"

Saffron pointed at the dazzling sky. "You see those vultures up there?"

The Londoner followed his finger and gave a contemptuous laugh. "Those aren't vultures. Vultures are big birds."

"They're vultures," Saffron said patiently. "They fly high and quarter the sky so if one of them spots anything dead or dying, the others spot its signals and follow it to the prey."

Bickers stared at him. "How do you know this?"

Saffron shrugged. "I must have read it somewhere. I wanted to see if I could fool them and bring them down. But I suppose they could see I was breathing or could see my eyes move."

Bickers gazed up at the tiny specks and then at Saffron again. "See your eyes? From thousands of feet up there? You have gone doolally, mate. They probably can't see the gas school from up there."

The Yorkshireman shook his head. "They've got both long range eyesight and microscopic lenses too. That's why they're so hard to fool."

Bickers was examining Saffron with some concern. "What do you want to bring 'em down for? For that matter, why do you want to waste time on our day off? Barron and Malcolm are asking if you'll make up a card school. What about it?"

Saffron picked up his gas cape from the ground. "Some other time. I feel like a walk today. The old bearer says there's a stream down on the other side of the plateau. Why don't you came with me? We could have a swim or at least a bathe down there."

Bickers drew back. "Don't you remember what happened the last time we took a walk? I'm not looking for trouble if you are, mate."

"OK. I'll be back before the gharry comes with our supper."

Bickers was looking worried. "You mean you'll hope you'll be back. Take the revolver with you. Just in case."

Saffron shook his head. "No. It's guns the tribesman go for. They say they can sniff 'em out from a couple of miles away."

"Then take something," Bickers urged. "Take a knife or a stick."

Saffron relented. "All right. I'll carry something. Remember you're in charge while I'm away, so don't let the men drift away in case McGrew decides to pay you a visit."

Bickers gave a sniff. "No one's going to drift away, Saffron. The rest of us have too much bloody sense."

Saffron heard the voices as he was approaching a bend in the stream. Bushes hid the speakers from him but although he could not understand their language the voices sounded both mocking and threatening.

Saffron had followed the stream for the last half mile. Flanked by the only vegetation he had seen in this part of the valley, it was less of a stream than a canal, running from the mountains to the east, where perpetual snow ensured a water supply even during the intense summer heat. According to the old bearer Moin, the canal had been cut to provide water for Shaman. At this point it was about eight feet wide but at the bend ahead it had broken its banks and formed a pool wide enough to allow a man to swim, the reason Saffron had been making for it.

The voices came again, harsh with laughter and menace. Common sense told Saffron he should retreat while he was undiscovered and he might have done this had he not heard a third voice replying in a way that suggested defiance.

Bending low to keep below the height of the bushes, he crept forward. He was carrying a four foot metal stay that, keeping his promise to Bickers, he had brought with him. Reaching a screen of bushes that ran to the water's edge, he parted them cautiously and saw a young man wearing only a loin cloth standing in a small clearing directly ahead of him. Two men barred his way both forward and back. Both were wearing the same head scarves and dress that Razim Khan's tribesmen had worn up the mountainside. Unshaven, villainous in appearance, they were brandishing long curved knives and it was apparent to Saffron they had caught the young man when bathing and were tormenting him before making their attack.

The young man, who was showing desperate defiance, looked familiar to Saffron. Puzzled for a moment, he then remembered he was one of the Ghurkas who was doing daily guard duty at the gas school.

Saffron knew he had only a moment to make a decision. The two tribesmen were drawing closer and the gestures they were making with their murderous knives could mean only one thing. Afraid of the knives, Saffron found himself wishing he had taken Bickers' advice and remained within the camp. Even then, as his instinct of self-preservation reminded him, it was not too late to retreat.

But Saffron had always suffered from a surfeit of remorse: a conscience whose daily scourging could inflict more distress than the blows of any enemy. Taking a deep breath, gripping the metal stay, he pushed aside the bushes and ran to the young man's side.

Taken by surprise, the two tribesmen jumped back and turned, clearly expecting more help to arrive.

But their uncertainty was soon over. Realising Saffron was alone and had no weapon but the metal stay, they turned back to the two men and with their knives making menacing patterns they began jeering and threatening them as they drew closer.

Their threats were all Saffron needed to fire his own aggression. As the nearer tribesman made a preliminary lunge at him, Saffron leapt to one side and brought the metal stay down on his extended arm with all his strength. As the man screamed and dropped the knife, the Yorkshireman swung the stay again and caught him full across the back. Seeing the man fall, Saffron snatched up his knife and turned towards the young Ghurka who was trying to evade the knife slashes of the second tribesman. As Saffron ran forward, the metal stay held out like a lance, the man realised he was outnumbered and fled into the bushes.

Saffron swung round. The first tribesman, clutching his back, was limping away. As the young Ghurka snatched the knife from Saffron, the Yorkshireman checked him. "No, let him go," he panted.

To his relief the Ghurka understood English. For a moment it seemed he would disobey. Then he nodded and turned back to Saffron. "Thank you, sergeant."

Saffron was still struggling for breath. "What happened?"

The Ghurka pointed at the stream. "I was taking a bath when they came. I could do nothing. My clothes and kukri are over there," and he pointed to a heap of clothes at the foot of a bush. "I would have been dishonoured but for you, sergeant."

Saffron thought what a quaint way it was of putting it. "Why did they want to kill you?"

The Ghurka smiled. "We are friends of the British, sergeant. So they hate us."

Saffron was recovering fast. "It's a reason, I suppose. How is it you speak such good English?"

The young Ghurka was busy climbing into his shirt and shorts. "We are taught it when we are recruited. All our officers are British."

"You've learned it well," Saffron said. "How long have you been in the Army?"

"Since I was a boy, sergeant."

"Do you like it?"

The young man's eyes glowed. "Very much. It is my life."

"What's your name?"

"Pemba, sergeant."

"Well, Pemba, I wouldn't come swimming again on my own. I know I shan't."

For a moment the Ghurka's face betrayed his shame. "I will not be caught again, sergeant. The next time it will be the tribesman who will face death."

Saffron believed him. He picked up the metal stay from the ground. "I'll have to go now. I'll see you the next time you're on duty."

To his surprise the Ghurka stepped in front of him. "No. You cannot go yet, sergeant."

"Why not?" Saffron asked.

"You have saved my life. I must give you my blood."

"Blood? What are you talking about?"

"Our blood must mingle, sergeant, so you become my brother."

As the Ghurka dropped his hand to his leather belt, Saffron noticed for the first time that there were two knife scabbards hanging from it, one on the left side and the other on the right. Then he remembered reading that Ghurkas were forbidden by their religion to draw their sacred kukris unless they drew blood, which made a second kukri necessary for the mundane tasks of military life.

Saffron noticed the Ghurka's hand was resting on his sacred kukri. "You don't owe me anything, Pemba. You would have done the same thing for me."

"Please, sergeant. Let my blood mingle with yours. Then I shall always be there to protect you."

"But I don't want protection," Saffron protested.

"But you have saved my life. So my life is yours whenever you need it."

"I don't need your life, Pemba. You're making too much of what happened just now."

The young Ghurka's head drooped and he turned away. "You are right. A man who allows two pigs to ambush him like that is not worthy to be your brother."

"Don't be stupid," Saffron said. "What happened to you could have happened to anybody." Then, seeing the young man's intense disappointment, he hesitated, then frowned. "Just what had you in mind?"

His face brightening, Pemba swung round. "It is nothing. It will be over in seconds." Explaining the ceremony, he then dropped a hand hopefully on the haft of his sacred kukri. "You will do me this honour, sergeant?"

Knowing once the kukri was drawn there would be no turning back, Saffron fought back his queasiness. "Yes, all right. Let's get it over."

Showing both gratitude and delight, Pemba drew his sacred kukri and approached the frowning Yorkshireman.

Bickers looked relieved. "Where the hell have you been? We thought the tribesman must have got you."

Saffron dropped on a bench left outside the lecture hut. "They nearly did."

About to question him about tribesmen, Bickers noticed Saffron's right hand around which a handkerchief was wrapped. "What's happened to your hand?"

Saffron told him the story. "The kid wouldn't let me go until he made us blood brothers. So I had to let him cut our thumbs and press them together."

Bickers was looking aghast. "You risked your life for one of these Ghurkas? Are you out of your mind, Saffron? What would have happened to us up here if they'd killed you? Don't you ever think of anyone but yourself?"

Saffron grinned. "Do you know something? That was the first thing that came to my mind when that tribesman came at me with his knife. What would my mate Bickers do if I wasn't around to keep pulling him out of the brown stuff?"

"It's all right you laughing, Saffron, but who's the first one to talk about responsibility? Why wouldn't you carry the gun? You promised me that you always would."

"I didn't think it was wise to go out of camp with it but I will in the future," Saffron promised.

"I should bloody well think so. You ought to have more sense going walkabout in this country."

"I was safe enough coming back," Saffron told him, aware that beneath the Londoner's bluster there was genuine concern for his safety. "Deciding a metal stay was no protection, the kid insisting on escorting me almost all the way."

Bickers sniffed. "Someone who gets caught like that doesn't sound much of an escort to me."

"Don't you believe it. Everyone round here is scared of the Ghurkas. You ought to see one of those sacred kukris. You could have shaved with this one."

Bickers' eyes dropped to Saffron's hand. "How deep did he cut it?"

"Quite deep," Saffron admitted. "But it'll soon heal."

Bickers looked queasy. "You're mad, Saffron. A guy who

lets a wog slash his thumb that way has to be. What about infection?"

A distant squawking attracted Saffron's attention. He rose to his feet. "What's that noise?"

"Vultures," the Londoner said.

"Vultures?"

"Yes. They're lining up on the wall of the rifle butt."

Moving round the lecture hut, Saffron saw he was right. At least a dozen vultures were perched on the high wall, squabbling and pecking at one another as they fought for position.

Saffron frowned. "What's brought them down?"

"It must have been you. That clowning you did earlier on must have alerted them." Bicker grinned. "Why don't you get over there and say you're sorry? Or lie down and let 'em have a feed? They're getting on our nerves. Particularly as more of 'em are coming."

Saffron saw he was right. As he watched, two more of the huge birds came swooping down, squawking and squabbling with the others as they landed. "Are you sure there's nothing in the butts?," Saffron asked. "No dead birds or animals?"

"No. Barron went to look. He's says there are some old bones mixed in with the sand but nothing a vulture could eat."

Saffron frowned. "Then I don't understand it. I couldn't get a single bird to come down earlier on."

Bickers glanced down maliciously at Saffron's hand. "Maybe it's something to do with that cut. Maybe they know the knife was infected and you're going to die. Have you thought of that?"

"You're a real funny man, aren't you?," Saffron said. He turned towards his billet. "I'm going to make myself some tea. You coming or not?"

The mystery of the vultures was settled early that evening. As the sun was setting over the western mountains, Malcolm appeared at Saffron's open door. His sensitive face had a puzzled, disturbed appearance. "Can you spare a moment, sergeant?"

Saffron, sitting on his bed reading, glanced up. "Yes, Malcolm. What's your problem?"

"There are half a dozen Indians at the rifles butts, sergeant. They've brought an old camel with them."

"A camel? What for?"

"I think they're going to kill it, sergeant."

Saffron laid down his book. "I'd better come over."

The first thing Saffron noticed as he rounded the lecture hut was the high wall above the butts. Every inch of its length was now packed with vultures, squawking and biting viciously at one another with their yellow beaks. Below them were half a dozen Indians, two of them with knives in their hands, and a feeble camel standing on spindly legs.

As Saffron reached the far end of the hut he saw Bickers and Barron standing there. The Londoner turned to Saffron. "Do you know anything about this, Saffron?"

The Yorkshireman shook his head. "No. But it must account for the bones in the sand. The Indians must use the butts to shoot or slaughter their old animals."

Malcolm had his eyes fixed on the row of squabbling vultures. "But how did the vultures know this was going to happen, sergeant?"

Before the Yorkshireman could reply, he saw one of the Indians tug on the camel's bridle. Obediently the old camel sank down in the sand. A moment later two men bent over it and slashed at its neck. As blood spurted out, the animal's legs kicked out, quivered, then lay still. At the same moment the row of vultures began a hideous squawking, some flapping their wings and swooping impatiently down, only to fly back to the wall when the Indians waved and shouted at them.

Alongside Saffron, Malcolm looked as if he were going to be sick. Across at the butts the Indians were removing the bridle from the old camel. As they moved away there was a great clattering of wings and in seconds the camel's body was covered by ripping, tearing carrion.

Bickers was looking almost as pale as Malcolm as he turned to Saffron. "I don't get it, do you?"

Saffron shook his head. "No, I don't."

"Those birds knew hours before that something was going to be killed here. They must have done."

Saffron's eyes were on Malcolm who was still staring at the butts as if hypnotised. "Rubbish," he said curtly. "One bird must have thought there was something to eat down here and the others just followed it."

"What – with those binocular eyes you were talking about? They knew something was going to die here, Saffron. Why don't you admit it?"

Giving Bickers a warning glance, Saffron took Malcolm's arm and found it was trembling. "It was only coincidence. Nothing more."

Shaken himself, Bickers was in no mood to comfort others. "This a damned creepy place, Saffron. Murderous tribesmen, live gas, man-eating spiders and now vultures who can see death coming. They shouldn't put men up in a place like this."

Concerned about Malcolm, Saffron found his temper snap. "Why don't you shut up and go to your billet? I don't want to listen any more to your stupid crap and neither do the rest of us."

The Yorkshireman half expected an indignant reply. Instead Bickers stared at him and then walked sullenly away.

Chapter Eighteen

"Saffron. What are you doing?"

The Yorkshireman, kneeling down in the doorway of his billet, looked back over his shoulder at Bickers. "I'm feeding Horace."

"You're what?"

"I'm feeding the spider. Come and look."

Bickers moved cautiously forward, keeping well behind the kneeling Saffron. Peering over his shoulder, he saw the Yorkshireman breaking up a biscuit and sprinkling it on the floor of the billet. In front of him Horace was sweeping up the crumbs with his pincers and pushing them into his gaping mouth. "My God, you are," Bickers said.

"You want to give him something too?" Saffron asked. "He'll be your friend if you do."

"Friend? Who wants to be friends with him?"

"He might patrol your billet then. Keep all the nasty creepy crawlies away."

Bickers shuddered. "What could be a worse creepy crawlie than that?"

"Scorpions could," Saffron told him. "Those things with the big tail that whips up and bites you."

"I don't believe that thing kills them, Saffron. I think Moin was just pulling your leg."

"Wrong. He killed one yesterday. I found the bits lying all over the floor of the billet."

"How do you know it was a scorpion?"

"There was a bit of its tail left. I don't think Horace cares for the tail."

Bickers glanced around uneasily. "I haven't seen any scorpions around."

"You will," Saffron assured him. He glanced back at Horace who was sweeping up the last of the biscuit. "You missed a good thing here, buster. You'll wish you hadn't been so fussy when you crawl out of bed one morning and find a scorpion slavering to bite you. Don't howl for me to come and kill it."

Bickers scowled. "Trust you to spoil a man's sleep. Isn't it bad enough thinking about the Mad Mullah without making things worse?"

About to reply, Saffron heard the distant sound of an engine. Rising, he glanced at his watch. "Dinner's early tonight, isn't it?"

Both men moved to gain sight of the dusty road. A minute

later a Bedford crested the hill and headed towards them. "Maybe it's not soya links and cabbage tonight," Bickers said hopefully. "Maybe the Navy have run out of the stuff at last."

The Londoner's complaint derived from the somewhat astonishing fact that military camps in Baluchistan came under the victualling province of the Royal Navy. As a consequence men believed that they were saddled with the food that the Senior Service rejected. Certainly the almost daily ration of the almost unpalatable soya sausages and boiled cabbage seemed to justify this belief.

The two NCOs watched the Bedford draw up before them and the muscular figure of Cornwall jump out. As he pulled out a cardboard box, Bickers frowned. "That doesn't look like our grub. So what's he bringing?"

The pugilist was grinning as he approached the two airmen. As he lowered the box at their feet, both men heard the clank of glass. "Hello, sergeant. Hello, corporal. I hope the news has made you both happy."

Saffron frowned. "What news?"

Cornwall showed surprise. "Don't say you haven't heard it."

"Heard what?"

"The European war's over. The Jerries have surrendered."

Both NCOs gaped at him. Saffron's voice was hoarse. "Is this a joke?"

"No. We got the news this morning. Didn't the guy who brought the food at midday tell you?"

"Nobody's told us. Is it true? Is it really over?"

"Yeah. The CO gave everyone a day off. Didn't anyone tell you that either?"

Bickers found his voice at last. "The bastards! They've all been celebrating down there and no one's given a damn about us."

Cornwall grinned. "I suppose they forget you."

"What about the Jap war?" Saffron asked.

"That goes on just the same. So don't get too excited."

Bickers could not forget the perfidy of it all. "What a bloody outfit we're in. We've got parents and girlfriends back there and nobody bothered to tell us they're safe. I'll never forgive 'em for this, Saffron."

Cornwall gave a cynical laugh. "You expect anyone to care about things like that. Where have you been all these years? In a nunnery?" When Bickers made no reply, the pugilist pointed at the box at his feet. "Never mind. They've remembered you now. There's your bit of comfort."

Bickers bent suspiciously over the cardboard box. "What is it."

"Eight bottles of beer. Two per man."

"What!"

Indicating Saffron's brevet, Cornwall grinned again. "The RAF's thanks for your years of loyal and dedicated service in overcoming Hitler's hordes. Don't get pissed on it, will you?"

Bickers sounded faint. "This is all we're getting? What about the celebrations down in the camp? Aren't we invited to them?"

"What celebrations? We've only had two bottles a man ourselves. Most of the lads feel worse than they did yesterday."

"Why?" Saffron asked.

Cornwall shrugged. "While everyone back in Blighty is whooping it up, we've still got the Japs to sort out. So what do we have to celebrate?"

"That's true," the Londoner muttered.

Saffron nodded at the Bedford. "You'd better get back, Cornwall."

Cornwall gave him a mocking salute. "Yes, sergeant. I'll leave you to your celebrations." His laugh came floating back at he made for the truck. "Take it easy tonight. You've still got a long war ahead of you."

Bickers poured the last drop of beer into his mug and gave a heavy, painful sigh. "Think of it, kid. They'll be drinking champagne back there."

"That's a laugh," Saffron said impatiently. "They'll be lucky if they've enough beer to go round. It hasn't been an easy war for them either, you know."

Bickers was not listening. "They'll be in Piccadilly Circus and Trafalgar Square, dancing and singing and hugging one another. And all those girls, kissing every serviceman they can lay hands on. Vera Lynn singing her head off. Joy unconfined, Saffron. And here we are with just two bottles of awful beer."

Barron, a Londoner himself, joined in Bickers' nostalgia. "They'll be whooping it up along the Old Kent Road too, corp."

Bickers nodded. "That's for sure. Street lights on again. Crowds dancing in the streets. Packed pubs and cinemas. Bloody marvellous."

Saffron grinned. "And pickpockets having a field day."

"Listen to a bloody Yorkshireman talking? What do you know about London, Saffron? You haven't a clue what it's like to belong to the greatest city on earth. You tykes should keep to things you know. Like jam butties and Yorkshire pud."

Saffron winked at young Malcolm, the other member of the squad sharing Bickers' billet that evening. "That beer must be stronger than we thought."

Bickers was having none of that. "It's nothing to do with beer, Saffron. It's the thought of being unable to share the happiness with all those people."

Saffron winked at Malcolm again. "He means he's fed up because he's not getting his share of those kisses the girls are handing out. How do you feel about the news, Malcolm?"

The shy youngster managed a smile. "I'm glad for my parents, sergeant. I didn't like those buzz bombs coming over night after night."

"Where's your home, Malcolm?"

"Southampton, sergeant." Before Saffron could comment, Malcolm went on: "How long do you think the war out here is going to last?"

Saffron shook his head. "I can't help you there, Malcolm. I just don't know."

"Years and bloody years," Bickers broke in, his frustration hiding from him the youngster's misgivings. "Those little bastards aren't going to quit. They'll fight to the last man."

Saffron gave him an angry glance. "Don't you believe it, Malcolm. They're fighting three nations on their own now. They must crack sooner or later."

Realising he had blundered, Bickers sniffed and changed the subject. "At least the grub was better tonight. What do you think it was? Camel meat?"

"It was spam," Saffron told him. "You've tasted spam before, haven't you?"

Bickers gave a grunt. "Oh, is that what it was? I thought there was something familiar about it. Only we've had so many soya links since we've been here I'd forgotten what other food tastes like."

The four men chatted for another hour before Saffron glanced at his watch. "I think we'd better break it up now. We've got twelve thick armourers to put through their paces in a few hours time." His eyes settled on Malcolm as the two aircraftmen rose. "At least you can go to bed tonight knowing one war is over. Let's hope this one ends soon too."

He waited until the two men had said goodnight and left the billet before turning to Bickers. "Ken, I want you to go easy with young Malcolm. He's a bright lad and learning fast but he's very tightly strung. Keep an eye on him and try to make sure he doesn't get depressed. OK?"

Bickers frowned. "I know. I shouldn't have said that about the war. But it's only what everyone else is thinking."

"It's not just the war. Don't talk in front of him about Razim Khan or the tribesmen. I've a feeling he might crack if he dwells on the danger too much."

The Londoner gave a sarcastic grunt. "All right. I'll tell him he's the luckiest lad in the world to be out here in all this sunshine and among all these friendly faces. And being looked after so well by the RAF. How will that do?"

Saffron grinned and clapped him across the shoulders. "Tell him that and you might convince yourself too. Then we'll all be happy."

Chapter Nineteen

Cornwall pressed the Bedford's hooter and then leaned from the open window of his cab. "Your grub's here, sergeant. Come and get it."

Saffron appeared at the door of the lecture hut. Seeing the Bedford, he turned back to his class of armourers who were already on their feet. "Take it easy. It's not going to run away." He nodded at the two men detailed for the task. "All right. Go and bring the food in. The rest of you dismiss and fetch your eating irons."

In the time honoured way of servicemen, there was a clatter of benches and then a rush for the door. As the hut emptied and Saffron began collecting his notes, a muscular figure appeared in the doorway. "How's it going, sergeant? You enjoying it up here?"

Saffron glanced at the grinning Cornwall. "I'm loving it," he said shortly.

"I take it you haven't seen anything of Razim Khan yet?"

"No."

"Do you expect to?"

"I don't know. I'm not a prophet."

Cornwall's grin spread at the Yorkshireman's brusqueness. "How's your corporal liking it?"

"Why don't you go and ask him?"

"Maybe I will. Where is he?"

"In his billet, I suppose."

Cornwall fished into the pocket of his shirt and pulled out an envelope. "I've got a letter for him."

Saffron showed surprise. "A letter? Why didn't it come with the other mail?"

147

"It didn't arrive with the other mail. It was dropped off at the guardroom last night."

Looking puzzled, Saffron held out his hand. "Let me see it."

Cornwall drew back his hand teasingly. "Naughty, naughty. It's addressed to Corporal Bickers."

"Let me see it," Saffron demanded.

Saffron examined the envelope as the grinning Cornwall handed it over. Pink in colour, it was made of quality paper and addressed in elegant handwriting to Corporal Ken Bickers. Saffron turned it over but could see no mention of the sender.

"It's from a woman," Cornwall said.

Although Saffron was certain he was right, he had no intention of giving Cornwall the slightest advantage. "What makes you think that?"

"The poncy envelope. The handwriting. That mate of yours must have been on the ran tan at the dance the other week. And it's been a white woman too. He must be getting it off with one of the officer's wives."

Saffron wondered why he was defending Bickers' peccadilloes. "What, and risk it being censored? Don't you know incoming mail as well as outgoing mail is censored here?"

Cornwall grinned again. "The woman knows that too. That's why she didn't post it but asked the guardroom to get it straight to Bickers. She must either know that Canadian SP or know he's an easy-going guy."

"Barlow gave it to you to deliver, did he?"

"That's right. With a big grin all over his face."

Saffron decided it was the moment to terminate the discussion. "All right. I'll see Bickers gets it. You'd better get back to Long Barracks."

Cornwall's smile was mocking. "Will you be in on this too?"

"In on what?"

"I mean when the two of you have finished with her, are you going to think of your old pals? There's a hell of a shortage of white women in these parts, in case you haven't noticed."

After Cornwall's commendable behaviour during the Razim Khan incident, Saffron was almost relieved to find that his one-time dislike of the man was justified. "Get back to Long Barracks, Cornwall. You bring a bad smell up here."

Cornwall's mocking laugh was almost drowned by the clank of metal cans as the two armourers entered the hut with the lunchtime meal. Telling them to start distributing it, Saffron went looking for Bickers. He found the Londoner in his hut, lying on his charpoy clad only in his shorts. "Gawd, it's hot, Saffron. It must be well over a hundred today."

"It is. It's a hundred and ten."

"White men shouldn't have to work in this heat, Saffron. It's all wrong."

"I notice you're putting in a hard stint. It must be murder lying there on that charpoy."

Bickers sniffed. "There's no need to be sarcastic, Saffron. Out here a wise man takes it easy when he can."

"So I've noticed. Do you know the grub's here?"

Bickers showed little interest. "Yes, I heard the gharry. What is it? The same old soya links and cabbage?"

"I suppose so. But there also a letter for you."

At that Bickers sat up sharply. "A letter?"

"Yes. Delivered to the guardroom. Here."

Bickers snatched the pink envelope from Saffron's hand. Tearing it open he drew out a single sheet of paper. Scanning it quickly, he gave a yelp of delight. "You know who this is from, kid?"

Saffron gave a curt nod. "I can guess."

"It's her, Lavinia. She's given me an address and the time she wants me round. Isn't that marvellous?"

"Wonderful," Saffron said. "She's like Salome. She wants your head on a plate."

Bickers was almost hugging himself with delight. "I thought she might have had second thoughts after the dance. But no.

She's got it all organised. Think of it, Saffron. A white woman after all this time."

"I am thinking about it," Saffron said. "I'm thinking about a red-faced old colonel with a gun in his hand."

For the briefest of moments, Bickers faltered. Then his euphoria returned. "No, she's got it all worked out. In two weeks time the old boy will be at the college for the entire weekend."

"Two weeks!" Saffron said. "The war could be over by then."

"Fat chance," Bickers grunted. "It's a long time to wait, I know, but at least it takes care of her old man."

"What about neighbours? They're sure to see you. What happens if they tell him?"

Bickers winked. "That's all taken care of. I'm not seeing her in her bungalow. I'm meeting her at a friend's place."

"What friend?"

"A young woman whose husband is away somewhere."

"Was she at the dance too?"

"No, she couldn't get that night. But Lavinia says she's a good sport."

"She must be. What's she running? A brothel?"

"Don't be stupid. She's just helping out a friend, that's all."

"What's she going to do while you're rogering Lavinia? Twiddling her thumbs or joining in?"

Bickers smirked. "That'd be fun, wouldn't it?" Then his tone changed. "No. She's going to have company too. Lavinia wants me to bring a friend."

"A friend? You mean for the other woman?"

"That's right." Bickers was looking pleased with himself, "It couldn't have worked out better, could it? Lavinia for me and the other woman for you. I've done you another favour, kid."

Saffron frowned. "Me? What are you talking about?"

"I've got you a date. With a pretty European woman."

The Yorkshireman's reply was emphatic. "Oh, no. I've

been caught with your blind dates before. Lavinia's not bad looking, I'll give you that, but that kind always have an ogre for a companion. You're not landing me with one of those again, buster. Not on your life."

"No, it's not like that," Bickers protested, handing the sheet of notepaper to Saffron. "This one's pretty. And she's young. Look what Lavinia says about her."

Saffron read the few terse lines. "She would say it, wouldn't she?"

"I don't see why. In any case, what have you got to lose? If you don't like the look of her you can always pack it in and leave."

It would be a lie to say Saffron was not tempted. Like many other wartime servicemen and women, he had discovered that the mere absence of social contact with the opposite sex was in many ways as unsettling as the lack of sex itself. After months of harsh masculine life, the Yorkshireman knew it would be a pleasure just to sit in a civilised living room and talk to an attractive woman.

Then he shook his head. "I don't think so. These snooty, toffee-nosed mensahibs don't appeal to me. And if she's a friend of Lavinia's she's bound to be like her."

"You don't know that. In any case," and Bickers gave a lecherous leer, "who cares whether they're toffee-nosed or not. The rest of them's just the same, isn't it?"

"You're nothing but a randy old tom cat. In any case, what about the gas stores up here? We can't both go off duty the same evening."

"Why not? There'll still be Barron and Malcolm up here plus the Ghurkas."

"I mean someone in charge. If McGrew or Prentice found out we were both missing, there'd be hell to pay."

Bickers was looking dismayed now. "But I was banking on you. You've got to come, Saffron."

"Did you plan this at the dance?" Saffron asked suspiciously.

Bickers' brief hesitation told all. "Not exactly. But I never thought you'd object. You're a spoilsport, Saffron. In fact, come to think of it, you're a mean bastard too."

Saffron grinned. "That's more like it. I'm so mean there's something you've totally forgotten."

Bickers stared at him. "What's that?"

"I haven't made out the leave roster yet. What if I don't let you off that Saturday night?

Bickers looked horrified. "You wouldn't do that. You couldn't."

"Couldn't I? It might be my duty as a friend. To save you from Lavinia and the glasshouse."

Bickers looked aghast. "That's terrible, Saffron. Terrible. A man has a chance to be a human being for a few hours and you'd snatch it from him. Even Hitler wouldn't do that."

Saffron grinned, then relented. "All right. You can have your Saturday night off. But don't blame me if it all goes wrong."

Bickers made a miraculous recovery. "I knew I could depend on you, mate."

"Don't thank me yet. Wait until you get back here in one piece."

Uneasiness took the shine off Bickers' euphoria. "I wish you'd come with me. Think what a change it would be."

"You mean you'd like me along in case it all goes wrong and you need help?"

The Londoner looked indignant. "I wasn't thinking that at all. I was thinking of the good it would do you. Aren't you sick to the back teeth of living with hairy-kneed men and hearing nothing but barrack room jokes? Don't you long for a pretty woman, a comfortable chair to sit on, and a decent drink or two?"

"And afterwards a night in bed with her, married or not?" Saffron said.

"When have you been so fussy about married woman?" Bickers demanded. "What about those two at Clifton in South Africa? I don't remember your being so fussy then."

"True," Saffron admitted.

Seeing he had the initiative for the moment, Bickers stepped on the pedal. "What if this woman is married? You'll be doing her a favour, that's all. It's odds on she's just as frustrated as we are and if you don't help her it'll be someone else."

"You should have been a lawyer," Saffron said.

"But it's true, kid. In any case, aren't we entitled now and then to the same thing that millions of lucky bastards back in the UK are getting every night? Why must we, the ones who're risking our lives for 'em, always be the losers?"

Saffron grinned again. "Don't overplay your hand."

"But I'm right, aren't I? We deserve a break now and then. You must feel like a civilised evening after all these months of living with bush apes like Cornwall and Wilkinson?"

"I can go better than that," the Yorkshireman said. "I've forgotten what a civilised evening feels like."

"Then there you are. You've a chance to remember in two weeks time. You can sort out the problem of the gas stores easily enough. Ask that blood brother of yours to bring a few of his friends up here. They'll take care of the gas better than we ever could."

Saffron eyed him admiringly. "And all this to get me along so I can guard your back in case of trouble."

"It's not that at all," Bickers said stiffly. "It's to help you, Saffron. You need to relax. It's been obvious for a long time that you're under stress."

"That's the joke of the year. You've been peeing yourself every minute we've been up here that Razim Khan will come and cut your throat."

Bickers had the grace to compromise. "All right, we're all under stress. That's why we should let these women help us. What do you say, kid? Let your hair down and give it a whirl."

"I'll think about it. There's still plenty of time. Now are you coming to eat? The food'll be getting cold."

Looking brighter, Bickers rose from his bed. "Those soya links are killing me. But I suppose a man has to keep his strength up."

Saffron grinned. "A man has. Lavinia will expect nothing less."

Chapter Twenty

Barron tapped on the billet door. Bickers raised his head from the crate he was using as a card table. "Come in."

Barron ducked under the low lintel and entered the hut.

"Where's Malcolm?" Bickers asked, seeing he was alone.

Barron pulled a face. "He's not feeling too good tonight, corp."

Saffron, sitting opposite Bickers, frowned. "You mean he's not well?"

Barron hesitated. "No, I don't think it's that. He just seems very depressed."

Saffron rose. "Where is he? In his billet?"

"No. He's sitting outside. Over near the rifle butts."

The Yorkshireman glanced at Bickers. "I'd better have a word with him."

As he made for the door, Barron's voice checked him. "He's had a drink or two, sarge."

Saffron turned. "Is he drinking much these days?"

"He does take a little rum at nights," Barron confessed. "He says it helps him to sleep."

"How little is little?"

Barron's hesitation told Saffron a great deal. Bickers broke in before he made a comment. "He hasn't taken to the bottle in a big way, has he?"

"No, not really, corp. He doesn't drink during the day but he has a few before he goes to bed."

Saffron made for the door again. "OK, I'll talk to him. I'll be as quick as I can."

Outside a full moon, floating near the crest of the southern mountain, was making it almost as light as day. To the east the peaks of the Hindu Kush were jet black silhouettes against a limitless sky. To the west the lights of Shaman were fireflies dancing in the dark depths of the valley. The great plateau that stretched out beyond the huts was no longer a hot barren wilderness. With its rocks and boulders bathed in the ghostly light it was a plain of awesome silence and mystery. It was, Saffron thought, a night of haunting but savage beauty.

He found Malcolm sitting on a low, crumbling wall that stood at the near end of the rifle butts. Hearing his footsteps, Malcolm turned sharply, to relax when he recognised the Yorkshireman. As he began to rise, Saffron waved him back. "It's all right. I've not come about the card game. Mind if I join you?"

The youngster looked embarrased. "I'm sorry, sergeant. I didn't feel like playing tonight. But I'll come if you want me to."

Saffron offered him a cigarette and then sat down alongside him. "No, it doesn't matter. I'm tired of cards myself. What are you doing? Enjoying the view?"

He thought he noticed a slight shudder run through the youngster. "It's quiet, isn't it?"

Saffron nodded. "It's always quiet except when we have courses up here. Does it worry you – the quiet, I mean?"

Malcolm drew in smoke. "Sometimes. I notice it more at nights. It's like a loud noise then. Have you noticed that?"

Saffron remembered Bickers saying a similar thing. "It's worse if you're used to big cities, Malcolm. You're from Southampton, aren't you?"

"Yes, sergeant."

"I've never been there. You were heavily bombed, weren't you?"

"Oh, yes. Very badly."

"So was my home town, Hull. Being on the river, they couldn't miss hitting it. How long have you been in the RAF, Malcolm?"

"Just over nine months, sergeant."

Saffron, barely twenty-five, suddenly felt old. An aircrew volunteer in 1939, he had already served over six years and with war turning every year into an eon, the gap in his service time and the youngster's seemed enormous. "How old are you, Malcolm?"

"Nineteen, sergeant." Then, as if ashamed of his confession. "Twenty next month."

Saffron was studying the youngster's face. He had noticed before that he had the features of a sensitive man but tonight in the moonlight it looked almost aesthetic. The Yorkshireman had also noticed that the young man spoke better than his colleague, Barron. "What were you doing before the war?"

"I was in an office. In a shipping company."

"Did you like it?"

"It was all right. Boring sometimes but not too bad."

"Are both your parents alive."

"Yes, Dad's also in an office."

"What about brothers and sisters?"

"I've got one of each. My brother's two years younger than I. My sister's eighteen months older."

"Did you get on well with your mum and dad?"

Malcolm looked surprised at the question. "Yes. Why?"

"I just wondered. Some men don't."

"Did you, sergeant?"

"Me? Oh, yes. We had our arguments now and then but it turned out they were usually right."

Encouraged to talk, Malcolm was beginning to look more relaxed. "Our trouble was always money. Dad doesn't earn much, so it was always a bit of a struggle for my mum to manage."

"I know," Saffron said. "It was the same for my family. But we never let it come between us."

The young man was looking both pleased and surprised at Saffron's disclosures. He indicated the aircrew brevet on Saffron's bush jacket. "When did you get into aircrew, sergeant?"

"In '39. I was in the RAF Volunteer Reserve."

"Were you on operations?"

Saffron nodded. "Until I was wounded. Then I was sent over to South Africa to train aircrews."

"Barron and I have often wondered what happened. So you were wounded in action?"

Seeing more than a hint of hero-worship in the youngster's eyes, Saffron dealt with it tersely. "There's nothing clever about being wounded, Malcolm. It just means you were a bloody fool to get in the way. What I'd like to know is why you became an armourer. It can be a nasty, dangerous business."

"I hadn't any choice, sergeant. I wanted to be a wireless operator but they said they had enough of them. So I was sent to an armament school."

"And now you're up here with us. How do you feel about that?"

Malcolm glanced away. "It's all right, sergeant."

Saffron decided it was time the preliminaries were over. "Don't give me that, Malcolm. You aren't a bit happy up here. A blind man could see it."

The youngster looked upset. "Aren't you satisfied with my work?"

"Your work's fine. You and Barron have picked everything up very well and you're a big help to me and Corporal Bickers. That wasn't my question. I said you weren't happy up here. Aren't I right?"

A full five seconds passed before Malcolm gave an ashamed laugh. "It's so lonely here, sergeant."

"Yes, I know that. But I can't think how many thousands of men would give their rights arms to swop places. Remember you could have been sent to Burma with the danger of the Japs capturing you. In war terms we're four lucky men."

The youngster made no attempt to argue. Instead he drew on his cigarette before asking his question. "Is it right what they say down in Long Barracks? That Razim Khan swore to kill you and Corporal Bickers?"

Saffron knew there was no point in denying it. "Yes, it is. But you mustn't take it too seriously. His brother had just been blown to pieces by one of our bombs so he hardly knew what he was saying."

"Yet everyone who's been here for any length of time say he's ruthless. They say he masses his tribesmen round Shaman every April and September in the hope there's an earthquake so he can sack the town."

Saffron smiled. "If he goes for a prize as big as that, he's hardly likely to worry about Bickers and me. Anyway, nothing's happened to us so far, has it?"

"But he might not know you're up here yet, sergeant."

While knowing it was quite possible, Saffron had no intention of admitting it. "They say he's got tribesmen everywhere. So that's pretty unlikely. I think you can forget about his threat. I certainly have."

"But we've no weapons, sergeant. We'd all feel better if we'd a rifle apiece."

Saffron nodded. "I can understand that. But the law doesn't allow our troops to carry arms in case an Indian civilian gets shot."

"But there'd be no danger of shooting any civilians up here. We'd just feel safer at nights, that's all."

Saffron changed the subject. "Are you having difficulty in sleeping?"

Malcolm glanced away again. "Just a little, now and then."

"Are you drinking rum to help you sleep?"

A hesitation followed and then a nod. "Sometimes."

"Sometimes," Saffron said. "I think you're drinking a lot more than that. So listen to me. That Indian rum is poison. It'll not only rot your guts, it'll affect your mind. The way to survive this place is to keep a clear head. If you fuddle yourself with drink, everything will get worse and worse for you. It will, believe me."

When the youngter made no comment, Saffron went on: "I can't stop you drinking in your free time, Malcolm, but you'll be a bloody fool if you drink that rot gut every night. It's likely to put you into hospital."

When Malcolm again remained silent, Saffron wondered for a moment if hospitalisation was what he wanted. "What about Barron? How is he taking it?"

Malcolm sucked on his cigarette. "I think he's all right. But, like me, he wishes he had a rifle."

Saffron gazed at him for a moment, then rose to his feet. "What are you going to do? Stay here or come and play cards?"

"I think I'd rather stay here, sergeant, if you don't mind."

Saffron shrugged. "No. You're free to do as you please." Hesitating a moment, he reached down and gave the youngster's slim shoulder a friendly squeeze. "Remember to watch that drinking, Peter. I don't want to lose you."

His use of Malcolm's forename clearly pleased the younger man. "Thanks for spending the time with me, sergeant. I enjoyed talking to you."

"Any time," Saffron said. "You know where to find me." With that he nodded and walked away, the crunch of his footsteps drilling holes in the silence. Above, the sinking moon was now dipping behind the southern mountain. As the first dark shadow of its demise appeared on the plateau and began moving towards the camp, Saffron felt an odd shudder of apprehension. Although shaking off the mood quickly, he was glad to enter Bicker's billet and to let the mellow light from its oil lamp wash over him.

Preston brushed a fly off his balding head. "Have you seen Warrant Officer McGlew about your request, sergeant?"

Saffron shook his head. "No, sir."

Preston's florid face showed curiosity rather than irritation. "Why not?"

"Because I know he won't agree to it, sir."

"Are you sure of that?"

"As sure as I can be of anything, sir. It would be a pure waste of time."

Preston frowned. "All the same, I don't see how we can go over his head. We don't want bad feeling in our section, do we?"

Saffron thought that was the joke of the year. When he neither moved nor spoke, Preston changed the subject. "How are you getting on up there otherwise? Are the arrangements we made working out all right?"

The Yorkshireman hesitated a moment, then nodded. "Reasonably well although I'd like more furniture for the billets. At the moment the lads are sitting on old wooden crates."

Preston made a note on a pad. "All right. I'll see what I can do there. How many courses have you taken so far?"

"We've completed one and are half-way through the second."

Preston brushed away another fly. "Are you finding a fortnight long enough to teach them all they need to know?"

"I'd like longer with them, sir, because we've only time to give them practical work. But Mr McGrew says a fortnight is all the time we can have."

"I'm afraid that's true, sergeant, SEAC are scared to death that gas is going to be used, so Mountbatten wants armourers trained in its use as quickly as possible."

Saffron returned to his initial request. "I understand that, but my instructors must feel reasonably secure or their work might suffer in the weeks ahead."

Preston drummed his pudgy fingers on his desk. "And you think it might help if we meet your request?"

"It'll do something to help, sir. I also feel the lads ought to get more than one night a week off duty. At the moment they've nothing to do when the day's work is over but feel sorry for themselves or examine their navels."

Preston gave a fruity laugh. "Their navels! You have a quirky turn of phrase, sergeant. But I take your point. I'll try to get a dartboard for you and talk to Mr McGrew about an extra night off duty. Mind you, it'll mean extra transport to carry the men back and forth and that might be a problem."

"Unless you can get bicycles for us," Saffron suggested.

"Bicycles. Well, I can try. Is that all?"

"All but my first request, sir."

"Ah, yes. Your request. Very well. I'll speak to Mr

McGrew." Before Saffron could protest, Preston had picked up his telephone. "Give me Warrant Officer McGrew, will you? Hello, Is that McGrew? Yes, Preston here. I'd like to see you in my office. Right away if you can. I've got Sergeant Saffron here."

As Saffron expected, once his name was mentioned McGrew was in the office less than a minute later. "Yes, sir. What is it?"

Preston indicated the erect figure of Saffron. "The sergeant here is asking that his men be given four rifles and equivalent ammunition. He says it will make them less nervous in their isolated position."

The glance McGrew gave Saffron was akin to a dagger thrust. "Why hasn't he put the request through to me, sir?"

"I did put it to you," Saffron said before Preston could reply. "And you turned me down."

Although his cheeks flushed with anger, McGrew pretended not to hear the Yorkshireman. "The sergeant should know that all requests must go through the proper chain of command. He has no right to see you without my permission, sir."

Preston glanced back at Saffron and raised a quizzical eyebrow. "I told you you were out of line, didn't I, sergeant?"

"Yes, sir. But what alternative did I have? My men are isolated and it's my duty to do all I can for them."

Preston glanced back whimsically at the angry McGrew. "He does have a point there, Warrant Officer. If he has approached you already, there isn't much point in approaching you again, is there?"

McGrew's voice sounded like a steel file being dragged across sandpaper. "This is the Royal Air Force, sir, not some undisciplined civilian rabble. Sergeant Saffron should learn its rules and regulations. Otherwise he is not fit to hold the rank he does."

Preston made a half-amused grimace. "You hear that, sergeant?"

"Yes, sir. But it's also an NCO's duty to look after his

men's welfare. I can't look after mine when they feel exposed and insecure."

Preston turned back to the warrant officer. "As I just said, he has a point, Warrant Officer."

McGrew was simmering now. "No, sir. He hasn't a point at all. I explained to him that airmen are not allowed to carry weapons because of the risk to Indian civilians. That isn't my directive. I understand it comes from the SEAC Commander himself."

"You heard that, sergeant? It doesn't give Mr McGrew any choice in the matter, does it?"

McGrew came back before Saffron could reply. "In any case, how could four men hold off a tribesmen's attack if one were made? Much more likely, they'll bring tribesmen down to steal the rifles."

Knowing McGrew was right, Saffron tried to calm the situation. "I do understand the problem. And it's true we couldn't defend the gas canisters if an attack came. It's the psychology of the thing. My men go to bed every night not knowing if some tribesman might break into their billets and cut their throats. A rifle beside them will make them feel that much safer."

McGrew gave a sarcastic laugh. "Safer? You'd draw every tribesmen in the territory when they found out what you'd got."

Saffron kept his eyes on Preston. "We wouldn't let anyone know, sir. I'll guarantee the rifles would be kept in the billets and chained to the beds during the day."

"What about your bearers?" McGrew demanded. "They'll know and they'll talk for money."

"Our bearers won't talk," Saffron said. "They hate the tribesmen."

Preston's eyes, which had been moving from one man to the other, paused on Saffron. "Are you sure of that, sergeant?"

"Yes, sir. Quite sure."

Preston's fingers drummed on the desk again. Then he threw a semi-apologetic glance at McGrew. "I wouldn't like to be out there on my own, McGrew, and I don't suppose you would either. It's a damn lonely place and two Ghurkas can't give the men much protection. So I think this is one time we can turn a blind eye to the directive, don't you?"

McGrew looked as if he could not believe his ears. "But the tribesmen will attack men for empty cartridge cases, sir. They'll hone in like bees when they see a tiny isolated group of airmen with rifles."

"I'm sure the sergeant is fully aware of this, McGrew. Just as I'm sure he won't let his men swagger about with rifles like a bunch of cowboys. I'm going to let him have four rifles and some ammunition." With McGrew looking as if he had been sandbagged, Preston turned to Saffron. "How many rounds would you like?"

Saffron kept his eyes off the stunned McGrew. "I'd think fifty would be enough, sir."

Nodding, Preston scribbled on a piece of paper and handed it to the Yorkshireman. "There's your authority. As you haven't a telephone connection to the main camp, I've also included the Very pistol you requested and half a dozen red flares. Take the chit to the armoury and the Station armourer will arrange for the rifles and sundries to be sent up to you. All right?"

Saffron took the chit and saluted. "Thank you, sir."

McGrew was waiting for him outside. His hairless eyes were bloodshot. "You've done it this time, Saffron. By the living God you have."

Fully aware that in this case much of the warrant officer's opposition had validity behind it, Saffron's reaction was mild. "I've got three nervous men up there, sir. I had to do something to calm them down."

"So you go over my head and make a fool of me. No one does that to me, Saffron. No one. I'm going to break you if it's the last thing I do."

With that McGrew strode away on stiff legs like an enraged bantamcock. With the humorous thoughts Saffron occasionally had in moment of stress, he wondered what

Bickers would make of this new confrontation with authority. Decided it might be policy to keep it quiet, Saffron made his way to the station armoury.

Chapter Twenty-One

The distant laughter was keeping Saffron awake. He had believed at first that it came from Barron and Malcolm but then thought it unlikely that the highly-strung Malcolm would be heralding their presence by making such a noise. Nor was Bickers likely to be involved because the Londoner had always insisted that the four of them kept as quiet as possible when darkness came.

The laughter came again. Listening to it carefully Saffron imagined he detected drunken elements in the outbursts. Unable to bear the mystery any longer, he lit a torch he had obtained from the Long Barracks' store and climbed into his shorts. As he walked quietly from his hut, he heard Bickers' nervous voice. "That you, Saffron?"

Saffron swung the torch round and saw the skinny, dishevelled figure of Bickers emerging from his hut. Before he could speak, the Londoner's alarmed voice came again. "Who is it, Saffron?"

"I don't know. That's what I've come to find out?"

Bickers moved closer to him. "You don't think it's tribesmen, do you."

"I've just said, I don't know. But whoever they are, they sound drunk to me."

"When are they sending us those bloody rifles?" the Londoner muttered?

"We couldn't bring them out even if we had them," Saffron pointed out.

"Then what about my revolver? I hope you're still carrying it on you?"

As Saffron patted the pocket of his shorts, another bellow

of laugher broke the silence. "Whoever they are, they hardly sound threatening. Do you want to come with me or stay here?"

With the prospect of being left alone, Bickers looked uncertain before making his decision. "No, I'll come with you."

As the two men approached the gas store, two other shadowy figures appeared. Barron and Malcolm had also heard the laughter. Behind the gas store Saffron could see a red glow. Barron pointed at it. "Someone's got a fire going over there, sarge. That's where the laughter's coming from."

At that moment one of the Ghurka guards came round the perimeter of the huts. Saffron checked him. "You speak English, soldier?"

The man hesitated. "A little, sergeant sahib."

"Is Pemba on duty tonight."

"No, sergeant. He come later."

Saffron pointed at the red glow. "Do you know what's going on over there?"

The Ghurka shook his head. Then, as another burst of laughter echoed back, his white teeth showed in a grin. "They are having fun, sahib."

"Yes, but what kind of fun?"

When the Ghurka shrugged, Saffron turned to the airmen. "I'm going to find out. Are you three coming or staying?."

As he expected, Barron moved forward. Bickers and Malcolm glanced at one another, then joined him. Saffron extinguished his torch. "It might be better if they don't see us coming," he explained.

A moment later he led the party across the plateau, the light from the stars helping them to avoid the occasional stones and boulders. Once clear of the huts Saffron could see the fire and estimated it was about a quarter of a mile away.

Bickers' nervous whisper sounded alongside him. "How many do you think there are?"

Saffron had been trying to count the occasional silhouettes that swam before the fire. "I'd say no more than four or five."

"Let's hope the buggers aren't armed," Bickers muttered.

Saffron shrugged. "What if they are? They might even be a party of Ghurkas. Not everyone's our enemy out here."

Bickers gave a sceptical grunt. "You could have fooled me, Saffron."

The laughter died down as the four airmen approached the fire. But when they were less than fifty yards from it, loud cheers broke out again. Barron touched Saffron's arm. "What's that over the fire, sarge?"

Saffron was wondering himself. A large tray of some kind, standing on four supports, appeared to be suspended over the fire and as the four airmen watched one of the spectators rose and dropped something on to it. The other men rose with him and as they peered into the tray another burst of drunken laughter broke out. Malcolm sounded relieved. "They're having a midnight feast, sergeant. They're cooking something. That's all it is."

More relaxed now, the four men drew nearer the fire. Still unseen by the men standing around it, they were within thirty yards of it when a thin, high-pitched screaming sounded through the drunken laughter. It was then the truth hit Saffron. "Oh, my God, no! They can't be."

Bickers looked startled. "Can't be what?"

Saffron began running. The madness that came over him gave no concession to fear or caution. Reaching the fire he kicked at the red hot tray of corrugated iron and sent it toppling to the ground. As it fell, two creatures were flung from the tray and tried to crawl away. One succeeded, the other's burned legs collapsed beneath it and it lay whimpering on the ground. Leaping through the fire, Saffron bent down and snapped the animal's neck. He then turned back to the fire where the four drunken men, all wearing the bandanas and dress of tribesmen, were staring at him.

Startled by his appearance and sudden attack, two of them snatched out knives from their belts. But as Barron appeared in the firelight, followed by Bickers and Malcolm, one tribesman called something to the others, pointed at Saffron, and shouted some derogatory remark. It was a signal for all four men to drop their threatening postures and break into mocking and derisive laughter.

Saffron never remembered what abuse he shouted back at them. All he remembered was Barron taking his arm and drawing him away. As the four airmen started back to the huts, there was a retching sound from Malcolm and the party had to pause while he vomited. Too shocked to talk, they reached the huts before Saffron turned to Barron and nodded at the trembling Malcolm. "Share a hut tonight, Les. Don't worry about McGrew's orders."

When Barron nodded, Saffron led the shaken Bickers away. As they reached their billets, the Londoner turned to Saffron. "Can I come in for a while?"

Without a word, Saffron led him into his hut. Lighting the oil lamp, he nodded at the wooden crate. "Sit down and have a cigarette."

Bickers' eyes were still huge with horror. "My God, Saffron. I still don't believe it."

Saffron discovered his own hands were still trembling as he lit both cigarettes. Pushing one between Bicker's bloodless lips, he sank down on his bed. As he sucked in smoke, Bickers stared around the billet. "I need a drink. You haven't got anything, have you?"

Saffron fumbled in his side pack and pulled out a half flask of whisky. He poured out a large dram into his mug and handed it to the Londoner. Gulping it down, Bickers slumped back on the crate. He looked dazed with disbelief. "They were laughing, kid. They thought it was funny."

Saffron nodded. "I know."

Bickers had all the symptoms of a man in shock as he repeated himself. "They were burning living creatures alive and they were laughing! Laughing, Saffron!"

The very heat of Saffron's fury had led to its dissolution, leaving him drained and uncharacteristically bitter. "Isn't that what human laughter is all about? Cruelty?"

Bickers' bloodless face stared at him. "What are you talking about?"

"Human laughter was always cruel. That's why animals fear it. It's only in recent years we've sanatised it. Those men out there are like we were a few hundred years ago."

Bickers shuddered. "If I thought I was like those bastards I'd shoot myself."

Saffron drew in smoke again. "Given the right circumstances you would be. So would we all. Hasn't this war taught you that we're the savagest creature on this planet?"

Bickers' refusal to take offence was a measure of the shock he had received. "You hardly acted as if they were brothers of yours. I thought you were going to attack them all bare-handed."

Remembering his hatred and his behaviour, Saffron shook his head and made no reply. In the silence that fell another distant outburst of drunken laughter could be heard. Bickers' cry was pure torment. "They're doing it again, Saffron! Christ, we can't stay in this place. We'll go mad if this goes on night after night."

Saffron surprised himself by his sudden offer. "You can go to Lavinia Oldroyd's place at the weekend if you want. And I'll come with you."

If he had expected a revival of Bickers' spirits at the offer, he was disappointed. The Londoner was showing only surprise. "What's changed your mind about coming yourself?"

Saffron hardly knew. "Does it matter?"

"But what about our leaving the gas store?"

"One of the Long Barracks' armourers told me today that McGrew's been called up to the college for the weekend. If I speak to Pemba I think he'll bring up an extra guard or two to look after the store. Then everything should be all right."

The scene he had just witnessed had driven all thoughts of pleasure from the Londoner's mind. "God, that was horrible, Saffron. The worse thing I've ever seen."

Saffron poured him another drink and took one himself. As he swallowed and felt the neat rum burning his stomach, another burst of drunken laughter sounded. It brought another shudder from Bickers. "The bastards! How are we going to sleep knowing what's going on out there?"

Saffron had the same thought. "Why don't you kip down in here tonight?"

Bickers rose unsteadily to his feet. "Thanks. I'll fetch my mattress."

Helping him pull the mattress inside, Saffron was thinking nothing could have underlined the extent of the Londoner's shock more than his ignoring or forgetting the presence of the scorpion spider. Although the Londoner was soon asleep, his twitching and delirious mutterings made it clear his dreams were full of horrors.

Saffron himself did not sleep at all. He lay listening to the drunken laughter until it ceased just before dawn. By that time he was too wide awake to contemplate sleep before it was time to begin a new day.

Chapter Twenty-Two

The road the two airmen were taking was narrow and flanked by naphtha-lit stalls, shacks, and dilapidated buildings. Crouched or standing over their wares, Indians were hawking food and trinkets. Barefooted children kept running up to the two men and begging for coins. The air rang with entreating voices and stank of sweat and curry.

Bickers turned his head uneasily. "He's still following us."

Saffron took a look himself. Thirty yards back along the dusty road the khaki-clad figure of a man could be seen, pausing as the two airmen paused. "I keep telling you it's all right," Saffron said impatiently. "It's only Pemba."

"Yes, but why the hell is he following us like this? I thought he was supposed to be guarding the gas store."

"He's brought plenty of his friends to do that. He begged me to let him come with us. He said it's far too dangerous for two unarmed airmen to wander about the town at night. Too many people in these parts don't like the British. So he's keeping an eye on us. It's part of this blood brother thing of his."

Bickers glanced uneasily at the naphtha-lit stalls around them. "Nobody told me it was that dangerous," he muttered.

Saffron started down the road again. "You should read standing orders. These frontier towns are like powder kegs, full of Indians, Muslims, Afghans, tribesmen, and God knows what else. If they aren't cutting each other throats, they'll enjoy cutting ours. In any case, compared with the average townsman, we're as rich as princes. So we're a nice juicy targets for thieves and vagabonds."

"Lavinia never told me this," Bickers muttered.

"Of course she didn't. She's one of the protected species who travels everywhere in a car with an escort. I told you you were out of your depths, buster."

"Why the hell couldn't we get a tonga tonight? Most of the time they're queuing up for our business."

"They'll all be busy taking the Top Brass up to the college. That's where the money is."

With his highly sensitive antennae alerted to danger, Bickers was seeing it everywhere now. "Maybe your Ghurka's one of those who doesn't like the British. He could have conned you with that blood brother crap."

"Don't be stupid. He's a member of one of the loyalist regiments in the British Army." Saffron gave a sarcastic grin. "I'm surprised he's making you uneasy. I'd have thought a brave character like you would be glad to have his back covered."

Bickers sniffed. "I don't see what protection a little guy like that could give us."

"Don't you believe it. Even the tribesmen are scared of the Ghurkas. Some think they're the world's best fighting men. I wouldn't argue with that."

Still not convinced of the Ghurka's purpose, Bickers took another glance back down the naphtha-lit road. "Then why doesn't he come up and join us?"

"He's obeying the protocol. He thinks it might get us into trouble with the military authorities if he's seen in our company."

"So you're telling me that wherever we go in this one-eyed town we'll have that little character following us?"

Saffron shook his head. "Not you. You're not his blood brother. Just me."

Bickers scowled. "That's just favouritism, Saffron. I'm as much entitled to protection as you are."

Saffron grinned. "Not to Pemba. In his book you're expendable."

"Bastard," Bickers muttered.

They reached the cantonment ten minutes later, an assortment of neat bungalows surrounded by a high chain link mesh fence. A tall elderly Sikh was standing sentry at the entrance. He came to attention as the two NCOs approached him but his rifle barred their entry. "What now?" Saffron asked Bickers.

"Lavinia said I had to mention her name," Bickers said. He turned to the tall sentry. "Me see Mrs Oldroyd. Me come through gate. You savvy?"

The Sikh's lined face showed no sign of understanding. Muttering something, he turned to Saffron. "We've come to see Memsahib Oldroyd," the Yorkshireman explained. "Hasn't she told you to expect Corporal Bickers?"

The Sikh's face brightened immediately. "Ah, Memsahib Oldroyd and Corporal Bickers. Yes, sergeant sahib. She is expecting you both. Please come inside."

With that he opened the gate and waved the men through. Bickers glanced back irritably. "Why didn't he open the gate for me?"

Saffron grinned. "It was that pigeon English of yours. Haven't you twigged yet that most of the older Indians here have been speaking English longer than you have?"

"How was I to know that?" Bickers grumbled. He jabbed a finger at a solitary figure just visible at the far side of the road. "What's does your blood brother do now?"

"He waits for us."

"Waits? But we could be hours."

"I told him that but he just shrugged and said it didn't matter." Saffron eyed the letter Bickers was pulling from his shirt pocket. "What's the address?"

"Azalea Cottage," Bickers told him.

"No number."

"No."

Saffron nodded. "That's typical of the Oldroyds and their like. Everyone's supposed to know where they live. All right. Let's go looking for Azalea Cottage."

For the next five minutes the two airmen walked up and down the rows of assorted bungalows. Lights were shining through some windows, others had blinds drawn. Radio or gramophone music could be heard and occasional voices and laughter reached the two men. Bickers was scowling. "Listen to them. It's another bloody world from that camp of ours, isn't it?"

Saffron shrugged. "I told you not to expect the memsahibs of the Raj to mix with us unwashed soldiery, didn't I?"

Reminder of their mission revived the Londoner's spirits and brought a chuckle from him. "And I proved you wrong, didn't I? They're going to mix with us in a few minutes, Saffron."

Azalea Cottage proved to be a small neat bungalow with stone steps leading to a verandah. Looking like a tom cat expecting a bowl of cream, Bickers paused on the bottom step. "You ready, Saffron?"

Saffron laughed at his expression. "I'm ready. Go ahead."

A dog began barking as the two men ascended the steps. As Bickers pressed a bell, the barking turned into a deep growling and snarling at the other side of the door. Bickers looked startled. "It sounds a big bastard, Saffron. Let's hope she can control it."

A woman's voice sounded a few seconds later. "Down, Churchill! Down!"

"Churchill," Bickers muttered. "Christ, it must be a bulldog."

The snarling sank into a low menacing growling. Then the door swung open and a woman appeared. With the hall light behind her, Saffron could only see her silhouette but her slimmer figure told him she was not the buxom Mrs Oldroyd. Alongside her, held in check by the woman's hand on its collar, was a large menacing shape.

The woman's voice was upper class and sharp. "Yes. What do you want?"

The growling dog was unnerving Bickers. "I'm Ken Bickers and this is Alan Saffron. I was told you were expecting us."

"Expecting you? Why should I be expecting you? Who are you?"

As Bickers was about to repeat their names again, there was a shout from inside the bungalow. "Is that the corporal, Mavis?

The woman's tone changed. "Are you the friend of Mrs Oldroyd?"

Bickers nodded. "Yes."

"Why didn't you say so? You'd better come inside."

Bickers took a step forward, only for Churchill to let out an explosive snarl. As the Londoner jumped back, Lavinia Oldroyd appeared in the hall. Her imperious order brought Churchill to heel in a flash. "You wicked dog! Go into the sitting room!. At once!"

With a last resentful look at Bickers, the dog slunk away. Waving her companion to one side, Lavinia swept forward. "Come in, Kenneth. And bring your friend in with you."

The two men found themselves in a sitting room lined with portraits of stern-faced Army officers with topees on their knees. A stuffed tiger's head and a pair of crossed kukris gave evidence of Mavis's background. A cocktail cabinet, a large sofa, and armchairs completed the furniture.

Lavinia introduced Bickers to her companion. "This is the man I spoke about who danced so well at the Station dance the other week, my dear. Kenneth Bickers."

Mavis, a slender and elegant woman against Lavinia's more

voluptuous charms, nodded at Bickers but did not offer her hand. "Hello, Kenneth."

Lavinia turned to Saffron. "And you must be the friend he was talking about that night."

Watching her slightly protruding eyes moving over his muscular body, Saffron had the thought of a farmer assessing a stud bull. It brought out the egalitarian that was never far below the surface in the Yorkshireman. "I suppose I must be, Mrs Oldroyd."

Lavinia turned to Bickers. "What does he mean, he must be? Is he your friend or isn't he?"

Bickers glared at Saffron. "Of course he is."

Lavinia gave Saffron a cold stare. "Then what did you mean? Don't you know if you are someone's friend?"

"No. I let other people decide if I am their friend or not, Mrs Oldroyd. I only know those who are friends to me."

Surprise at such a response from a mere sergeant brought a frown from Lavinia but her bullying tone faded. "Yes, of course. I do see what you mean."

Having made his point, Saffron decided the situation called for a softer approach. He pointed at the bulldog that was still staring balefully at Bickers. "Is that your dog, Mrs Oldroyd?"

"Bitch," Lavinia corrected, "Bitch, not dog."

"Churchill?"

"In the circumstances we thought it fitting, sergeant."

"I see. So Churchill is yours?"

"Yes. Do you like dogs?

Saffron nodded. "Very much."

"That's to your credit, sergeant." Lavinia turned to Bickers. "What about you, Kenneth? Do you like dogs?"

With Churchill's baleful eyes watching his every move, Bickers needed to call on all his powers of Thespianism. "Oh, yes. I love them. Big or small."

Lavinia gazed at the crouching dog. "Yet he doesn't seem to like you. I wonder why."

No doubt thinking the doggy conversation was bringing up

unexpected problems, Mavis interrupted it. "Would you two boys like a drink?"

When both men nodded, Mavis motioned at the sofa, then walked over to the cocktail cabinet. "Do sit down. I suppose you both prefer beer. I do have some."

Before Bickers could reply, Saffron shook his head. "I'd rather have a whisky myself."

Mavis's well-bred face showed surprise. "Whisky? You prefer it to beer, do you?"

"Always," Saffron said, ignoring Bickers' kick on his ankle. "I never drink anything else. Beer has such a nasty common smell, don't you think?"

"I suppose it has," Mavis said doubtfully. "What about you, Kenneth?"

"I don't mind," Bickers said hurriedly. "But I'll have a whisky if Alan is."

While the drinks were being poured Saffron was able to pay more attention to Mavis. At least seven or eight years younger than Lavinia, she was a young woman who carried her slender figure well. Her features were attractive if not beautiful and her long blonde hair swung about her face in the Veronica Lake fashion of the time. Like Lavinia, who in spite of her memsahib manner, was a sexually attractive woman, Mavis was undoubtedly a gift to men who had been starved of female company for months. By the time Saffron had downed a second large whisky he was no longer sorry he had agreed to keep Bickers company.

Although etiquette demanded some conversation before the more serious business of the evening started, it was soon clear that Lavinia and Bickers, with their libidos stimulated by drink, were losing patience with it. As an onyx clock on the mantelpiece struck eight, Lavinia lifted her statuesque figure from her chair and fixed her eyes on Bickers. "Kenneth! I've brought some photographs of Kashmir that I took last year. Wouldn't you like to see them? They're in the other room."

Relieved the foreplay was over at last, Bickers leapt to his feet. "Kashmir? Oh, yes. I'd love to see pictures of Kashmir."

"Then come along," Lavinia ordered. As she swept into the adjacent bedroom, Churchill rose on her bow legs and followed her. Checked in his stride, Bickers threw a dismayed glance at Mavis. "Does she have to go to?"

Mavis nodded. "She'll howl her head off if she doesn't. In the cantonment she goes everywhere with Lavinia."

There was an impatient cry from the bedroom. "What are you doing, Kenneth? Come along!"

With a helpless glance at Saffron, Bickers followed the dog through the door. A few seconds later it closed firmly behind him. Mavis turned to Saffron with a giggle. "She's a bit overpowering, isn't she?"

Saffron grinned. "Who? Lavinia or the dog?"

Mavis, who had had two very large gins herself, giggled again. "Both, I suppose." Rising, she took the empty place on the sofa. "Isn't that better than shouting across the room at one another?"

"Much better," Saffron agreed.

She snuggled closer to him. "How long have you been here, Alan?"

"Only a few weeks."

"Do you like it?"

Saffron nodded. "I do tonight."

"Why?"

He smiled. "Can't you guess?"

She put a hand on his arm and lifted her face to his. "I think so. But show me."

After a moment's hesitation, Saffron kissed her and the result astonished him. It was like applying a match to the touch paper of a rocket. Her slim body convulsed and her arms closed around his neck. For endless seconds her lips bruised his own and then, sobbing for breath, she broke away and began fumbling at his shirt and shorts. Accustomed to be in control of his sexual encounters, the Yorkshireman was thrown off balance by her enthusiasm. He gave an embarrassed laugh. "Just a minute. Let me get my breath back."

She either never heard him or took no notice. Her hand

was in his groin, nipping and massaging as her moist mouth returned to his lips. Her voice was throaty with all its earlier accent missing. "Take me, Alan. Quickly. Do what you like but take me."

For the briefest of moments Saffron thought what a leveller sex was. Then her fingers were squeezing and probing again and he decided that only fools dithered and refused the fruits that life was offering them.

Chapter Twenty-Three

As the bedroom door closed behind Bickers, he found himself in darkness. Pausing a moment to accustom his eyes, he heard a cooing voice from the bed. "I'm here, Kenneth. Come and join me."

Bickers could now see a white shape on the bed and a pile of discarded clothes hanging over a nearby chair. As he started forward, a low growl pulled him up short. At the same moment Lavinia's cooing voice came again. "You've still got your clothes on, Kenneth. Take them off and make yourself comfortable as I have."

Bickers could now see that she had. Her voluptuous charms were seen swelling above the bed sheet. Given another time and place the Londoner would have hurled his clothes to the four winds and reached the bed in one bound. But tonight there was a problem. "What about Churchill, Lavinia? She definitely doesn't like me."

"Never mind Churchill, dear. She's just a silly jealous old thing. You want to take me into your arms, don't you?"

"Yes, of course I do."

"Then don't worry about Churchill. Just take off your clothes and come over to me."

With his libido and apprehension locked in combat as the growling continued, Bickers managed to pull off his shirt and began unbuttoning his shorts. In musical terms the growling became *agitato* when he dropped his shorts and stood in his underpants. Acutely conscious of the truth that a man feels vulnerable when unclothed, Bickers hesitated.

Lavinia was growing impatient. "What on earth are you doing? It doesn't take all night to take off your shirt and shorts, does it?"

Bickers cleared his throat. "I'm coming, Lavinia." Steeling himself, he moved towards the bed, trying to ignore the warning growls that were giving him goosepimples.

He had barely reached the bedside when he gave a yelp of surprise. Reaching out, Lavinia grabbed him and with surprising strength pulled him on the bed. "There. Isn't that what you wanted?" Then she gave a cry of vexation. "Good God, man, you've still got your underpants on! And your socks and shoes! What's the matter with you? Are you stupid?"

Bickers' temper almost broke at this. "Why don't you blame that dog of yours? She sounded as if she wanted to bite something."

"Rubbish. Anyway, you can take everything off now. I don't want your shoes scratching my legs."

Muttering to himself, Bickers wriggled out of his underpants and then threw off his socks and shoes. As the latter hit the floor he heard a growl and then a champing sound. He sat up sharply. "God, she's eating my shoes!"

Lavinia sounded shocked. "Your shoes! Is that all you can think about at a time like this?"

Bickers gazed at the pulchritudinous figure beneath him and decided chewed-up shoes would have to wait. "Sorry, luv. But Churchill's thrown me right out of my stride."

With her libido aroused, Lavinia could show forgiveness even if she was terse with it. "Stop talking, man! Put your mind on what you're supposed to be doing."

Bickers' reply died into a muffled mumble as her arms went round his neck and drew his face between her huge breasts. "There," she said. "Isn't that better than talking?"

Her act resurrected Bickers' libido but denied him breath. After a minute he had to come up for air. He was allowed only a couple of gasps before his face was buried again. Beneath him Lavinia gave a throaty laugh. "You know what they say, Kenneth. You could go deaf and blind having this done to you."

Coming up for air again, Bickers could believe it. As he struggled for breath, Lavinia caught the lobe of his ear in her teeth and tugged. Giving a startled yelp, Bickers ran a hand down her body and then between her thighs. She gave a gasp of pleasure. "Yes! Do that again. Oh, yes, yes."

Bickers did it again and she tightened her arms around him. "It was clever of me to choose you, wasn't it, Kenneth?"

Still short of breath, Bickers could only hope she was right. As he nodded, she gave another throaty laugh. "I like a man who is sure of himself."

Seeing how sex was transforming a formidable memsahib into a pliable if demanding woman, Bickers found his confidence restored. "And I like a woman who knows what she wants," he panted.

She drew his hands to her breasts. "Then give me what I want."

She gave a long, drawn out gasp as Bickers obeyed. Her legs closed around him and the springs of the bed began a rhythmical protest. As their breathing quickened and both felt Nirvana was close at hand, there was a sudden heavy thump on the bed and then a startled yell from Bickers. "Get off, you brute! Get off me!"

High in the heights of ecstasy at one moment, Lavinia was shocked by Bickers' sudden withdrawal. "What on earth's the matter? What's happened?"

The panting Bickers was in no mood for niceties. "It's that dog of yours. She's jumped on the bed and she's rubbing herself up and down my leg."

"Does it matter? Can't you just carry on?"

"Of course I can't carry on," Bickers yelled. "She weighs a ton. Get her off me before she does some damage!"

Extracting herself from beneath him with some difficulty,

Lavinia reached down for the panting dog. "Come on, Churchill. This isn't the place for you."

The grunting animal paid no attention. With the dog on his thigh and close to parts that were precious to him, Bickers dared not move. "What's the matter with the brute? What's come over her?"

Lavinia had to grab the dog's collar with both hands before it released Bickers and jumped down to the floor. Sitting up, Bickers stared at it with acute dislike. "I thought she didn't like me. Instead she tried to rape me. Why?"

Ordering the dog to stay in one corner of the bedroom, Lavinia sank down on the bed alongside Bickers and ran a hand through his lank damp hair. "It's that sex drive of yours, darling. Even the dog feels it."

Somewhat mollified, Bickers fumbled in his shirt pocket. "I need a smoke. What about you?"

She nodded, her voice sympathetic. "You poor darling. Just as it was all going to happen. I'm just as disappointed myself. But never mind. We've got plenty of time ahead of us, haven't we?"

Bickers pointed at the snorting dog. "Not while that thing's in here. Or she'll do it again."

She put a arm around his naked shoulders. "It'll be all right the next time, darling. We'll put Churchill into the kitchen. She'll howl but we can put up with that, can't we?"

"I suppose so," Bickers muttered. He nodded at the closed door. "I wonder how those two are getting on?"

"They've been very quiet. So I suppose they are liking one another."

Bickers couldn't resist the dig. "Mind you, they haven't a dog to spoil things, have they?" Then he gave a start. "Wait a minute. What's that?"

Lavinia listened, then heard a woman's upraised voice. "It's Mavis. She sounds angry about something."

As they listened the younger woman's voice grew louder and shriller. Then there was a heavy bump that shook the floor. Lavinia looked startled. "That friend of yours isn't a woman beater, is he?"

"Course he's not," Bickers muttered. "They're just having a quarrel of some kind, that's all."

More feminine cries followed and then there was a crash of glass. Bickers jumped to his feet. "Christ! She's throwing things at him now. Shouldn't we got in and see what's happening?"

Lavinia pushed him back. "No. Give them a few minutes more. It might just be a lovers' quarrel."

"Some quarrel," Bickers muttered uneasily as Mavis's voice rose again. "If it goes on they'll wake up the entire cantonment."

Saffron sank back on the sofa. Mavis snuggled against his tanned body. "Wasn't that nice?"

Saffron sighed. "After six months, you can't imagine how nice. Was it nice for you too?"

Her eyes shone. She reached up and kissed him. "It was marvellous, darling. I'll never be able to thank Lavinia enough for bringing you round. Would you like another whisky?"

"Yes, thanks. I would."

Her slender, naked body rose and crossed over to the cocktail cabinet. Watching her, Saffron found he was having kindly thoughts about Bickers and his peccadilloes. As she returned with two half filled glasses, he offered her a cigarette. "Did you hear the dog growling in the other room?"

She smiled. "Yes. I hope it hasn't spoilt things for Ken."

Saffron offered her a match. "He's none too happy with big snarling dogs. I half expected him to run back in here."

"Thank goodness he didn't. Think what he might have seen."

Saffron grinned. "It doesn't bear thinking about, does it?"

She gave a humorous grimace. "You needn't have worried. When Lavinia gets her hands on a man, he doesn't have much chance to escape."

"Have you known her long?"

"About eight months. Since we came here."

Saffron wanted to ask about her husband but she gave him no time. Putting aside her whisky and cigarette she leaned against his naked shoulder. "Were you serious just now? Was it really six months since you last slept with a woman?"

Saffron shrugged. "Six months, eight months, I don't remember. We've been in transit most of that time and there's been no chance to meet women."

She put a hand on his naked thigh. "I don't know how you're able to stand it."

"Neither do we," Saffron said. "But we haven't much choice, have we?

She reached up and kissed him. "Poor darling. But never mind. You've got me now, haven't you?"

"Have I?" Saffron said.

Her hand moved further up his thigh. "Of course you have. You know where I live and you can come here any time you like. You would like to come, wouldn't you?"

Saffron, who found his passion was rising again, drew aside her blonde hair and gave her a kiss. "What do you think?"

She drew him over her and reached down with her hands. "Then you must come," she breathed. "Whenever you want. You don't need to ask."

It was Saffron's chance and he took it. "But what about your husband? Doesn't he work in Shaman?"

She shook her head. "No."

"Then doesn't he come to see you?"

"No."

"Then what is it? Are you divorced or getting divorced?"

Her voice turned impatient. "Stop talking about him. Make love to me again."

Saffron wanted nothing more but found his questions needed answers. "I must know something about him, Mavis. Where is he?"

Her arms tightened around him and she gave a gasp as their naked parts touched. "He's in Assam or is it Burma? Anyway, it's far away. Stop talking and make love to me again. Please, Alan, please."

Saffron suddenly felt very cold. "Are you saying your husband's on active service?"

Her eyes were closed and her voice dreamy. "Yes, I think that's what they call it." Then, as Saffron gave a sudden groan and rolled away, her blonde head lifted. "What are you doing? What's the matter?"

Saffron had never felt more sober in his life. "Don't you know?"

"Of course I don't know. Is it something I've said?"

Wincing again, the Yorkshireman rose from the sofa and picked up his clothes. Mavis was sitting upright now. "What on earth are you doing?"

"I'll have to go," Saffron muttered. "I'm sorry."

"But why? A moment ago you couldn't leave me alone. So why are you acting like this."

Saffron drew on his shirt. "You really don't know, do you?"

"That's what I keep on telling you. Why have you become so horrible all of a sudden?

Hating himself, Saffron pulled on his shoes. "You've a husband fighting the Japs and likely to get killed any day and you don't know what's wrong with sleeping with me? So what can I say to you?"

Her attractive face suddenly thinned. "So that's it? You've suddenly become conscious stricken, have you? But not until you've had your way with me."

Saffron slid on his shoes. "I didn't know about your husband, Mavis. I thought he was like Lavinia's husband, based nearby. I'm desperately sorry."

Her lips curled in a sneer. "So it would have been all right if he was a clerk or a lecturer?"

"Yes," Saffron said. "It would."

"Then you're a hypocrite, aren't you? A damned hypocrite."

Saffron finished lacing his shoes and rose. "You're probably right. But I wish you'd told me about him earlier."

Her voice rose. "How was I to know you were so damned choosy?"

Disgusted with himself and goaded, Saffron made the mistake of striking back. "Some men are. I'd suggest you tell the next man the truth in case he's one of them."

Her eyes blazed. "The next one? Are you suggesting I have men in here every night?"

"No. But equally I don't flatter myself that I'm the first."

"You bastard," she screamed. "How dare you talk to me that way."

Saffron sighed. "I'm going now. I'm just very sorry I didn't know beforehand."

Glancing round, Mavis saw her whisky glass on a nearby table and hurled it at the Yorkshireman. Ducking, he went to the closed bedroom door and banged on it. "Ken! I'm leaving. And if you've any sense you'll do the same."

Saffron's bang on the bedroom door came as Bickers and Lavinia heard startled voices outside the bungalow. Lavinia jumped to her feet and snatched up her clothes. "You're right. It is alarming the neighbours. Get yourself dressed! Quickly!"

Bickers, with his mission as yet unfulfilled, showed disappointment. "The neighbours aren't likely to come into the bungalow, are they?"

"Don't be such a fool." Lavinia's memsahib persona was was back with a vengeance. "To the cantonment we have been giving a treat to a couple of other ranks. If neighbours tell my husband there has been some funny business going on, God only knows what he'll do. Get your clothes on! At once!"

Bickers needed to hear no more and shouted back to Saffron. "I'm coming, kid. Just give me a minute."

There was another crash of glass before he heard Saffron again. "Hurry up or she'll smash the place up."

Still in darkness, Bickers searched for his shoes. "Can't we put the light on?"

Lavinia dragged on her dress, then clicked on the switch.

Her statuesque figure, topped by a flushed anxious face, came into focus in front of the Londoner. "Why are you taking so long?"

Bickers was on hands and knees on the floor. "Your dog's run off with my shoes," he complained.

Outside startled voices were growing louder. Giving a cry of impatience, Lavinia bent down and threw two gooey pieces of leather at the Londoner. "Get them on and go before someone phones my husband. Hurry, hurry!"

No threat could have electrified Bickers more. Dragging on the chewed up shoes, he yanked the door open. At the same moment another glass from Mavis soared across the room and missed him by inches. The Londoner blinked at Saffron. "What the hell's going on, Saffron? Why is she chucking things at you?"

"Never mind," the Yorkshireman panted, dragging him across the room. As they passed Mavis she took a swing at Bickers that caught him on the right ear. Running down the verandah steps outside, the two airmen saw half a dozen men and women gathered in the front garden of a bungalow opposite. Seeing the airmen, a couple of the men ran to the gate as if to pursue them. Saffron grabbed the Londoner's arm again. "Keep going! Run!"

Bickers needed no telling. The two airmen fled down lane after lane until they saw the cantonment gate ahead. "Go steady here," Saffron panted. "We don't want that Sikh to get suspicious."

Dishevelled and breathless as the two men were, they received a puzzled look from the elderly Sikh but he let them through the gate without asking questions. Even so, neither man felt safe until the huts and naphtha flares of the merchants lining the road hid the cantonment from sight. Then Saffron took a deep breath. "Don't you ever do that to me again? Do you hear me? Never again."

Nothing could have brought Bickers' indignation to the boil more. "Me? To you? You ruined everything, Saffron. Everything."

"Do you know who Mavis's husband is?"

"No, I don't. And I don't care, even if he's the bloody Viceroy. I got you a date and you blew it for both of us."

Saffron gritted his teeth and tried again. "He's on active service in Burma. Now do you understand?"

"Understand what? He didn't come home and catch you, did he?"

Saffron groaned. "You're just like her, aren't you?"

"What do you mean – just like her? What did you do to her? It must have been bad because she took a swing at my ear. I think it's swelling, Saffron."

"Sod your ear," Saffron snarled. "I wish she'd taken your head off. I should have known that any date you get for me would be a disaster. God knows, it's happened often enough in the past."

"That's gratitude for you. I get you a date with a good-looking woman and because you can't handle it, you put the blame on me."

Saffron glared at him. "Can't handle it! You unprincipled moron. You couldn't care about anything as long as you get your oats, could you?"

And so the altercation raged on. With both men incandescent and the night air full of recriminations that went on far into the night, in no way could it be said that Bickers' first date with Shaman's memsahibs had been an unqualified success.

Chapter Twenty-Four

Six more weeks passed. Although the intense heat remained, everyone in Quetta knew that the earthquake period was drawing closer. A routine general alert was sent to Long Barracks and the Ghurka camp and adjutants reminded commanders of the precautions required of them.

It cannot be said that commanders or their officers allowed the threat to overshadow their daily routine. Committed to producing trained soldiers and airmen for the desperate battles being raged against the Japanese, most officers tended to regard the alert as a disruptive nuisance rather than a major threat. Only the few men who had known the great earthquakes of the past were less sanguine.

Nevertheless, platoons of Ghurkas were issued with transports and briefed on their duties should Razim Khan's tribesmen attempt a major raid on the town. In Long Barracks machine guns posts were re-equipped and armourers detailed to man them in case of an emergency. All personnel, regardless of rank, were told that if an earthquake occurred when they were outside the camp, they must report back at all haste to receive their orders.

This being said and done, men settled down to their tasks again in the stoical way of the serviceman. But most men lived in a large base with hundreds of comrades around them to offer security. The same could not be said about the four men up on the eastern plateau. All were fully aware that if the tribesmen did threaten the town, no matter what other success they might achieve, it was certain they would overrun the lonely outpost.

Because of this and the danger of tribesmen capturing the stocks of gas, Saffron had tried to obtain a more formidable security guard. But although he had put in petition after petition, all had been rejected on the grounds that the Ghurkas were fully stretched, both in their intensive training programme and their commitments to the town in the case of an emergency. Because he had no liaison with Ghurka officers, Saffron had been forced to send his petitions through the standard RAF channels and he had no doubt whatever that they had been stifled in one way or the other by McGrew.

In some ways this puzzled him, for although he had no illusion about McGrew's feelings for him, he could not believe any officer of McGrew's standing would risk the loss of dangerous stores because of a personal grudge. His personal belief was that, unlike rifles, automatic weapons, and high explosives, McGrew genuinely believed that tribesmen would steer well clear of the lethal and less manageable chemical gases.

This view was not shared by his three men who were viewing the possibility of an earthquake with apprehension. Another factor wearing their nerves thin was the heat. Although throughout the summer it had been intense, it seemed to grow even hotter as the season drew to a close, making the wearing of gas capes and gas masks, even for a few minutes, an ordeal to be dreaded.

Nor was there any relief at night. Naked beneath their mosquito nets, men would lie soaked in sweat and the temptation to throw off the protective nets in an effort to gain a breath of cooler air was almost overpowering.

It was on such a night that Saffron heard drunken laughter again. Although this time he guessed its origin and cause, he found little comfort in the knowledge. Nor it seemed did Bickers, for after a few minutes his voice sounded at the billet door. "Saffron, Are you awake?"

Sighing, Saffron reached down for his torch. "Yes, I'm awake. What do you want this time?"

Bickers was standing in the open doorway. Shiny with sweat, wearing nothing but a pair of service underpants, he made a comical figure in the torch light. "Those bastards are out there again, Saffron. Have you heard them?"

"Of course I've heard them. Who couldn't?"

"What are you going to do about them?"

"What can I do?" the Yorkshireman asked bitterly. "I can't stop these sadistic bastards from having their fun. From all we know it's the popular sport around here."

"You stopped 'em the last time," Bickers accused.

"No I didn't. I just saved a couple of animals from more pain. The sods started it again as soon as we left. In any case, this is probably a different gang."

Bickers picked up the Yorkshireman's bush hat and wafted his perspiring body. "God, it's hot, Saffron. You said it would get cooler this month but it's got worse and worse."

"So I was wrong," Saffron said irritably. "Is that what you've come to tell me?"

Another burst of drunken laughter sounded. Bickers winced. "No, I came about those bastards. We can't let them go on doing it, Saffron. It's too horrible."

"So what do we do? Go and shoot them?"

Bickers' reply came from the heart. "Oh, wouldn't that be marvellous? I'd love to, kid. Gawd, how I'd love to."

"Who wouldn't? But as we can't, what else can we do?"

"We've got rifles now. Can't we just go over and put the fear of God into them?"

"We've got rifles but we're only allowed to use them in self-defence. If we use them to threaten tribesmen, there'll be hell to pay."

There were screams of laughter now, giving both men visions of the horrors being perpetrated by the revellers. Giving a groan, Bickers clapped his hands to his ears. "I can't take it, Saffron. I can't, honestly. We can't be expected to. We've got to do something."

Saffron lifted the torch beam to the Londoner's face and saw the acute distress there. "It's really got to you, hasn't it?"

Bickers nodded jerkily. "I can't spend the night listening to those bastards and imagining what they're doing. It'll drive me crazy."

"So what's your plan. To take a rifle and go over to them?"

Bickers' face suddenly set. "If you won't come with me, yes."

Saffron grinned. "That'll be the day."

"I mean it, Saffron. Those aren't men. They're fiends. Sod McGrew and his orders. We've got rifles. I'm going to put mine to some use."

Saffron had never seen the Londoner in this mood. As Bickers moved towards the door, he threw back his mosquito net. "We mustn't fire on them or all hell could break loose. But maybe we can scare them off."

Bickers' expression changed from defiance to relief. "Does that mean you're coming with me?"

Saffron climbed into his shorts. "What do you think? Go and get your pants on and I'll see you outside."

Bickers ran to his billet. A minute later both men found Barron and Malcolm standing at the far side of the huts gazing at the distant campfire. With the night dark and men little more than shadows, neither armourer noticed the rifles the two NCOs were carrying. Malcolm sounded distressed. "They're at it again, sergeant."

"We know," Saffron said tersely. "And we're going to break up their party. Do you want to come along with us or not? You don't have to."

Barron replied immediately. "Let's do it, sarge."

"And you, Malcolm?"

The youngster's hesitation lasted no more than a second. "Yes, all right, sergeant."

"Good. Then go and fetch your rifles."

When both men gave a start, Saffron nodded grimly. "I know the orders but I'm waiving them tonight. But remember, you don't load them. Whatever happens we mustn't open fire. Now get the rifles and let's get over there."

Within minutes the four men were closing on the fire. This time they counted six tribesmen clustered around it. All were in some stage of intoxication and too engrossed in their entertainment to notice the four men approaching them. One tall tribesmen, who appeared to be the master of ceremonies, had a large sack which in the flickering firelight appeared to be squirming at his feet. Reaching into it, he drew out a large animal and before Saffron or the others could prevent him, threw it into the red hot tray above the fire. The high-pitched screaming that followed brought a gasp of horror from Bickers. "That's a cat! God, Saffron, we've got to stop this."

With the agonised, spitting cat trying to leap out of the tray and the laughing tribesmen driving it back with sharpened sticks, the four armed airmen remained unnoticed. Although hatred was jetting like a blowtorch in his mind, Saffron managed to control his emotions this time. Shouting at the others to cover him, he was about to run forward and smash the tray from the fire when a single rifle shot rang out. The tall tribesmen who had thrown the cat into the tray gave a cry, dropped to his knees and rolled over.

For a second the Yorkshireman was stunned. The rifle shot seemed to reverberate around his brain as if he had been shot himself. Then he recovered and ran to the fire. With its tormentors forced to abandon their game, the tormented cat had escaped but Saffron could see the charred remains of other creatures inside the tray. Driving the abominable creation away from the fire with his rifle butt, he smashed the sides to render it useless and then attacked the posts that had supported it over the fire. Only then was he able to give attention to the six tribesmen.

With three rifles covering them and one man shot, all of them were very sober now. Telling his party to keep them covered, Saffron approached the wounded man who was now sitting upright with two of the tribesmen bending over him. Although their looks were venomous, the two men drew back as Saffron reached them. The wounded man had a hand pressed to his left shoulder and as Saffron bent down he could see dark blood trickling through his fingers. "How badly are you hurt? Can you tell me?"

For an answer the man spat right into his face. Taking a deep breath, Saffron wiped the spittle away and gazed round at the other five threatening faces. "This man ought to go to hospital. Do any of you speak English?"

"I do." The voice came from one of the two tribesmen who had examined the man's wound. Rising, Saffron saw a heavily built man with a face bearing the scars of smallpox. For a moment he believed he had seen him before but the urgency of the moment drove the thought away. "He should be taken to hospital to have this wound treated. If you bring him to our camp I'll make the arrangements for him."

The wounded man at his feet spat again, this time on Saffron's dusty shoes. The scarred tribesman shook his head.

"He does not want your hospital. We shall take care of him ourselves."

"But the wound might be serious. It should be treated as soon as possible."

"It will be treated. By our own people, not yours."

A growl of assent went around the scowling tribesmen. Unsure what to do next, Saffron stood back. "Will you be able to get him to your people?"

Recovering from the initial shock of the rifle bullet, the wounded man was now stumbling to his feet. As Saffron tried to help him, his hand was thrown savegely away. The pock-marked tribesmen spoke for him. "He will walk with us. He is not a soft Englishman."

"I'm sorry it happened," Saffron said. "But my men could not bear to see you torturing animals like that."

His interpreter said something to the others, who broke into mocking laughter. "My friends think you are women, Englishman. Are you?"

Whatever the circumstances, Saffron was never a man to retreat from a challenge. "Your friends have poor eyesight. We believe that men who hurt and torture weaker creatures than themselves are bullies and cowards."

The man's eyes burned at him. "You are calling us cowards, Englishman."

Conscious of the absurdity of a slanging match at such a time, Saffron bit back his reply. "So you don't want your friend to go to hospital?"

The wounded man shouted something at him and spat again. Saffron shrugged. "All right. Then there's nothing we can do. I'm just sorry it happened."

He had no doubts that the shouts that followed him as he joined the three airmen were heavy with abuse and threats. Motioning to his men, he led them back towards the huts. They had almost reached the billets before he spoke. "Who fired the shot?"

When no one replied, he swung round on Bickers. "Was it you?"

The Londoner looked hurt but made no reply. Saffron's voice rose. "I'm going to find out. Who was it?"

A frightened voice answered him a few seconds later. "I did it, sergeant. I'm sorry. I know it was wrong of me."

Saffron gazed with astonishment at the ashen-faced Malcolm. "Wrong?" Have you any idea what you've done?"

Malcolm sounded as if he were crying. "I couldn't help it, sergeant. When he threw that cat into the tray I think I went crazy."

"You did go crazy," Saffron said grimly. "That shot could bring the hills on top of us. I shall have to report you, Malcolm. It isn't as if I didn't warn you."

A grunt of protest from Bickers made Saffron say more than he intended. "I know how you all feel. Do you think I didn't feel it too? I'd have liked to have shot all the bastards. But we've got those rifles for protection only. I told you that before we set out."

There was a sob from Malcolm. Frowning, Saffron turned to Barron. "Get him to his billet. We'll talk about it in the morning."

Leaving Barron taking the sobbing youngster's arm, Saffron made for his own hut. Bickers followed him inside. "You're not going to report him, are you?"

His nerves on edge, Saffron swung round on him. "Don't you start! If you hadn't wanted to be St Francis of Assisi tonight, none of this would have happened."

"Oh, come off it, Saffron. You hated it as much as I did."

Saffron lit the oil lamp, then sank down on his bed. "Maybe I did but I never thought anybody would go over the top like that."

"I didn't either," the Londoner muttered. "Did you notice who that character with the smallpox scars was?"

"No. I thought I'd seen him before but I couldn't remember where."

Bickers was looking very pale in the lamp light. "He was in Razim Khan's gang when they attacked us on the mountainside."

Saffron felt someone had hit him in the stomach. "Are you sure?"

"Too true I am. I'd know him anywhere. Razim Khan's sure to know about us now." Seeing Saffron's shocked expression, Bickers' voice petered out. "It's bad, isn't it?"

Saffron took a deep breath. "Bad? That's the understatement of the year." Then he rallied. "But what the hell. Khan's probably known all along that we're up here."

"If he has, he hasn't known we've got rifles and ammunition and are prepared to use them against his men. He does now."

Saffron badly needed a target for his resentment. "Could neither of you stop that young fool from firing?"

"We didn't know he'd a bullet up the spout. He just suddenly raised his rifle and fired." Bickers' voice shook with emotion. "His mistake was not killing the bastard. Isn't that what we all wanted?"

"Thank God he didn't. Things are bad enough now. In fact I don't know what the hell to do."

Cast in the unaccustomed role of adviser and commiserator to his usually capable friend, Bickers handled it clumsily. "I'd keep my mouth shut if I were you. Otherwise McGrew will make a meal of it and punish the lot of us." Seeing no change in Saffron's expression, the Londoner tried a little mordant humour. "That hoodoo of yours has done it again, mate. In fact it's having a bloody field day out here."

Sensitive about his luck as Saffron was, it would not have been the wisest of remarks at the best of times. Tonight it brought a vivid curse from him and a shout that made Bickers blink in dismay. "That's all I need. Stop talking a load of crap and get out of here. Go on. I've had a bellyful of you and everyone else tonight."

Bickers retreated to the door. "I was only joking, mate. I was trying to help you."

"Help me?" Saffron choked. "A lot of help you are to me. You couldn't even stop that stupid kid firing his rifle out there. Piss off. I don't want to see you again tonight."

Unused to seeing the Yorkshireman in such a temper, Bickers was about to reply, then decided against it and vanished.

Left alone, Saffron found sweat was pouring from him. Drying himself with a towel, he tried to calm himself by having a cigarette before climbing back into bed. But although there was no drunken laughter to keep him awake, he found his thoughts were an equal enemy to sleep. He was blaming Malcolm for the incident but wasn't he, Saffron, equally to blame for giving into Bickers' request and taking the guns over to the tribesmen? Could the youngster be blamed for doing what all of them had wanted to do? Was it wise, even although it was his duty, to inform McGrew of the night's happenings when it was certain McGrew would take all the guns back from them and leave them disarmed just when the weapons might be needed? For that matter why had he snapped at Bickers so harshly when it was patently obvious the Londoner was trying to help him? Was he going like the others and finding his nerves beginning to snap?

With one question bringing another in its wake and the heat seeming to grow as the night wore on, Saffron both longed for the morning and dreaded it because of the decision he would have to make. Switching on his torch, he saw only two hours had passed since the incident with the tribesmen. As he dropped back on his abrasive, sweat-soaked blanket, an odd sound in the silence made him lift his head and listen.

It came again. It had a vague resemblance to the bark of a dog but Saffron was certain the sound was not canine. As he listened the sound changed into an eerie howling. Knowing he would have to investigate, Saffron groaned and threw back his mosquito net. As he was pulling on his shorts, he heard footsteps running past his hut. A few seconds later startled voices could be heard, then a shout. "Go and get the sergeant!"

Outside the moon has just risen, its slanting rays throwing silver patches and dark shadows. As the Yorkshireman reached the hut doorway, a breathless Barron came running up, his usually cheerful face showing both alarm and fear. "It's Malcolm, sarge. God knows what's happened to him."

Saffron ran after him. Near the crumbled wall before the rifle butts a figure was crouched on the ground with Bickers standing well clear. The Londoner gave a sigh of relief as the two men ran up. "Look at him, Saffron. He's gone mad or something."

Pushing past him, Saffron knelt down over the crouched figure. "What is it, Peter? What's happened?"

When the crouching man neither moved nor spoke, Saffron reached out a hand to take his arm. The effect was instantaneous and shocking. With a sound that was a cross between a growl and a snarl, the man turned his head and snapped with his teeth at the Yorkshireman's hand. As Saffron snatched his hand away and Malcolm tried to follow it, the moonlight fell on his face.

Bickers gave a horrified cry. "Oh, dear God! No!"

Malcolm remained on all fours, snarling at the three shocked men. Still unable to believe what he was seeing, Saffron bent forward again. "If this is some kind of a game, Peter, it's not amusing anybody. Pull yourself together and come back with us to the billets."

For an answer Malcolm bared his teeth threateningly. Feeling he was experiencing some bizarre nightmare, Saffron turned to the other dismayed men. "We can't leave him here. Let's get him to his billet."

Looking as scared as they were feeling, the three airmen gingerly approached the snarling youngster. As they tried to catch his arms and legs, he kicked and fought like a wild animal. Cursing, frightened, they somehow hung on to him although he kept trying to bite them, and began dragging him to his billet. "Have we got any rope?" Saffron gasped as a kick almost winded him.

"There a coil in the store," Barron panted.

"Then go and fetch it. Hurry, for Christ's sake."

By this time the Ghurka guards had heard the outcry and were gazing at the struggling youth in astonishment. Seeing one of them was Pemba, Saffron waved him over and the three men dragged the frenzied youngster to his bed and held him there until Barron ran in with the rope. It was only when his legs were tied to the bed and his threshing arms safely secured that the man could pause to catch their breath. Even then the youngster's head kept snapping up in a savage attempt to bite them.

Bickers' face was ash-grey as he sank down on a crate. "In God's name what is it, Saffron? What's happened to him?"

Saffron's hands were trembling as he lit a lamp. "I don't know. Unless he's got hydrophobia."

"Hydrophobia? Because he's acting like a mad dog?"

The Yorkshireman approached the threshing youngster again. "It could be, I suppose. But I don't know. I'm not a doctor."

He held the lamp over the youngster, careful to keep it out of reach of his snapping teeth. Then he gave a start, closed his eyes for a moment, then looked again. Bickers saw his expression and rose to his feet. "What is it?"

Saffron knew he would remember what he was seeing for the rest of his life. For a moment he could not speak. Then he pointed down at the youngster's contorted face. "Look at his eyes!"

Bickers did and gave a gasp of horror. "But that's not possible."

Barron was at Saffron's side now. He looked as shocked as Bickers. "It's the lamp light, sarge. It must be."

Saffron moved the lamp but the youngster's eyes still burned up at him like miniature searchlights. "No," he said. "The irises of his eyes have changed colour. They were blue before, weren't they?"

Barron nodded shakily. "I think so."

"Well, they're not blue now, are they?"

The horrified men saw two yellow eyes glaring up at them. "It's not possible," Bickers muttered again.

"Possible or not, it's happened. You're both seeing it."

Bickers shivered. "What are we going to do with him, Saffron?"

To everyone's relief, the youngster's staring eyes closed. As his body relaxed, Saffron gave a sigh of relief. "I think he's going to sleep."

Pemba's voice broke the shocked silence that followed. "I do not think it is the water sickness, sergeant sahib."

Saffron turned, to see the young Ghurka at his elbow. "Why is that?"

"The way he acted, sergeant. And his eyes. It is not the way of the sickness."

"How can you tell?"

"I have seen the water sickness in my country, sergeant. Try to give him water when he wakes up. If he drinks it, it is not the sickness."

"I think he could be right, sarge," Barron said before Saffron could reply. "Maybe it has something to do with booze."

The Yorkshireman swung round on him. "Was he drinking tonight?"

"He was after we got back from the fire. He swigged back nearly half a bottle of rum. Take a look under his bed."

Saffron bent down and saw half a dozen empty bottles standing there. "Why didn't you tell me he's been drinking as heavily as this?"

Barron looked crestfallen. "I didn't like to give him away, I knew he couldn't sleep without it."

"But booze wouldn't do that to him," Bickers protested. "He was acting like a wild animal out there. And what about his eyes?"

Saffron gazed down at the twitching, unconscious youngster. "God knows. We'll just have to wait and see how he is later." He turned to the young Ghurka. "You'd better get back on duty, Pemba. And you get some sleep, Barron. We've a new course arriving in four hours' time."

Looking as if sleep were the last thing he could hope for, Barron nodded reluctantly and left the billet with the Ghurka.

"What about you?" Saffron asked Bickers. "You can go if you like. I'm going to stay with him."

Bickers sank down on a crate. "I won't get any sleep, Saffron. I'll be wondering what'll happen next."

Saffron sat on the foot of the bed. "It has been quite a night, hasn't it?"

The Londoner groaned. "Why just tonight? It's been a nightmare ever since we arrived. And it gets worse by the day. Who'd have thought that young kid would turn into a wild animal? What do you think it is, Saffron?"

The Yorkshireman shook his head. "If it isn't hydrophobia, it's some kind of personality change. Perhaps brought on by that damned rum."

Bickers looked dismayed. "Let's hope not because I've had a swig of it myself now and then."

Saffron tried to lighten the moment. "Don't you start taking bites out of me or I'll put you down."

Bickers shivered again. "It's not funny, Saffron. I was terrified out there. And his eyes. Christ, they looked as if they belonged to the devil himself."

Saffron made no reply. His eyes had turned back to the bed where Malcolm had given a groan and tried to sit up. Rising, the Yorkshireman leaned over him. "Malcolm! Can you hear me?"

The youngster's eyes opened. Although befuddled with drink, they recognised Saffron, although his speech was slurred. "Hello, sergeant. Was'as happened? Why can't I move."

Motioning to Bickers, Saffron began untying the ropes round his legs. "It's all right, Peter. You've just had too much to drink, that's all."

Bickers, who had drawn nervously back on seeing Saffron releasing the youngster, now came alongside him. As Malcolm turned his head towards him, he gave a cry of astonishment. "Look at his eyes! They're normal again."

Saffron was beginning to think they had all been transported into some sinister Alice in Wonderland world. "Get me his water bottle," he muttered.

Bickers drew back. "You think it's safe to do that?"

"I've left his arms tied. Get me the bottle."

Bickers returned with the half-filled flask. As Saffron removed the cork, Bickers held his breath and moved behind him. His own heart pounding painfully, Saffron lowered the bottle to the youngster's parched lips. "Take a drink, Peter."

Malcolm shook his head. "Don't want a drink, sergeant," he slurred.

Fearful for him, Saffron tried again. "Take a drink, Peter. Go on. Do as you're told."

For a moment it seemed Malcolm would refuse again. Then, to Saffron's relief, he lifted his head and took a few mouthfuls before dropping back. Releasing his breath, Saffron passed the bottle back to Bickers. "It's not hydrophobia," he muttered.

Bickers wasn't convinced. "What if Pemba's wrong?"

"He isn't. Hydrophobia means a dread of water. He didn't show any reaction at all."

Afraid he might have been overheard, Saffron glanced back but Malcolm, exhausted by his earlier frenzy, had fallen asleep again. Bickers was showing no relief at the news. "If it isn't hydrophobia, then it's even more scary. What the hell was it and how could his eyes turn colour like that? You don't think someone's put out a spell on us, do you? You don't think we're haunted?"

Seeing the look of disgust that Saffron gave him as he untied the youngster's arms, the Londoner defended himself. "You were as scared as I was when you saw those yellow eyes. Don't tell me you weren't."

Saffron could not deny it. "There must be some explanation. There has to be."

"You can't think of one. And neither can anyone else. I'm going to remember those eyes for the rest of my life, Saffron." Then the Londoner's tone changed. "When are they going to repatriate us?"

The Yorkshireman shrugged. "When our four years is up. Hopefully in another two or three months. Why? What brought that on?"

"I was wondering what all this is doing to us. Have you ever had that thought, kid?"

Saffron frowned. "What do you mean – doing to us?"

"Seeing all this cruelty. Seeing what human beings can do to animals and to themselves. Being told as kids that human beings are God's finest creation and then seeing what awful sods we really are. And now seeing this kid go crazy. Isn't that going to affect all kinds of beliefs we once had?"

Saffron gazed at him and for a moment the only sound in the hut was the heavy breathing of Malcolm. Then the Yorkshireman took a deep breath and nodded at the door. "You'd better go and get some sleep. I'll stay here with Malcolm."

Bickers shuddered. "No, kid, I'm staying with you. As far as I'm concerned you're the last sane person left in this crazy, blood-stained world."

Chapter Twenty-Five

To Saffron, the days that followed Malcolm's night of rash and mystifying behaviour were like the remorseless ticking of a delayed action bomb. Or, more accurately, a straddle of such bombs. Malcolm's precipitous action had greatly increased the threat from Razim Khan; it would be a minor miracle if McGrew did not hear from one source or another about the wounded tribesman; and on top of everything else there was the possibility that Malcolm would make his astonishing transmogrification again. In addition a faint but alarming trembling of the ground one morning suggested that the warnings about autumn earthquakes were anything but alarmist.

Saffron had fretted for hours over Malcolm. Although the

youngster's hangover had been severe enough to keep him in bed most of the following day, he had remembered only his shooting of the tribesman and nothing of what happened afterwards. Moreover, once the effect of alcohol had worn off, he had appeared his old self again, apologising time and again for his rash behaviour. He had also promised never to touch rum again when the Yorkshireman had warned him about his heavy drinking.

In the end Saffron decided not to charge or report him. With tribesmen involved, he knew McGrew's punishment would be severe. Also, it was likely the warrant officer would withdraw the rifles so bitterly obtained, just at a time when they might be needed most. A further inducement to keep silent was Malcolm's welfare. He seemed to have recovered from whatever trauma had struck him and yet if the details of his night's behaviour were given to the Medical Officer it was more than likely he would be considered a psychiatric case and sent off to some mental care unit. Saffron felt he could not do that to the youngster.

Not that Saffron's decision was purely altruistic, as he was the first to admit to Bickers. "McGrew would love it. He's been waiting all this time to get me. So if he hears what happened, he's sure to make the most of it."

At first Bickers had second thoughts. "Are you sure? We don't know the kid won't have another fit. I think I'll go round the bend myself if I catch him howling at the moon again."

Saffron shrugged. "If it happens again, we'll have to mention it but let's keep our fingers crossed."

"There's another advantage in telling all," Bickers pointed out. "If they hear we had a ding dong with tribesmen it might make 'em bring us down from here and put us in a safer place."

"Where is a safer place?" Saffron asked. "They can't put us anywhere near Long Barracks or the Ghurka camp, so we'd still be relatively unprotected."

"There must be somewhere better than this," Bickers

grumbled. "You're not just thinking about the bollocking you'll get from McGrew, are you?"

Saffron decided it was an accusation that called for a little malice. "Not in the way you mean. You forget there isn't much McGrew can do to me while this gas scare is on. Who else is there to take my place? No, all he'd do is take our rifles away and punish us by deferring our repatriation on the grounds we can't be spared. Is that what you want?"

Bickers looked horrified. "Are you saying he'd lump me in with you?"

"Of course he would. He has so far, hasn't he?"

Bickers needed to hear no more. "Then you mustn't say a word to the bastard. Another year out here would finish me off."

Saffron grinned. "I thought you'd see it my way."

A week of tension passed. Feeling it was almost inevitable that Razim Khan would take some action against the outpost, men dreaded the end of each day and the long dark hours that had to be endured before dawn. Finding it impossible to snatch more than a few hours sleep at a time, men became irritable and found faults with one another and the courses they were tutoring. It was, Saffron thought, like the atmospheric build up before a violent storm.

The storm broke when it was least expected. During daylight hours, the four men had felt relatively safe, feeling, perhaps more instinctively than logically, that Razim Khan would use the cover of darkness to make an attack. In the event Khan deceived everyone.

It happened two Sundays after Malcolm's strange fit. With the training camp allowing men one day a week from their labours, Sundays were the chosen days when trainees were not brought up for their gas lessons and Saffron and his men were allowed time either to visit Long Barracks or to take a trip into Shaman. Nevertheless McGrew had made it clear that two of the four instructors must always remain with the gas stores and with Bickers showing no inclination to visit Shaman alone after hearing about its perils, he chose to make any excursions out of camp only when Saffron and the inevitable Pemba could accompany him.

The result of all this meant that, apart from the Ghurka guards, he and Saffron were alone in Hill Camp every second Sunday and it was on such a day that Razim Khan made his move.

It happened during the lunch hour. With no facilities to cook their own food, the instructors were still reliant on food being brought up to them from Long Barracks and although other drivers were occasionally used, in general it was either Wilkinson or Cornwall who made the three times a day delivery.

On this particular Sunday Cornwall was the driver. The day itself gave a hint of the storm to come. Unusual for the plateau, a steady wind was blowing from north to south and although not chilly enough to make the airmen slip on pullovers, it was a reminder that in a few weeks that same wind would be carrying from Siberia cold so bitter that it could frostbite a man's lungs if he wore no protective face guard.

Bickers' first reaction was relief at the drop in temperature. "This is more like it, kid. A man doesn't feel like a blob of grease paint all the time."

"Make the most of it," Saffron said. "Because if the old sweats are right it'll be so cold in a few weeks you'll be howling for long johns and a couple of dozen blankets."

Bickers looked sceptical. "Don't old sweats always exaggerate?"

"It's not just the old sweats who say it. That book I read says it's the sudden weight of icy air coming after the intense summer heat that triggers off the earthquakes."

With little or nothing to do that day, the two men were standing at the end of the dirt road from Long Barracks, awaiting the arrival of their lunch. The only other occupants of the camp were Pemba, who was on duty that morning, and another of his fellow Ghurkas. With eight days having elapsed since Malcolm had shot the tribesman, Bickers was markedly less pessimistic than he had been earlier in the week. "With any luck our repatriation papers could be here before the winter and we could be saying goodbye to the place."

Having read how suddenly and fiercely the winter arrived in that part of the world, Saffron had his doubts but he had no wish to bring on another of Bickers' doom and gloom moods. "Let's hope so. I've had enough of you moaning about the heat. Having you bellyaching about the cold would be too much."

About to make an indignant reply, Bickers paused. "That's the truck, isn't it?"

Saffron listened and then frowned. "That's funny. It sounds like a number of trucks. One coming up the hill and the others from over there," and he pointed in the direction of the huts.

As he spoke a Bedford crested the hill and accelerated towards them. Bickers' face cleared. "It must be the wind carrying the sound over there."

Saffron was gazing at the huts and still listening. On the road ahead the truck was gathering speed and growing larger as it neared the two NCOs. "He's in a hurry this morning, isn't he?" Bickers complained. "Or is he playing silly buggers and pretending to run us down?"

Saffron turned back to him. "Who is it? Cornwall or Wilkinson?"

Bickers shaded his eyes. "I can't tell yet. The sun's on the windscreen." Then his tone changed. "There are two other men in the cab with him. Do you think it's McGrew?"

The words had barely left his mouth when a couple of rifle shots came from the direction of the huts. They were followed by harsh shouts and three more shots. Saffron spun round on the startled Bickers. "They're here! Come on! Get your rifle!"

Ahead, the Bedford was less than thirty feet from the two NCOs. As it screamed to a halt, its tailgate dropped and armed tribesmen began jumping down to the road. Saffron grabbed Bickers' arm. "Your rifle! Run and get it!"

Seeing Bickers was paralysed by the suddenness of it all,

Saffron had no option but to leave him. But as he sprinted for his billet, four armed men emerged from the huts and barred his way. One was Razim Khan and his bearded face wore a triumphant expression as he advanced on Saffron. "We meet again, sergeant. And this time you will wish you had never been born."

Cornwall, his square face shiny with sweat, edged up against Saffron as the two men heaved a carboy of mustard gas towards the narrow entrance of the gas store. "What's the bastard's game? Why is he taking all the gas and equipment away?"

"He's hoping to blackmail the camp," Saffron told him. "When the wind's in the right direction, he's going to threaten to smother it with gas unless they give him all the guns and ammunition in the armoury."

"Will it work?"

"It might. He must have found out no one has any gas masks down there."

"Is that why he's kept you and Bickers alive? So you can handle it for him?"

Saffron grimaced. "So he says."

Cornwall stared at him. "What are you going to do?"

The Yorkshireman shrugged. "I don't know. I can only play it by ear."

There was a harsh shout from the tribesman at the gas store entrance. "Sod you," Cornwall muttered as the man threatened them with his rifle. At that moment Bickers edged by the tribesman and entered the hut. Saffron caught his arm. "Are you all right, Ken?"

The Londoner was looking grey with fear. His voice was little more than a croak. "What happened to Pemba?"

Saffron shook his head. "I don't know. Unless they shot him and left his body in a billet."

There was another threatening shout and this time a rifle muzzle was driven painfully into Saffron's ribs. Catching his breath, he tried to give Bickers some reassurance. "Keep your chin up. Khan won't do anything to us while we have this gas to handle."

Leaving Bickers lowering a phosgene bomb into a sack, Saffron and Cornwall manhandled the large carboy from the store and towards the trucks that were now waiting at the south side of the huts. On their way they had to pass the body of the young Ghurka who had been shot outside the gas store. Not content with shooting him, the tribesman had also slashed his throat from ear to ear. It was a sight that made even the tough Cornwall avert his eyes each time he passed by.

Razim Khan was standing alongside the trucks when Saffron and Cornwall arrived with the large carboy. Some thirty yards away at least twenty of his followers were squatting in a large circle. Although laughing and talking as if they hadn't a care in the world, the occasional uneasy glances they threw at the trucks told Saffron they were fully aware of the danger poison gas presented.

As the two men lowered the carboy to the ground for a moment, Khan's fierce voice struck at them. "You are wasting time. Hurry or you will be punished."

The sweating Cornwall answered back before Saffron could speak. "If you're in such a hurry to get away, why don't you tell some of your men to help us?"

Without warning, Khan slashed a hand across his face. "Don't talk that way to me, you dog, or I'll have your tongue cut out."

Saffron, who knew something about men and their reactions, saw the pugilist's face turn white and knew what it signified. Grabbing the man's powerful arm, he answered for him. "We can't work any faster. Why don't you give us some help? We'll make sure no gas is spilled."

The tribesman's fierce eyes turned on him and for a moment the Yorkshireman believed he was going to receive the same treatment as the simmering Cornwall. "You will load up all the gas yourself. My men will take care of the equipment."

At that moment two distant rifle shots were heard, followed

by two more. Seeing the look on the two airmen's faces, Razim Khan shook his bearded head. "You need not look so hopeful. It is only my men killing your other guard."

For a moment Saffron felt a twinge of hope. "Then he got away?"

Khan showed his white teeth in a grin. "Only because the dog was relieving himself in a hut when we arrived. But he could never hope to escape from my men. They know this country far too well than those mercenaries you British pay to fight for you."

Although Saffron felt his hope dying, he had no intention of letting his defiance die with it. "You do realise all this shooting might be heard down in Long Barracks or in the Ghurka camp. If it is, you could have patrols coming up to see what's happening."

Khan made a derisive gesture. "Both sides will only think the others are having exercises. But they are too far to hear. You are not going to be rescued, Englishman. At least not until you are dead." His eyes, black and mocking, turned to Bickers who was staggering towards the truck with a loaded sack over his shoulder. "Look at your friend. He is working harder than either of you. Do you think it is because he is afraid?"

Making no reply, Saffron nodded at Cornwall and climbed into the truck. A moment later the pugilist swung the carboy up and Saffron slid it forward towards the others. As the panting Bickers came alongside Cornwall, the pugilist was about to take the sack from him when the Londoner checked him. "No," he panted. "It's two of the phosgene bombs. Leave them to Saffron."

Drawing back, Cornwall watched Saffron lean down and take the sack from the Londoner. Khan's voice was harsh with impatience as the Yorkshireman jumped down from the truck. "How much more is there to bring?"

Cornwall, still simmering with rage, turned on him before Saffron could reply. "Why don't you come and look yourself instead of throwing your bloody orders about?"

As fast as a striking snake, Khan swung his rifle butt round and caught Cornwall full in the stomach. Dropping on his knees with a gasp, the pugilist retched for a moment, then struggled to his feet. Seeing Khan's face as he waited, Saffron jumped in front of the enraged airman. "Stop it, you fool! Can't you see it's what he wants?"

Seeing Cornwall's expression, Saffron braced himself for clubbing fists. For an endless moment he saw his face reflected in the man's bloodshot eyes. Then the madness begin to dim and ebb from them. A second more and Cornwall took a deep breath and turned away. Khan's mocking laugh followed him. "You are wise, Englishman. I would have slit your belly open like a paper bag." Waving a hand, he motioned an armed tribesman towards him. Saying something to him, he turned back to the three airmen. "Bring the rest of the gas over before I set my men on you."

The detailed guard rammed his rifle into Saffron's back. Turning and catching sight of his pock-marked face, the Yorkshireman recognised him as the tribesman who had attended to the man Malcolm had shot. As he stumbled forward, Cornwall came alongside him, his voice low. "What the hell are we going to do, Saffron?"

Remembering the scarred man spoke English, Saffron warned the pugilist with his eyes. "We can't do anything at the moment except get the gas into the truck. How were you ambushed?"

"The bastards had laid stones across the road. When I pulled up, they jumped me."

On the other side of Saffron, Bickers was clutching at straws. "Do you think there's a chance Pemba got away?"

Saffron wanted to believe his own words as much as he wanted to encourage the Londoner. "There's always a chance. I didn't see any of Khan's men return, did you?"

"If he did get away, the Ghurkas are taking a hell of a time to get here, aren't they?"

"I don't think we can hope for that," Saffron told him.

"Khan's sure to have scouts out watching for any help coming."

Bickers groaned. "Then what are we going to do? Just wait until they cut our throats?"

Hearing voices behind him, Saffron glanced back and saw the scarred tribesman was talking to a colleague and had fallen back a few paces. He lowered his voice to a whisper. "If possible we must all be in the same truck when we drive away. And we must try to have all the gas masks with us."

Cornwall gave a start. "You thought of something?"

Seeing the scarred tribesmen finish his conversation and approach them again, Saffron gave him a warning glance. "I'll explain later. Just try to do as I say."

Chapter Twenty-Six

With his shirt black with sweat, Saffron jumped down from the truck. "That's all the gas," he told Razim Khan.

Khan glanced at the pock-marked tribesman. When the man nodded, Khan turned and shouted an order to his waiting men. When they began running towards the huts, he turned back to the three airmen and pointed at Bickers who was approaching the truck with a number of gas masks strung around his neck. "Why is he carrying those masks? I said all the other equipment had to go into another truck."

"When you're handling live gas you always keep masks close by," Saffron said.

The tribesman stared at him. "Does that mean you are afraid of your own gas, Englishman?"

Knowing their only hope rested on his powers of persuasion, Saffron fought to keep his voice steady. "Everyone who has any sense is afraid of poison gas. That's why we are trained never to move the gas unless we have masks with us."

Khan's lips twisted mockingly. "I am not interested in your welfare, sergeant. If you were to be gassed it would be no more than you deserve. My concern is for my men." He turned to the sweating Bickers. "Put those masks in that other truck."

Saffron felt his heart miss a beat. "I thought you wanted to use us to threaten the camp. We'll be no use to you if we're dead."

Khan's lips twisted mockingly. "You're not likely to release the gas and kill yourselves, sergeant. So your little melodrama does not impress me."

Dismayed, Saffron could only hope the man knew little about gas weapons. "You don't understand. We have phosgene bombs in there. They can leak during transit, particularly when jolted about in rough terrain like this. I take it you won't be travelling on any of the recognised roads?"

The man laughed and pointed at the mountains to the south. "No, Englishman. We are going over there to a village of my people. Miles from here."

"With no roads?"

"We don't need roads. We can find our way without them."

"Then that's my point. If we're going to drive over rough country, the bombs could leak and if they did they could kill us all, your driver and guards as well as us." When he saw Khan hesitate, the Yorkshireman played his last card. "You didn't believe me when I told you those bombs up the mountainside were dangerous and look what happened. You have to believe me now or you could put all your men in danger. Because leaking gas wouldn't only contaminate our truck. In this wind it could reach the rest of your men."

There was a frown on the man's bearded face now. "What are you telling me? That if the bombs began leaking, you could stop them?"

"Yes. But only if we have masks to protect us." Feeling the pendulum was swinging his way now, Saffron took heart. "What do you have to worry about? There'll be guards on our truck, won't there?"

The man's lips twisted again. "Be sure of that, sergeant. With orders to shoot you if you make one false move."

"Then what's your problem? We wouldn't be able to tinker with the bombs if that's what you're afraid of. Not even if we wanted to."

With the man's fierce gaze eyeing him suspiciously, Saffron knew his life and the lives of Bickers and Cornwall might depend on the next few seconds. He felt his entire body relax as Khan turned to Bickers and made an abrupt gesture at the truck. "Very well. Put them in! My guards will take care of them."

As Saffron hid his relief by turning away, he caught Cornwall's glance, a mixture of congratulation and puzzlement. Ignoring it in case of awakening Khan's suspicions, he helped Bickers store the masks inside the truck.

With plenty of helpers to bring out the rest of the equipment, the gas store was quickly emptied and the three trucks ready to move off five minutes later. No doubt due to Saffron's mention of a possible gas leakage, all three airmen were bundled into the truck carrying the chemicals, much to Saffron's relief. Two heavily armed guards climbed in with them, one positioning himself just behind the cab and the other near the tailgate. Both carried knives and revolvers as well as rifles and from their looks and gestures would be only too happy to use them. Three equally well-armed tribesmen, one of them the driver, occupied the cab.

With Razim Khan's truck in the lead, the three vehicles pulled away. Cornwall, sitting on one of the truck's side metal benches, edged nearer to Saffron, his voice low. "What's your game, Saffron?"

Not knowing whether the guards knew any English, Saffron answered with a question. "I wonder where we're going?"

"We're going south across the plateau," Cornwall said as the truck rumbled and shook over the stony ground. "You heard Khan. He's got a camp somewhere out there." He turned to the guard behind the cab. "Where are we going, Genghis Khan?"

The man stared at him stonily. Cornwall winked at Saffron and tried again. "Where are we going, you bloody wog?"

Although Bickers, sitting at the other side of Saffron, looked horrified at the insult, the tribesman's only reaction was a shrug of his shoulders. Cornwall then turned to the tribesman sitting near the tailgate who was chewing betal nut. "You're an ugly bastard. Do you know that?"

Although the man scowled, he continued to chew. "What do you think?" Cornwall asked Saffron. "Does he or doesn't he?"

When Saffron shook his head, Cornwall tried again. "You're as ugly as a pig. In fact you're the ugliest pig I've ever seen."

Bickers gave a yelp of protest. "That's the worst insult you can give him! Stop it or he might shoot us."

Cornwall grinned. "Look at his face. He doesn't understand a word. It's OK, Saffron. You can talk."

Still unsure of the guards, Saffron turned to Bickers. "Do you remember that thing I took from you at Worli?"

With his mind clouded by fear, Bickers took a moment to remember. "What thing?"

"The thing you wanted to take back the first night we were up here."

Bickers's face then showed enlightenment. As he seemed about to name the revolver, Saffron broke in quickly. "That's it. The thing you wanted me to carry at all times. Well, I have it. Do you understand?"

Bickers' voice was hoarse. "You mean now?"

"Yes. Now."

Cornwall was showing intense curiosity. "What thing? What are the two of you talking about?"

A harsh shout interrupted Saffron's reply. Showing suspicion at the airmen's conversation, the nearer guard was threatening them with his rifle. Knowing he had to answer Cornwall, Saffron tried to think of a word the tribesmen were unlikely to know. Ignoring the threatening rifle he spelt out the word: "A sort of d.e.r.r.i.n.g.e.r."

A vicious job into his ribs with the rifle made him catch his breath. Recovering, he turned to Cornwall, whose expression

213

made him fear for a moment that the pugilist did not know the word. Then the man's face lit up. "You've got one? With you?"

With the guard threatening them both, Saffron could only nod. Showing his excitement Cornwall drew out a packet of cigarettes from his stained shirt and offered it to the guard. Bickers shook his head. "It's no good. They don't smoke."

Cornwall grinned as the man took the packet from him. "This one does."

The tribesman took a light from him and then shoved the packet into his baggy trousers. At the same time he showed less aggression when Cornwall addressed Saffron again. "What's your plan, Saffron?"

Saffron knew he could wait no longer if his plan was to work. Faking a smile, he gave a warning to the eager Cornwall. "Don't look so pleased or these guards will suspect something."

The pugilist nodded. "OK. But let's have it."

Smiling at the quaking Bickers, looking as if he were talking about the weather, Saffron quickly outlined his plan. When he finished Bickers' eyes were huge in his pale lugubrious face. "It's hellishly dangerous, Saffron."

Saffron gave his false smile again. "It's our only chance. And stop looking so scared. The guards have their eyes on you."

Bickers' Adam's apple could be seen rolling beneath his open shirt. Before he could speak, Cornwall gave an approving grunt. "When do we do it?"

"We'll have to wait until the other trucks are well ahead of us. They are gaining on us all the time."

Peering round the side of the open truck, Cornwall saw he was right. Warned not to travel fast over the rocky ground because of the truck's gas contents, the driver was falling behind the other vehicles. Saffron waited another two minutes and then, afraid Razim Khan would notice the wide gap and order his front trucks to slow down, he gave Cornwall a slight nod.

It was the signal for Cornwall to make an exclamation and

move over to the sacks of phosgene bombs on the truck floor. Sniffing at them, he glanced at Saffron and gave a cry of warning. Showing alarm, Saffron turned to the guard who was smoking and pointed at the sacks. "It's gas! We think it's escaping!"

Although his words probably made no sense to the two tribesmen, his tone and actions did. Showing alarm, the guard dug his rifle into the Yorkshireman's ribs and pushed him towards the sacks. Edging past the mustard gas containers, Saffron reached one sack and opened it. Sniffing its contents, he glanced up urgently at Cornwall. "It is escaping! Get the masks on!"

Showing the necessary urgency, Cornwall and Bickers snatched up masks and offering them to the two guards. As both men hesitated, Cornwall pushed a mask at the guard near the tailboard. "Go on, you bastard! Put it on or you'll choke to death." He followed the words by clutching his own throat and pretending to choke.

Both guards were deceived by the mime. The front guard climbed over the tanks and carboys and reached for the mask Saffron was offering him. At the same moment Saffron's other hand was fumbling in his shorts for the tiny revolver. As the guard took the mask, the Yorkshireman pulled the revolver out and rammed it into his startled face.

The second guard was deceived in a similar fashion. As he lowered his rifle to take the mask Cornwall was offering him, the pugilist hit him with a vicious blow to the jaw. The man's head snapped back and he slid stunned to the floor of the truck.

Cornwall swung round to Saffron. "What shall I do with the bastard? Throw him out?"

Saffron still had the revolver pressed against the other guard's forehead. Although the man was making no sound, his eyes were feral and hating as they glared at the Yorkshireman and his hands were still clutching his rifle. Not daring to take his eyes off him for a moment, Saffron shouted at the petrified Bickers. "Ken! Get his guns and his knife. Quickly, for God's sake." As Bickers rallied and edged past the carboys to obey, Saffron answered Cornwall. "No. Keep your man here. If you throw him out the others might see him."

With the three men in the front cab having no cause for suspicion, the truck was still lurching on. Checking the rear guard was still unconscious and taking his weapons, Cornwall edged past the gas stores to reach the two NCOs. His square face was glinting with triumph and excitement. "What's the next move, Saffron?"

The Yorkshireman pointed at the cab in front of them. "I'll stop the truck by banging on it. When they get out to see what's happening, you cover them with the rifles. Don't fire if you can avoid it because it might alert Khan." His eyes moved to Bickers. "OK?"

Bickers' Adam's apple did another roll as he nodded.

"Then get into position and be ready. One of you on each side because that's how they'll probably come out. OK?"

Cornwall pointed at the second guard. "What about him? He's sure to warn 'em when they come out." Before Saffron could think of an answer, Cornwall grabbed the man's revolver from Bickers and smashed it on the tribesman's head. As the unconscious man collapsed on a row of carboys, the pugilist grinned. "He won't shout out now."

He's enjoying all this was Saffron's thought before circumstances drove all other thoughts from his mind. He waited until Bickers and Cornwall were in position of both sides of the truck, then took a deep breath. "Ready?" When both men nodded, he picked up the guard's rifle and banged it half a dozen times on the back of the metal cab.

The truck slowed at once, making all three airmen cling to the sides for support. Saffron, who had positioned himself at the same side of the truck as Bickers, glanced back at the Londoner. "It'll be all right, Ken. Just take it nice and steady."

Looking too scared to reply, Bickers only jerked his head as the truck slowed and then juddered to a halt. Saffron felt the Bedford sway as the cab doors were flung open. A moment later there was a questioning shout. Heart thudding like a drum, he waited as another shout came. Praying the three tribesmen would not become suspicious and drive off again, the Yorkshireman heard puzzled conversation and then the sound of footsteps on the stony ground.

A couple of seconds later two tribesmen appeared below. Made suspicious by the absence of a reply from the airmen's guards, both had their rifles at the ready. Knowing he had only seconds to work in, Saffron thrust his rifle over the side of the Bedford and shouted for the men to drop their weapons.

One man did. But the other, a powerfully built tribesman, whipped up his rifle and fired, the bullet striking one of the truck's metal stanchions only a couple of feet from Saffron's head. As the bullet whined away, Saffron fired himself and saw the man clutch his side and fall. At almost the same moment another shot rang out, followed by Cornwall's shout of triumph. "I've got the bastard, Saffron. I think he was the driver."

The Yorkshireman felt little surprise. In his heart he had never believed the bloodthirsty Cornwall would obey his order and let a captor live. Keeping the remaining tribesman covered, he shouted his urgent order. "Take the wheel, Cornwall. At the double before Khan gets back to us."

Cornwall needed no prompting. Before the shooting, Khan and his men had already noticed the third truck had halted and had slowed down to investigate. Now, hearing the rifle fire, they were swinging their trucks round at speed. Jumping down from the tailgate, Cornwall ran round the side of the truck and grabbed up the remaining tribesman's weapons. Throwing them up at Bickers, he was about to club the tribesman with his revolver when Saffron gave a shout. "No, that's enough. He's unarmed. Leave him."

Cornwall hesitated, then with a grunt of disgust jumped into the truck and started the engine. As he swung the truck round, Saffron caught a glimpse of Khan's two vehicles. They were less than three hundred yards away and coming at speed leaving a smokescreen of red dust behind them. Bickers, clinging on a stanchion as the truck bucked and shuddered, showed dismay. "They're catching us, Saffron. They're faster than we are."

Knowing Cornwall might have difficulty seeing the other trucks because of the dust his own wheels were throwing up, Saffron banged on the back of the cab as a warning. The truck's engine note rose higher and with red dust blotted out their vision, the NCOs could only hope it was maintaining its distance.

That hope was soon dispelled as the truck began to climb a long incline. As it climbed higher, Khan's pursuing trucks became visible over the dust plume. The sight brought a gasp of shock from Bickers. "They're no more than two hundreds yards behind us, Saffron. We'll never make it to the main camp."

Saffron knew he was right. He also know that although the dust thrown back by his truck was acting as a smokescreen, some of Khan's men would already be firing into it and at any moment a stray bullet might strike them or one of the gas containers.

The incline was long and wide, its crest stretching far along the edge of the plateau. By the time the truck was nearing the crest its engine was screaming its protest. But a yell from Bickers caught Saffron's attention. The Londoner was pointing at a small vehicle standing on the very edge of the crest. "Look up there, Saffron. Isn't that a jeep?"

Saffron saw Bickers was right. Straining his eyes, he saw four men were standing alongside it, all wearing distinctive slouch hats. "You're right! They're Ghurkas!"

Bickers' prayer was heartfelt. "Thank God."

As he spoke, the truck swung towards the jeep. Cornwall had spotted it too and was making for it. Down the long incline the two pursuing vehicles slowed down and stopped as Khan and his men also spotted the military vehicle. Bickers slumped down on the metal bench. "We're saved, aren't we, Saffron? Pemba must have escaped."

Having the same thought, Saffron clung to the side of the

truck as it lurched over the hill crest and headed towards the jeep. Expecting to see other vehicles either parked or moving forward, he saw to his dismay that the stony ground was empty as far as the eye could see. Bickers, given only a brief sight of salvation, sounded shattered. "Surely this isn't all of them?"

There was no time for Saffron to reply. Cornwall was already halting the truck alongside the jeep. Catching sight of Saffron, Pemba ran towards him. "Are you all right, sergeant sahib?"

"Yes, but what's happened? Why are there only four of you?"

"There was no time to tell our officers, sahib. They would have asked questions and wanted a report and I believed Khan was going to kill you. So I called my three friends and we stole the jeep."

"You're crazy," Saffron told him. "There are well over twenty armed tribesmen down there. Once they find out you're alone, you won't have a chance."

As if to back his words, a bullet struck the truck and whined away. Although uncertain what lay over the hill crest, Khan was probing. Motioning the two NCOs and Cornwall to take cover behind the vehicle, Pemba nodded at his three comrades, who flung themselves down along the edge of the crest. The young Ghurka turned back to Saffron. "You must go, sergeant sahib, and take the gas with you. We can hold them long enough for you to get away."

For the first time Saffron noticed a stain of blood on the Ghurka's shirt. "You were wounded, weren't you?"

"Go, sahib. Please. They will soon realise there are only four of us."

Cornwall spoke for the first time. "He's right. It's our only chance, Saffron."

Below, the Yorkshireman could see tribesmen leaping from the trucks and spreading along the hillside to thin out the Ghurkas' fire. At a word from Pemba, the other three Ghurkas began firing on them. Although tribesmen flung themselves to the ground, the crackle of their rifles as they returned fire was a message in itself. "They have guessed there is no one else here, sergeant sahib. So you must go or you will be captured again. That must not happen."

The loyalty of the little Ghurka was too much for Saffron. "We're not leaving you or your men. We've got rifles too."

"Three more will still not be enough, sergeant. There are too many of them."

At that moment an extra gust of wind ruffled Saffron's hair and rocked the truck on its springs. About to address Bickers and Cornwall, Saffron gave a violent start and swung back to the small Ghurka. "Can your men hold them for a few minutes, Pemba?"

"Yes, sergeant. Longer than that if they have to."

Saffron took a deep breath. "Then I think I've got the answer."

Chapter Twenty-Seven

Saffron glanced at Pemba. "Are your men ready?"

The Ghurka nodded. "Yes, sergeant."

The Yorkshireman turned to the truck which was now drawn back from the ridge and so out of sight of Khan's riflemen. Seeing Cornwall give him a nod, Saffron took a deep breath and then shouted at the top of his voice. "Razim Khan! Can you hear what I say? If not, you can come closer. No one will shoot at you."

For a moment all the listening men could hear was the sound of the wind and the dying echoes of the question. Then a distant harsh voice sounded. "I hear you, Englishman. What do you want?"

"If you value your life and the lives of your men, you will drive away at once. Otherwise you will die a painful death."

Once again the echoes came reverberating back. Then Khan's contemptuous reply. "What nonsense are you talking, Englishman. You have only a few men up there. In a moment my men will sweep you away like a wave washing away a sandbar."

"You are wrong, Khan. Because if you don't withdraw I am going to let loose some of this poison gas. It will burn your lungs like fire and send you to hell."

This time all the echoes had died away before Khan answered. "You are bluffing, Englishman. You will kill your own men if you release the gas."

"No, Khan. We have the gas masks and the wind is blowing towards you. Put your hand up and feel it."

A full ten seconds of silence followed. Bickers, standing alongside Saffron, began looking hopeful. "Do you think he's fallen for it?"

The Yorkshireman motioned him to be silent as Khan's harsh voice sounded again. "You are not escaping, Englishman. I swore your death on Allah and on my brother's grave. Those few Ghurka dogs will not save you."

"Your men won't follow you, Khan. Not when they catch the smell of newly mown hay and know that a few lungfuls of it will kill them."

"My men will do as I tell them, Englishman. They do not speak English, so your words mean nothing to them."

Bickers showed dismay. "That means we can't bluff them, Saffron."

Saffron realised he was right. His face tightened. "Then we'll have to do it. We've no option."

The idea of releasing poison gas was unnerving the Londoner. "What if something goes wrong?" He glanced at the waiting truck. "Wouldn't it be safer to run for it?"

"We were running and they were catching us. In any case, we can't leave Pemba to cover our backs."

"Can't they run with us?"

"Pemba won't do that. You heard him."

Bickers was about to point out that that was the Ghurka's problem when the cough of an engine sounded below the ridge. As Pemba turned and shouted at him, Saffron crawled alongside the prostrate Ghurka and saw the foremost truck had started up again and was making for the hill crest. At the same time the tribesmen strung out along the hillside began firing. As bullets hummed over the ridge it was clear that Khan's assault had begun.

"The truck," Saffron yelled, grabbing his own rifle. "Get the truck first."

Pemba and his men were already firing at it. As Saffron set his rifle sights on it, he saw its windshield shatter and then its nearside front tyre collapse. A moment later it slewed round and stopped.

But the tribesmen were now on their feet and swarming up the hillside. Conscious his bluff had failed, Saffron turned and yelled at the ashen-faced Bickers. "Get the masks out of the truck and give them to the Ghurkas! Then put yours on. At the double."

Anticipating the order, Cornwall had already started the truck engine and moved the vehicle nearer the prostrate men. Jumping out, he helped Bickers to throw masks at the Ghurkas, then he crawled forward and handed one to Saffron. "You're really going to do this, Saffron?"

The panting Yorkshireman was already slipped the mask straps over his head. "I've no choice, have I? The bastards will be up here in another minute or two."

Gazing over the rim, Cornwall saw he was right. Showing fanatical courage, the tribesmen were already half-way up the hillside and although the rifle fire from the four Ghurkas was taking its toll and forcing them to dive behind rocks and boulders, it was clear that the losses a few rifles could inflict would have no chance of stopping them for long.

Closing the mask over his face, Saffron could taste metal and rubber as he drew in breath. Alongside him, Cornwall and the Ghurkas became equally grotesque figures. Drawing back from the ridge, hearing his breath sobbing in his ears, Saffron ran towards the truck and waved frantically at Bickers. "I want the phosgene bombs. Get them down."

Bickers gave a start. "Phosgene?"

"Yes. And throw me down a revolver at the same time. Move it, for God's sake, or they'll be up here."

Moving quickly for once in his life, Bickers swung down a sack of the 25lb bombs and then a captured revolver. His bewildered question reached Saffron as the Yorkshireman dragged a bomb from the sack. "How are you going to blow it open? They're not fused with exploders or detonators, are they?"

Saffron had no time to explain. Seeing Cornwall had followed him, he handed a bomb to the man. "Set it down over there on its side," he shouted. "Behind the Ghurkas."

To his relief, Cornwall asked no questions and ran off. Grabbing a second bomb, the Yorkshireman ran towards the other end of the ridge. After he had covered thirty yards, sobbing for breath through the hose of his mask, he laid the bomb on its side and drew back a couple of yards. He then pointed the revolver at the bomb's nose and fired.

Nothing happened. Cursing his trembling hands, he fired again and saw only a small cloud of dust rise around the bomb. Gritting his teeth, he moved right up to the bomb, pointed the revolver with both hands, and fired again. This time when the dust cleared away he could see through the goggles of his mask that the nose of the bomb had been blown away and a yellow pressurised mist was hissing out.

There was no time to see more. Climbing to his feet, cursing the mask that was making breathing such a lung-tearing effort, he ran back to the bomb that Cornwall had laid behind the Ghurkas. Waving the four men back from the ridge, he knelt down and fired the revolver again. He missed the first time but his second shot was successful and again a sinister yellow mist begin hissing out and blowing over the brow of the hill.

With the possibility that some of the tribesmen might have spread further along the hillside and so outflanked the gas, Saffron needed to see what was happening below. As he flung himself down and began crawling towards the ridge, he felt a restraining hand on his shoulder. Glancing up he saw two huge insect eyes gazing down at him. It was only when the Ghurka spoke that he realised the man was Pemba. "No, sahib. It is dangerous. They are still firing."

He shook off the Ghurka's hand. "Let me go. I must see if it's having any effect."

Realising he would not be stopped, Pemba waved his masked Ghurkas forward and, ignoring the gas that was billowing over them, all four took positions alongside Saffron.

The Yorkshireman's first reaction was dismay. Because the two bombs had not contained explosive charges, the gas was being released only by pressure and so spreading less quickly than he had hoped. Moreover the wind had dropped again and at the moment was little more than a slight breeze. Accordingly, the two translucent yellowish clouds, although heavier than air, had not yet drifted down the hillside and the tribesmen, unaware of their danger, were less than sixty yards from the summit. Over to the right, forced to leave the first crippled truck and finding the second one was also damaged by rifle fire, the tall, bearded figure of Razim Khan could be seen leading his men on foot. Catching sight of him and his fanatical gestures, the Ghurkas took turns at firing at him but because of the range he was not hit until he was well up the hillside. Only then did he stumble, clutch his leg, and fall to the ground.

Saffron's hope that his fall would discourage his followers was shattered immediately as vengeful shouts sounded below and men rose from behind boulders and rushed recklessly forward. Their headlong rush was checked for a moment by the fire of the rock-steady Ghurkas but it was obvious enough that one more attack would sweep the defenders off the ledge unless the gas stopped them first.

As the translucent clouds were now sinking down the hillside, it seemed likely the gas would do this and the thought of so many men dying an agonising death dismayed Saffron. Glancing at Pemba he drew back from the ridge and ran behind the still smoking bomb. There, breathing a silent prayer the air was not contaminated, he pulled off his mask and shouted at the top of his voice. "You must go back! Your leader has deceived you. The cloud drifting down to you that smells like newly mown hay is poison gas. It will burn your lungs and kill you unless you go back. I swear it in the name of Allah."

The firing had stopped during his warning. In reply he heard another shout coming from below. Replacing his mask, he crawled back to the ledge and saw a heavily-built man had risen from a boulder and was gesticulating at the mist that was descending the slope. As one of the Ghurkas took aim on him, Saffron knocked away the man's rifle. "No! Let him speak! He's warning them about the gas."

As the man's voice came echoed back, Saffron recognised him as the tribesman who had attended the man Malcolm had shot. As his warning rang out, shouts were heard and tribesmen were seen questioning one another. Then, as the word passed from mouth to mouth and men caught the first smell of fresh hay, alarm began to spread among them like a bush fire. Tribesmen who would face bullets and cold steel without flinching rose from cover and lifted their arms in a gesture of submission.

Meeting Saffron's eyes, Pemba ordered his men to cease firing. Below, with their fight clearly over, tribesmen picked up their wounded and began hurriedly retreating down the vast hillside.

They left one wounded man behind them, which made Saffron wonder if it was an act of revenge for their betrayal. At the far end of the hillside and only fifty yards from its crest, Razim Khan was struggling to escape the gas that was now beginning to spread along its entire length. Only one man, the one with the pock-marked face, had gone over to help him. With Khan's arms draped over his shoulders, he was struggling to get his leader away from the oncoming gas, but with Khan virtually helpless and the wind freshening again, it was clearly a hopeless task.

Behind Saffron, Cornwall had been watching the rout of the tribesmen. Jumping to his feet, Saffron drew the pugilist behind the still smoking bomb and pulled off his mask. At

Cornwall's questioning look, he nodded. "It's all right. It's safe back here."

Cornwall's square face was alight with triumph as he removed his mask. "You did a hell of a job, Saffron. That's taught the bastards a thing or two."

Saffron ignored his praise. "Listen. We can't leave those two men to choke to death. I want you to take me down to them. Right away. Before the gas sinks down there."

Cornwall's expression changed. "You gone doolally or something? The wounded one's Khan."

"I know that. But he's still a man." Saffron pushed the pugilist towards the truck. "Come on. Let's go."

Cornwall shook his head. "I'm not helping the bastard. He was going to cut our throats. Let him choke. I'll enjoy watching it."

"For Christ's sake, Cornwall, we can't leave him. It's a dreadful death."

"Good. That's what he deserves. I'm not going, Saffron." Cornwall gestured at the Ghurkas. "You go or let them go. But not me."

Bickers, who had come to see what the argument was about, added his own protest. "You're crazy, Saffron. They'll think you've come to capture them and shoot at you."

Although he knew it was only too likely, Saffron ignored the warning. "How many masks were left in the truck?"

"None," Bickers told him. "I gave them all out."

Saffron waved Pemba towards him. "Tell your men to draw back this side of the bomb. Then they'll be safe. I want two masks from them. Quickly."

The little Ghurka obeyed and handed Saffron two masks. Only then did he ask his question. "You are taking them to Khan, sergeant sahib?"

With no time to answer, the Yorkshireman swung round on Bickers. "Will you come with me? If they start shooting I might need some help."

Before Bickers could answer, Pemba stepped forward. "I'll come, sergeant sahib."

Saffron pushed him back. "No, you've done enough. We released the gas. It's our responsibility." He turned to Bickers again. "Are you coming or do I go alone?"

Bickers swallowed, then, to Saffron's surprise, gave a nervous nod. "I suppose so. What do you want me to do?"

Thrusting the two masks at him, Saffron ran with him to the truck. "Stay in the back and throw out the masks when I sound the hooter. Keep your head down in case they start shooting. But keep your mask on all the time because we'll be driving right through the gas."

As Bickers climbed over the tailgate, Saffron ran round to the driver's seat. Pulling on his mask, he started the engine and swung the truck round. As he passed the first bomb, which was still exuding gas, the sinister translucent cloud swept over the truck and deposited tiny yellow droplets on its windshield.

As the vehicle lurched over the hill crest and started downwards, Khan and his helper could be seen. Although the frantic efforts of the pock-marked man had taken them another hundred yards down the hillside, it was clearly only a matter of minutes before the gas cloud reached them. As Saffron stood on the accelerator and the truck bucked and rolled, he heard the clank of metal behind him and could only pray none of the mustard gas tanks split open.

Khan's helper had now seen the vehicle. Lowering the wounded man to the ground he began unslinging his rifle. Switching on his headlights, Saffron flashed them in the hope his message would be understood.

It was not. While the truck was still in the gas cloud, the tribesman fired and a bullet shattered the windshield. Cursing, Saffron was forced to swing the vehicle from side to side and as metal rattled and clanked he could only guess what was happening behind him.

A second bullet whined from the engine cowling but now Saffron was clear of the gas. Another forty yards and he estimated there would be time for the tribesman to collect the masks and get back to Khan. Accordingly he gave three blasts on the hooter. Ahead, the aggressive tribesman who was about to fire again, lowered his rifle, and began running.

Knowing Bickers must have thrown out the masks, the Yorkshireman turned for the hill crest again. Glancing in his mirror, he saw the tribesman picking up the masks and raising an acknowledging arm.

Relief was surging through Saffron's veins like some stimulating drug as he headed into the gas cloud again. In spite of all that had happened, it seemed luck had been with them. Neither his men nor Pemba's had suffered any casualties during the battle and Razim Khan had taken an ignominious beating and apparently lost credibility with his followers. Moreover, with Khan's life saved by his enemies, his religion would surely demand that he took no further punitive action against them. One way and another, when one considered how heavily the odds had been stacked against them at the onset, Saffron felt things could hardly have turned out better. In this euphoric mood, he drove the truck over the hill crest and out of the gas cloud to where the Ghurkas and Cornwall were waiting for him.

Pemba was at his cab door before he could jump out, his oval face full of admiration. "Well done, sergeant sahib. But if they had shot you we would have killed them both."

Saffron grinned. "I'm glad it wasn't necessary, Pemba." Then he heard coughing from the back of the truck. Giving a start, he ran round and found Bickers lying on the floor of the truck with his discarded mask alongside him. Climbing over the tailgate, Saffron bent over him. "What's happened, Ken?"

The Londoner's frightened, bloodshot eyes gazed up at him. "My mask, Saffron . . . I slipped and fell when we were going down the hill . . . it must have damaged it." He broke into a spasm of coughing, then tried to reach the mask. "I didn't notice until we were coming back . . . But then I got a lungful of gas . . ."

As the Londoner coughed and choked again, Saffron

snatched up the mask. He took one look at it and then gave a groan of horror. "Oh, my God, no!"

Chapter Twenty-Eight

Saffron turned to the hospital nurse. "How long has he been on oxygen?"

The nurse, a petite Anglo-Indian girl, glanced at her watch. "He's been on it ever since you brought him in, sergeant. At least two hours."

"Then I think we can remove the mask for a little while."

The girl showed hesitation. "I'd better see a doctor first."

Saffron nodded. "All right. But I don't think he'll argue."

Giving him an uncertain smile, the nurse hurried away. Left alone, Saffron turned back to the bed where Bickers was lying with an oxygen mask clamped over his pale face. Believing he saw the Londoner's eyelids flicker, he bent over him. "How are you feeling, Ken?"

Bickers' bloodless lips moved but Saffron could hear nothing through the mask. Wincing, he sank down on a bedside chair and waited for the doctor.

It had been Saffron who had brought the Londoner to the town's military hospital. Frantic for him to get urgent medical treatment, he had initially intended to drive him straight there in the truck until he realised its gas contents prohibited such a move. With no time to unload the poisonous contents, he had borrowed the jeep from the Ghurkas to make the journey.

It was only when reaching the hospital that he had realised the problems Bickers faced. Although the hospital was staffed by doctors capable enough to carry out routine medical therapy and surgery, none had the slightest knowledge of poison gas and the correct treatment for its victims.

As a result Saffron had been asked himself what should be done. Taught, as servicemen were, to use weapons with little regard to the survival of their enemies, the Yorkshireman only knew that phosgene victims should be given copious oxygen. When asked for how long, he had to admit the course he had been given had provided no further information.

The sound of footsteps broke into his thoughts. Turning, he saw an elderly doctor approaching. The man's tone was terse and unfriendly "What is it, sergeant? I understand you want to see a doctor."

Saffron, whose earlier encounters had been with two younger doctors, decided this one must be the officer in charge or the registrar. "Yes, sir. I suggested to the nurse that we remove the patient's mask for a while and she felt we should get your permission first."

The man's lined face frowned. "*You* suggested his mask should be removed! What are you, sergeant? A doctor in disguise?"

"No, sir. As I think you know, I'm the NCO in charge of the poison gas school."

"And that makes you an expert on its victims, does it?"

Upset by Bickers' accident, Saffron felt his temper fraying. "No, sir, I only wish it did. Only I'm told there isn't much known about phosgene poisoning in this hospital either. So I felt the removal of his mask for a time might be wise."

The doctor gave him a look of dislike, then swung round on the young nurse. "How long has his mask been on?"

"Two hours, sir."

"Two hours eh." The man bent over Bickers and ran his stethoscope over his chest. Straightening, avoiding Saffron's eyes, he glanced back at the nurse. "Very well. Remove the mask for half an hour but replace it at once if he shows any distress and call me." Still without looking at Saffron, he strode out of the ward.

Resentful, Saffron turned to the nurse. "He wouldn't admit he knows nothing about the correct treatment, would he?"

The girl, who looked too afraid of losing her job to criticise her superiors, began unfastening Bickers' mask. "I'm sure they're doing their best to find out more, sergeant. I believe telegrams have been sent to Cawnpore and Dehli."

Seeing Bickers' eyes had opened, Saffron leaned over him. "Can you talk, Ken?"

The Londoner's voice was little more than a croak. "Is that you, Saffron?"

"Yes. How are you feeling?"

"Bloody awful, mate. My throat feels like raw meat."

"That's because you've been coughing. It'll soon wear off."

Bickers' eyes were wandering round the ward, giving Saffron the belief he was still under shock and not yet fully aware of the danger he was in. His croak came again. "Where've Cornwall and the Ghurkas gone?"

"Back to their units, I suppose."

"Won't Pemba be in trouble for pinching a jeep?"

"I don't think so. I had to tell the CO everything after I got you in here and he promised to contact the Ghurka commandant. I'm hoping those lads get citations for what they did. They deserve it."

"What happened to me, Saffron?"

The Yorkshireman wondered whether to tell him or not. In the end he compromised. "You had a bit of a mishap, old lad. You slipped and fell down in the truck when we went to help Razim Khan. Nothing too serious but I thought it better to get you into hospital for a check up."

As the Londoner's bloodshot eyes gazed up at him, Saffron saw memory returning to them. With it came fear of a kind the Yorkshireman had never seen before. "I was gassed, wasn't I, Saffron? I'm going to die, aren't I?"

Saffron grabbed his hand. "No, you're not. The mask wasn't that damaged. You only got a whiff or two."

Panic brought a coughing fit to the Londoner. Helped by the nurse, Saffron raised his head and shoulders until the paroxysm ceased. Gasping for breath, Bickers dropped back on his pillow, his accusing eyes gazing up at Saffron. "They told us in South Africa that it doesn't need more than few lungfuls to kill a man. And you've been telling the courses the same thing."

"Yes, but you didn't have a few lungfuls. The tube from the purifier was only partially torn. You didn't get pure gas into your lungs."

Bickers' terrified eyes moved to the oxygen mask hanging beside his bed. "Then why have they been giving me oxygen?"

"Only as a precaution," Saffron told him. "Not for any other reason. You're still full of life, aren't you?"

His reassurance calmed Bickers but only for a moment. Then more memory returned and with it terror. "They told us this is how phosgene works. Gives a man hope for a few hours but then kills him. You're lying to me, Saffron. You know I'm going to die tonight or tomorrow."

Upset by his torment, Saffron glanced at the distressed nurse. Filling a glass with water she hurried towards the bed and picked up two tablets from a tray. "I'm to give him these if he becomes restless," she whispered. "Will you help me, please?"

With Saffron's help, the nurse managed to get the distraught Londoner to swallow the tablets. Saffron had no idea what they contained but they were powerful enough to calm Bickers and induce him to sleep. In the meantime the nurse brought back the elderly doctor who curtly informed Saffron he must now leave the hospital and could only return after 20.00 hours that evening.

With Bickers unconscious and his oxygen mask restored, Saffron had no case to argue. The long hours that followed were not ones he wanted to remember. Relieved by the CO of his normal duties, partly in recognition of what he had done that day and partly out of sympathy for his stricken friend, he had little else to do but hang around in the hospital grounds and wait for his visiting hours to arrive.

With the self-critical faculties that burdened the Yorkshireman, the outcome was inevitable. Question after brooding question poured into his mind. Had he needed to take Bickers down the hillside that day? Surely it would have been possible for him to have thrown the masks to the tribesmen himself without risking the life of an innocent man.

For that matter had he been right in the first place to help Khan? Had he been too squirmish: had Cornwall been right in refusing to go? To his great credit (and Saffron's surprise) Bickers had accepted the risk but because of it he might now suffer the same hideous death that had threatened a pitiless enemy. This unfair twist of fortune, Saffron thought, could be blamed on no one but himself.

There was yet another factor that was troubling him. The news had been given him by Fraser that afternoon and he had been so distraught over Bickers' accident that it had barely entered into the equation of his behaviour. Indeed he had forgotten about it when talking to the distressed Londoner earlier on. Now he had to decide his correct conduct when he spoke to Bickers again. Would the news encourage him and help him to fight the threat that was hanging over him? Or would it have the reverse effect and bring him despair that he might not live to enjoy its benefits?

Like as many rats in a cage, these and other thoughts were still wrestling and tumbling over in Saffron's mind when the long wait was over and he was allowed into the ward again. To his surprise the young Anglo-Indian girl was still on duty. "How is he?" he muttered as she hurried to his side.

"He's awake," she whispered. "But he's still under sedation. So you'll find him calmer than he was this afternoon."

"Has the doctor been to him again?"

"Yes, but not the major. He's off duty now. Dr Saunders has seen him a couple of times and taken off his oxygen mask."

Saffron remembered Saunders was one of the younger doctors who had openly admitted their ignorance of the correct therapy. Thanking the girl, he approached the bed. "Hiya, kid. How's it going?"

Bickers, who had more colour in his cheeks now, gave him a scowl. "What have you been doing all this time? Flirting with the nurses?"

Saffron grinned and dropped into the bedside chair. "That's

more like my laughing boy. No, I haven't. They kicked me out of here three hours ago and I've been twiddling my thumbs ever since. How are you feeling?"

"Bloody awful, Saffron. I've got a mouth like a gorilla's armpit. I keep telling 'em but they don't do anything about it."

Although Saffron knew the Londoner's change of mood was due to sedation, he could not help feeling encouraged. "I'll see you get some lemonade or something tomorrow."

Bickers' reply came like a sudden cold finger on the spine. "Tomorrow's no good, Saffron. You know that as well as I do."

Saffron pretended ignorance. "What are you talking about?"

"Don't flannel me, Saffron. You've told us about that delay in symptoms often enough. That's why I've stopped coughing. But in another twelve hours the gas will get me and that'll be that." Lifting his head, Bickers glanced round the small, private ward. "That's why they've put me in here by myself, isn't it? So patients won't see the way I go."

"But, kid, I don't think you inhaled pure gas. I think you're going to be OK. You're looking better already."

"There you go again. Why don't you shut up and let me talk? I've got things I need to say."

"What sort of things?"

"Things I must tell you before it's too late. Things I want you to tell Betty. Dozens of things."

Alarmed, Saffron half rose from his chair. "Are you sure you don't want to talk to a parson or a priest? I'm sure they'll find one if you do."

Bickers scowled. "I don't want some bloody sky lawyer to hear what I've done, Saffron. He'd probably shop me to the CO."

To his dismay Saffron felt he was going to burst into hysterical laugher. "All right. What do you want to say?"

Giving a lugubrious sigh, the Londoner sank back on his pillow. "I've been a bastard, Saffron. A real sod."

Saffron managed a grin. "So what's new?"

He received a hurt look. "You don't have to rub it in."

"Sorry, kid. Go on."

"I've been a sod with everyone, Saffron. But particularly with you. Did you know I've sometimes disliked you?"

"You don't say."

"But I have, Saffron. And do you know why? Because time and again you've made me feel like a coward and a prat. Yet I couldn't have managed without you. I want you to know that, mate. You've been a hell of a friend."

Saffron heard a muted sob and saw the young nurse had a handkerchief to her eyes. He turned back to the bed. "Is that it?"

"Christ, no. There are women too. I've been a bastard with them, Saffron. Everywhere I've been." Raising a hand, Bickers wiped a tear from his cheek. "And yet back home Betty's been waiting faithfully for me all these years. Isn't it awful?"

Saffron fought back hysterical laughter again. "Terrible," he agreed.

He received a reproachful look before the Londoner's remorse returned. "I want you to see and talk to Betty but I don't know what you should say. Is it fair to tell her what a bastard I've been or should I leave her with a happy memory?"

"Leave her with a happy memory," Saffron suggested.

"You don't think that's being deceitful?"

"It is but it's also kinder."

Bickers sighed. "I hoped you'd say that, Saffron." His tearful eyes moved to the nurse whose shapely body was shaking with emotion. "It's going to be hell leaving it all, Saffron."

"Leaving what, kid?"

With his eyes still on the girl, Bickers gave a tearful sniff. "Leaving the fleshpots. You don't think it'll only be men up there, do you? That would be the end."

"Why should there just be men? Women qualify too, don't they?"

"God, I hope so, Saffron. It'll be hellishly lonely if they don't."

Saffron grinned. "You're still at it, aren't you, you randy old tomcat?"

Bickers looked shocked. "Don't talk like that, Saffron. It's just so hard for a man to face the end of everything he's known and appreciated."

Without quite knowing why, Saffron decided it was the moment to break his news. "You've wasted your time making your confessions to me, buster. You'll be able to make them to Betty yourself in another few weeks. The CO told me today our repatriation papers have come through and we leave here at the end of the month."

Bickers gave a violent start. "Is it true or are you just saying it?"

"No, it's true. They're also winding up the gas school. They've decided the Japs aren't going to use gas after all."

For a moment Bickers forgot his despair. "What a bastard you are, Saffron."

"I am? Why?"

"You sat there and let me say all those things to you when you knew this all the time."

Saffron was taking heart by the minute. "So you've decided to return to Blighty with me after all, have you?"

Then Bickers remembered his accident and his role. His head sank back on his pillow. "My God, I won't be able to go, will I? I've looked forward to this for four years and now I can't go. Isn't it hellish, Saffron? Isn't it absolutely hellish?"

Still unsure of the Londoner's chances of survival, Saffron took his hand. "Just think about going home and seeing Betty again. Don't think of anything else."

Turning away, Bickers made no reply. Seeing his eyes were closing, Saffron gave a worried glance at the nurse, who hurried over. "Can I stay here tonight?" he asked.

Drying her eyes, she nodded. "Yes. I'm sure Dr Saunders won't mind."

"Then I will. Thank you."

Saffron was dreaming of Razim Khan when he heard his name called. "Saffron! What the hell are you doing? Let go of my hand!"

The Yorkshireman woke, to find his head and shoulders were slumped over the bed with Bickers' hand gripped tightly in his own. Releasing it, he sat back in the chair, wincing at the pain in his back. "Sorry. I must have fallen asleep."

Bickers' voice was testy. "I couldn't move when I woke up. What are you doing here anyway?"

Saffron saw sunlight was slanting through a nearby window. He fumbled to look at his wrist-watch. "What's the time?"

"Nearly seven," Bickers muttered. "And the bastards haven't come to feed me yet. You can tell it's a bloody military hospital, can't you?"

Memory was flooding back to Saffron now. "How do you feel?"

"I've just told you. Hungry. I didn't have a damn thing to eat last night. Won't you go and find out what the bastards are doing?"

Massively relieved, Saffron rose to his feet and grinned at a nurse who had appeared in the doorway. "He's hungry and he's moaning again. Welcome back to life and the world, Laughing Boy."

Chapter Twenty-Nine

Bickers took a sip of tea and grimaced. Turning, he gazed down the mess table. "Any sugar down there?"

Twenty odd stony faces gazed back at him. Bickers indicated his mug of tea. "Sugar? Have you got any?"

Twenty odd faces turned away and resumed eating. Bickers frowned but had the good sense to keep his voice low. "Friendly bastards, aren't they?"

Saffron, seated next to him, grinned. "What do you expect? Hugs and kisses?"

Bickers sniffed. "Is a civil answer too much to expect?"

"They haven't come from a civilised place. They've been in Burma, some of them for years. Not a place to polish one's manners in."

"It's nothing to do with that, Saffron. It's the old jealousy again. We're the RAF. The Navy hates us, the Army hates us. And all we've done is save their bloody skins."

Seeing the look the Londoner was receiving from a hard-nosed lance corporal sitting opposite him, Saffron gave him a warning nudge. "I wouldn't shout that too loud if I were you. Not to men who've been fighting the Japs in the jungle. They might think you're exaggerating a little."

Catching the tough swaddy's look of dislike, Bickers hastily tried to atone. "I wasn't meaning out here, of course. I was meaning back in the UK."

The soldier's big aggressive face pushed half-way across the mess table. "You know what you are, mate? You're a real funny man. All wind and piss, like the rest of your lot."

Seeing other swaddies turning towards them, Saffron decided immediate intervention was necessary. "He didn't mean any harm, corporal." He lifted a finger to his temple and waggled it around. "He's been ill recently and it's done things to him."

"You mean the bugger's doolally?" The lance corporal's voice sounded like steel balls rolling over corrugated iron. "You don't need to tell me that, mate. You can see it just to look at him."

Bickers blinked, too conscious of the threat of violence to show resentment. "I was only complaining about the sugar," he muttered. "Everything's sour on this ship. Haven't you noticed that?"

The corporal's lips curled. "You're soft, mate. Like the rest of your shower."

Saffron nudged Bickers again and rose to his feet. "Come on. Finish your tea and let get up on deck."

The two men were on board the SS *Lahore*, bound for the UK with a large contingent of time expired men. Ninety-five per cent were soldiers of the 14th Army, men who had fought the Japanese in some of the most brutal conditions known in the history of warfare. Some were drained by the experience and could be seen wandering around the ship as if unable to believe the hell was over at last. A number of others, due no doubt to the excessively savage engagements they had suffered, gave the impression of being brutalised by the experience and it was Saffron and Bickers' misfortune to be sharing a billet and mess deck with such a unit.

The disgruntled Bickers made mention of it when he followed Saffron on to the deck. "They're like animals, Saffron. Snarling and biting at everyone around them."

"They're victims," Saffron told him. "We might be like that ourselves if we'd been given a different kind of posting."

"Rubbish. Experiences don't change a man's basic personality like that."

Saffron gave him a look. "Don't they? How about a man who thought for years he was God's gift to women and then suddenly confessed he'd been a bastard to them. He made that change in just one day."

Bickers scowled at the reminder. "That was different. I expected to die."

"So did all those men. Not just one day but probably every day for years. I wonder what that would have done to you. You'd probably have come back as Dracula."

"You do talk the most awful crap sometimes, Saffron."

The Yorkshireman grinned. "Steady. I'm the man you're jealous of. Remember?"

Bickers scowled. "If I said that I *was* delirious. Clean out of my mind."

The men emerged from a companionway on to a deck packed tightly with troops. Pushing their way forward, they managed to reach a rail where Bickers gazed at the sunlit Indian ocean with suspicion. "Remember the last time? It looked just as innocent as this until that Jap sub nearly wiped us out."

Saffron nodded at a corvette stationed half a mile abeam. "I think it's safer now. The Navy must have cleaned up their act since those days."

Bickers, whose dislike of the Navy had begun during their enforced stay in Kenya and sunk to an all time low with the sinking of the *Kehdive Ismail*, gave a sniff of disdain. "That'll be the day. If they could let that sub get right into the centre of a convoy without being detected, they're capable of anything. I won't sleep at nights until we're safely out of here and in the Med."

When Saffron made no reply, Bickers gazed at him. "What are you thinking?"

The Yorkshireman smiled. "A hundred things. Like wondering if Moin will feed Horace now we've left. Like the big earthquake we expected but never had. Like that wonderful little guy Pemba. I hated saying goodbye to him. I was also wondering what'll happen to those kids, Barron and Malcolm, now we've gone."

"They'll be OK. They'll probably go back to the main camp armoury." Bickers' tone changed. "We never found out what caused Malcolm's fit, did we?"

Saffron shook his head. "No. And we probably never will. That's what war does. Answers some questions but leaves others high and dry. Take Cornwall. Look what a bastard he was in Kenya. And yet when it came to the crunch with Razim Khan he behaved well."

Bickers wasn't having that. "What do you mean – well? He wouldn't go down with you to give Khan a mask, would he?"

"No, but that's because he wasn't the forgiving kind. But he behaved well before that. It showed that not all bullies are cowards."

"You're going soft, Saffron. You're forgetting what he did to Merrow in Kenya."

"No, I'm not," Saffron said. "I'm just learning things from

this war. You should do the same. You'll never go to a better school."

Bickers gave a guffaw. "School? If it's a school it turning out some bloody funny pupils. Look at those sods we're billeted with. They look as if they'd cut our throats for a box of matches."

Saffron grinned. "I don't know about matches but I wouldn't trust one or two of 'em with our wallets. So you take yours with you when you go to the washroom and sleep with it under your pillow at nights."

The two airmen went down to their bunks an hour later. With the holds packed with double-tiered beds and with many men dozing on them, the air was fetid with sweat and unwashed clothes. Saffron, whose bunk was above Bickers', had his eyes on a bed not ten feet away on which a soldier was lying. A man with a mean, avaricious face, he had rolled over to watch the two airmen as they entered the hold and although he seemed to close his eyes on noticing Saffron observing him, the Yorkshireman knew that he was watching every move they made. Saffron drew Bickers to the other side of their bunks. "That's the little sod you've got to watch. He's the type who'd steal his grandfather's underpants."

"Why just him?" Bickers muttered. "They all hate our guts. Why had we to be the only airmen put in here among a mob of swaddies?"

Saffron grinned. "Don't get paranoid. They're tough but they're still on the same side as us. They won't give us any problems as long as you don't put your big foot in it again."

Bickers bridled. "What do you mean, my big foot?"

"Like calling them nice friendly bastards. Pointing out that you've won the war for them. Or even calling 'em savage animals. Tiny little things like that."

Bickers sniffed. "If the shoe fits, let 'em wear it."

Saffron tapped him on the shoulder. "There's thirty or more of them in this hold and I'm not getting myself torn into small pieces because you can't keep that tongue of yours quiet. So you watch it, buster."

* * *

Four uneventful days passed. To Bickers' relief the SS *Lahore* left the still perilous Indian ocean behind and passed through Suez into the Mediterranean. With its protective warships left behind, the *Lahore* proceeded unescorted towards the United Kingdom, with its repatriated servicemen growing more excited by the day. "Think of it, Saffron. In another week, maybe less, we'll be back in old Blightly again. Cosy pubs, home fires, friendly people, fish and chips . . . Won't it be bloody marvellous?"

"It will," Saffron agreed.

"Do you think we'll get a reception when we dock? You know, like you see in the movies? A band and girls waving handkerchiefs and things."

"What? Welcoming home the conquering heroes?"

"Why not? We've been away four years. We deserve a bit of a reception, don't we?"

Saffron grinned. "It'd be nice but I wouldn't bank on it. We're not the Yanks, you know."

Bickers' euphoria received a rude setback at reveille the following morning. The last to rise as usual, he heard a call from Saffron who was standing at the door of the crowded washroom. "Ken! My shaving soap's finished. Lend me yours, will you? If I come over I'll lose my place in here."

Grumbling, Bickers swung his skinny legs out of bed and rummaged in his side kit. Finding a bar of soap he padded to towards the Yorkshireman and handed it to him. Returning to his bunk, he remembered his wallet and jerked his pillow back. To his relief the wallet was still there and he was about to push it into his shirt pocket when something made him open it. A second later his startled yell turned every face in the hold towards him. "My money's gone! Saffron! Someone's stolen my money!"

Saffron, stripped to the waist and with half his face covered in shaving cream, came running out of the washroom. Bickers, looking pale and shocked, showed him his wallet. "It's all gone, Saffron! All of it!"

Spinning round, Saffron saw the rat-faced man on the opposite bunk turn quickly away and begin drawing on his socks. Certain he was the thief, the Yorkshireman ran over to him. "Give it back to him! Every penny."

He received a sullen stare. "What yer talking about? I haven't got his bloody money."

Saffron grabbed his shirt collar. "Yes, you have. Where is it?"

Cursing, the man tried to knee him in the groin. Expecting it, Saffron spun him round and drove his head against the upright beam of his bunk. "Give it back to him, you little bastard, or I'll break your neck."

Although in his anger Saffron ignored the danger, he half expected a dozen soldiers to descend on him as he shook the man like a terrier shaking a rat. Instead, although every solder present had stopped dressing and was watching the fracas, not a man spoke or moved against him. If the Yorkshireman had harboured doubts before of the man's guilt, he had none now. Driving his head once more against the beam, he threw him violently to one side and waved Bickers over. "Help me search his kit!"

As he half expected, they found nothing. Saffron turned to the soldier who had a large contusion on his face. "Where have you hidden it, you thieving little sod?"

He received a triumphant sneer. "I'm reporting you, sergeant."

"You do that," Saffron told him. "And I'll make certain that money's found and you're sent to the glasshouse if it's the last thing I do." He turned and shouted at the ring of stony faces. "Anyone that steals from his mates is scum. This friend of mine been saving his money for years to get married. Now it's gone. If you're the men I think you are you'll either get it back or take it out of his filthy hide."

Again no one spoke or moved. Giving a last shout of disgust, Saffron helped the shattered Bickers to get dressed. "Come on. Let's get out of this hell hole and find some fresh air."

They climbed up on deck. As they stood against a ship rail,

the Yorkshireman saw Bickers was still trembling. He put a hand on his arm. "I'm so sorry, Ken. I really am."

Bickers had never sounded more forlorn. "It's not just the money, Saffron, although that's bad enough. It's the fact your own mates could do a thing like that."

Saffron sighed. "It's another thing we can learn from this war. We were taught as kids that suffering brings out the best in a man's character. It might in some people but it sure as hell doesn't in others. You've just run into a typical case."

"But none of the others shopped him, Saffron. Wouldn't you have thought someone would have taken our side?"

"No, that's the code. For better or worse he's still one of theirs. But that doesn't mean he's getting away with it."

"Why? There's nothing we can do."

Saffron gave a grin of pure satisfaction. "We don't have to do anything, kid. Didn't you notice what was happening when we came out? Two of the biggest swaddies in the unit were going over to knock hell out of him."

The SS *Lahore* nosed towards Greenock six days later. With the ship tannoy booming out orders, men clattered down into the holds, swung up their kitbags, and prepared to set foot on British soil again. Loaded with their kit, as yet unable to see what was awaiting them ashore, Bickers and Saffron shuffled foot by foot along a hot, narrow passageway. Forgetting his troubles in the moment of euphoria, Bickers beamed at the Yorkshireman. "We've made it, Saffron. We're home again. Isn't it bloody marvellous?"

Winking at him, Saffron nodded at a commotion at the head of the queue. "What's happening up there?"

Bickers tried to peer past the line of shuffling men. "It looks as if the crew are selling things. Probably postcards or souvenirs."

With men up front having difficulty in climbing a steep companionway with their bulky kitbags, it took the two NCOs over five minutes to reach the two white-overalled crewmen standing at the junction of a side passage. One, huge and portly with an avuncular smile, held out a filled paperbag to Bickers. "Want to give your girlfriend a treat, corporal?"

Bickers peered at the bag. "What is it?"

"Something she hasn't had much of, corp. Sugar. Two quid a bag." The galley cook leered. "Give it to her and she'll look after you, mate. All night long."

Bickers turned to Saffron. "What do you think? Should we buy a bag?" Then the truth dawned on him. "That's it! That's why the grub's been so awful! They're selling us our own sugar, Saffron. The bastards!"

Bickers had barely recovered from the shock when they emerged on the deck fifteen minutes later. The *Lahore* had already berthed and gangways were clattering down. As men moved forward, an icy wind, laced with spots of rain, stung their cheeks. Shuffling along the lower deck, gazing hopefully for a reception committee, Bickers could see only a row of sullen-faced men lining the long concrete berth. As they stared across at the docking ship, Saffron grinned and nudged the Londoner's arm. "Can't you see the band? And the girls? It's just like the movies, isn't it?"

Bickers frowned. "It has to get better, Saffron. They must have a welcome somewhere waiting for us."

A booming megaphone provided that welcome half an hour later when all the units were formed in squares along the rainswept quayside. "All units hear this. The dockers are on strike for more pay, so all men trained in handling and unloading ship cargoes will report to the Shipping Officer on No. 7 berth. The rest of you will stand by for further orders."

The roar that rose at this announcement must have reached Glasgow itself. With the recalcitrant dockers still foolishly present, the 14th Army took one look at them and charged. In seconds hysterical screams were heard and bodies could be seen seen flying through the air and splashing down twixt ship and quayside. With the bedlam drowning the impotent bellows from the megaphone, Saffron drew Bickers back from the mayhem and motioned him to sit down on his kitbag. "How's that for a welcome, kid? Feel better now?"

Bickers took his eyes off the passing countryside and turned to Saffron. "Do you realise we haven't spoken to an English civilian yet?"

Saffron nodded. "That's right, we haven't. The pleasure's still to come."

"That's been the trouble so far, mate. We've still been in the hands of the bloody Services, bawling out orders, handing out train tickets, and cocking everything up as usual. It'll all be different when we get back among civilised people again."

Saffron grinned. "And I always thought you were the pessimist."

"Not any more, mate. I'm back in Blighty again. I'm a different man here."

"You certainly are. I'd have thought that welcome at Greenock would have soured you for the rest of your life."

Bickers turned back to the train window. "No. That was just one of those things. Thank God all the camps are full and we're going to a civvie billet." Bickers paused and glanced back. "For that matter where are we going?"

"West Kirby. I was billeted there in 1941."

"So was I," Bickers said. "And the people were marvellous. I can't wait, Saffron."

The train pulled in at 16.00 hours where transports were waiting to take repatriated airmen to RAF West Kirby. There, after being warned that they might be recalled to go on another overseas tour if the Japanese war didn't end soon, they were given civilian addresses as temporary billets. Bickers, initially horrified at hearing he might end up once again in the Japanese theatre of war, rallied after Saffron's comforting words. "It might never happen, Ken. And anyway we've four weeks leave to come soon. Live for today. Hasn't the war taught you that?"

The prospect of leave and homecoming did the trick and the Londoner was optimistic again when the two airmen searched through rainswept streets for their billet. "Think of it, Saffron. We're like people on holiday. A few days being spoiled by some kindly old landlady and then we'll be home. Isn't this something?"

They found the address in a backstreet near the sea front. As Saffron produced the military warrant from his greatcoat, Bickers rubbed his hands together. "This is it, Saffron. Our first real contact with a civilian. I can't wait."

Saffron rang the door bell. When a long silence followed, Saffron rang again. A few seconds later a tall, gaunt woman with a face like a butcher's cleaver snatched the door open. "What's the matter with you?" she snapped. "Can't you wait for people to get down the stairs?" Her intimidating gaze swept over them. "What do you want anyway?"

As Bickers' face dropped, Saffron handed her the warrant. If it were possible, the woman's frown hardened. "So you're the couple I've got to billet, are you? Then you'd better come inside."

The two men entered a hall furnished with a mahogany coat hanger and ancient prints. The woman faced them at the foot of a flight of stairs. "Before I take you to your room, I've this to say to you. This is a decent boarding house with paying guests. So they come first with me. That means you don't use the bathrooms in a morning until they've finished in them, you wait until they've eaten before you get your meals, and you're back every night by 10.30 or you'll be locked out. If I have any trouble from you, I shall report you to your commanding officer. Is that clear?"

Bickers' voice quivered. "But we've just come back after four years abroad."

The woman's eyes drilled through him. "Have you indeed? Then you've been on a good scrounge, haven't you, while we've been fighting the war for you. Wipe your feet on the mat before you follow me upstairs. I don't want boot marks on my carpets."

They followed the woman's skinny legs up three flights of steep stairs. Stopping on a small landing, the woman pointed at a door below the sloping roof. "That's your room. You'll keep it clean and make your own beds. And you'll play no music. I don't want my guests kept awake at nights. That's all for now."

She swept off down the stairs. Bickers opened the door and gave a gasp. "This isn't a room, Saffron. It's a bloody cupboard."

Entering, Saffron ducked his head to avoid the roof. Two single beds and one half size wardrobe completed the attic's furniture. There was no window, only an electric light dangling on a flex from the ceiling. Almost as shaken as the Londoner, Saffron sank down on a hard mattress. "Well. How did you enjoy your first talk with a civilian?"

Crushed by his final disillusionment, Bickers gave a deep groan. "I don't believe this, Saffron. What's happened to everybody since we left?"

Saffron lit a cigarette. Resilient though he was, it was a full minute before he took a deep breath and clapped Bickers' shoulder. "Let's be charitable, Ken. They've had a bad time back here these last six years."

Bickers was not to be comforted. "They don't need to treat us like untouchables, do they?"

Saffron crushed out his cigarette. "This is what war does to some people. Remember it if you and Betty get together and have kids. Tell 'em to be smart and make sure their generation aren't fools enough to have another."

The train was puffing out steam like an impatient animal as the two men clasped hands. "You will keep in touch, mate?" Bickers asked.

Saffron grinned. "I thought you were fed up with feeling like a prat."

Bickers frowned. "That's a lousy way to say goodbye, Saffron. But I always said you were an insensitive bastard, didn't I?"

"You did, mush. Often. Now get on that train before it steams off and I'm left with your moans again."

"When does your train leave?"

The Yorkshireman glanced at his watch. "14.15. Another thirty minutes. But you'd better grab a seat while you can."

Bickers patted his greatcoat pocket. "Hang on. I want some pipe tobacco for the journey."

He ran to a shop and returned three minutes later looking astonished. "You'll never believe this, Saffron! I've got forty quid in my wallet."

Saffron looked equally surprised. "You have? Where the hell did that come from?"

Then the penny dropped and Bickers' voice turned hoarse. "It's you, isn't it? That's what you did when I was in the bathroom this morning. You've given me your money."

"Rubbish. It must have been the old dragon. She must have had a change of heart and taken pity on you."

Bickers choked. "You old bastard. But I can't accept it."

A shrill whistle sounded. Saffron grabbed his arm and pushed him towards a carriage. "Get yourself on. Buy Betty a ring if she'll still have you. Go on! Jildi!"

The Londoner had to brush his eyes. "I'll pay you back, Saffron."

"Get in your seat before someone grabs it. Trains are hell these days."

Heaving his kitbag after him, Bickers vanished. A minute later a window dropped and his head and shoulders appeared. Unable to hear him for the hiss of steam, Saffron drew closer. "What is it?"

He caught the Londoner's words as couplings clanked and the train began to move forward. "It wasn't all bad, was it, Saffron? We had a hell of a friendship, hadn't we?"

Saffron reached up and gripped his hand. "We had, kid. I enjoyed it too."

The train began building up speed. The Yorkshireman stood watching it until it disappeared round a bend. Then, shaking his head, he turned and walked away. People crowded past him, some in uniform, some in civilian clothes, but at that moment he noticed none of them. His expression was humorous and whimsical, with a strong dash of regret. Without Bickers, Saffron was thinking, life would never be quite the same again.